Daniel M. Jaffe

The Limits of Pleasure

Pre-publication
REVIEWS,
COMMENTARIES,
EVALUATIONS . . .

"**R**eaders, grab hold of your joy-sticks (pun absolutely intended): Daniel Jaffe's Dave will take you on an unforgettable ride. What are the limits of pleasure, the limits of suffering, the limits of language? Hallucinatory, blasphemous, shamelessly erotic, unflinching, by turns wrenching and wildly comic, Jaffe's narrative stops at nothing in its exploration of what it means to be homosexual, Jewish, human; to survive. This is high-stakes, extreme fiction, whose rewards are as great as the risks it embraces. Just as Jaffe's tormented, irrepressible, and oddly endearing hero earns the 'redemption of risk,' so does his brilliantly fearless creator."

Ellen Lesser
Author, *The Blue Streak*
and *The Shoplifter's Apprentice*

"**V**acationing in Amsterdam, the American hero of Jaffe's coming-of-middle-age novel—orphaned, Jewish, gay—is a stranger in a strange land, a citizen of the New World, bound to the Old World by the forces of both history and memory. At breakneck speed, Jaffe charts this rake's progress—his sentimental, sexual education—in a narrative that's as smart as it is sexy. *The Limits of Pleasure* is a true page-turner, an invigorating exploration of the ways in which the past informs our present, and desire—both for the spirit and for the flesh—shapes our identity. Whether cruising for sex or communing with the spirits of his past, Jaffe's hero reminds us that the sometimes perilous path to self-discovery is a journey we do not, and cannot, make alone. Tremendously wise, hilariously funny, and supremely sexy, Jaffe's big-hearted novel affirms our faith in the power of the spirit, the glory of the flesh, to make us more fully human. A thoughtful, deeply satisfying novel, *The Limits of Pleasure* reminds us that, despite the various limits placed upon our spiritual and sexual identities, we must strive—in the words of E. M. Forster—to 'only connect.' "

Karl Woelz
Co-Editor,
Men on Men 2000

More pre-publication
REVIEWS, COMMENTARIES, EVALUATIONS . . .

"**W**e've heard of survivors' guilt, but Daniel Jaffe brings us a visceral understanding of its less understood concomitant, survivors' rage, in this extraordinarily fearless novel. His prose moves into the minds and cuts close to the bone of his characters as he explores the conflicted sites of contemporary identity. His novel walks mysterious paths to redemption and illuminates the paradox in which one must hold back to survive but risk all to live."

Diane Lefer, MFA
Author, *Radiant Hunger,*
Very Much Like Desire,
and *The Circles I Move In*

———❧❧———

"**T**he *Limits of Pleasure* explores a vast reservoir of possibilities that exists between the constrictions of psychic and emotional pain and the expansiveness of physical sensation and desire. With great wit, insight, and imagination, Mr. Jaffe reveals in his characters a stunning inner landscape that pits smoldering, down-the-throat sensuality against heartfelt nostalgia for cultural awareness and familial belonging. Keep this book by the nightstand for erotic and physical stimulation when the other side of the bed is absent a warm body to do the needful otherwise."

Ron Suresha
Editor, *Bearotica;*
Author, *Bears on Bears*

———❧❧———

"**A**geing, I've seen an attitudinal progression toward gay literature among influential book people. Responses have gone from homophobia (whether ugly or merely curious), to so-called 'tolerance' of so-called 'de-viant' writing, to endorsement of queer studies, etc. Whether such progression truly suggests the word it contains—'progress'—is too vast an issue for me to address in short compass. I can only testify to the riveting effect that Daniel Jaffe's *The Limits of Pleasure* has had on me.

But my testimony is not so simple a matter in an omni-politicized world, whose academic representatives would surely and accurately point out that I am straight, bourgeois, and (again and alas) ageing. Let them think what they think. Let them quibble or condescend at my notion that the truly groundbreaking work breaks its ground by virtue of its universality. I'd call it both mischievous and idle to speak of Jaffe's accomplishment in any sectarian way, just because this brilliant author's central figure Dave is every (wo)man's Every(wo)man. He's crude and sensitive at once; irreverent and deeply caring; sensual to the point of hedonism; he wears the literal bindings of self-denial (the tefillin, both as hot leather item and sign of tribal obeisance is nothing less than a miracle here).

Daniel Jaffe has done the great thing: made a fresh pilgrimage to the age-old human well, where sex and death, good-hearted secularism and the promptings of an ambiguous Higher Power, revolutionism and blood fealty, all roil the pond from surface to sediment. Let the knowing academics prattle on about 'the canon.' The canon itself quakes, shudders, and then invites the likes of *The Limits of Pleasure* in, as it so emphatically must. "

Sydney Lea
Founding Editor,
New England Review/
Breadloaf Quarterly;
Author, *A Place in Mind*
and *Pursuit of a Wound: Poems*

"Since people have been writing fiction, they have been trying to use the medium of untruth to tell the Truth—the truth about life, love, desire, joy, suffering, death, the world they live in, their families, and their communities, and by encapsulating them in words, describe the exact predicament that is the human condition. Since writers are human, however, they often fall short of their goal by leaving some essential part of themselves out of their work. Only a few writers are able to put their entire selves into their writing, not just those few portions that they are certain are likable and thus fit for public consumption. But Daniel Jaffe has succeeded. His *The Limits of Pleasure* examines not just the life of a gay Jew living at the end of the twentieth century, but his interior life as well, a life reflected in and lit by his earliest memories of his parents, his grandmother's community of Holocaust survivors, Boston's gay bars, and Amsterdam's canalled streets.

The Limits of Pleasure is as seamless as anything Christopher Isherwood, Toni Morrison, or Chaim Potok (admittedly, three very different writers) might write, a work where the visionary sits at the table with the mundane, where the divine sleeps in the same bed as the profane. The sexual self is integrated into the spiritual self, the Jewish into the queer, and as the disparate parts of the protagonist fragment they are just as quickly reassembled into one of the most complete, annoying, and lovable characters in the history of our literature, one who is familiar and believable, endearing but frustrating, and ultimately too human for words: A man who composes letters from his dead mother, has anonymous sex with an Arab in Amsterdam, argues with his grandmother at her graveside, wears phylacteries to a gay bar then uses them to flog another Jew in the bar's backroom, and waltzes with Anne Frank in her Secret Annex discussing what it means to be Jewish and queer in their overlapping worlds.

I finished the novel feeling breathless. I, who like all writers love words more than anything, was left without any. What more can be said than that?"

David May
Author,
Madrugada: A Cycle of Erotic Fictions

Southern Tier Editions
Harrington Park Press
An Imprint of The Haworth Press, Inc.
New York • London • Oxford

The Limits of Pleasure

HARRINGTON PARK PRESS
Southern Tier Editions
Gay Men's Fiction
Jay Quinn, Executive Editor

Love, the Magician by Brian Bouldrey

Distortion by Stephen Beachy

The City Kid by Paul Reidinger

Rebel Yell: Stories by Contemporary Southern Gay Authors edited by Jay Quinn

Metes and Bounds by Jay Quinn

The Limits of Pleasure by Daniel M. Jaffe

The Big Book of Misunderstanding by Jim Gladstone

This Thing Called Courage: South Boston Stories by J. G. Hayes

The Limits of Pleasure

Daniel M. Jaffe

Southern Tier Editions
Harrington Park Press
An Imprint of The Haworth Press®
New York • London • Oxford

Published by

Southern Tier Editions, Harrington Park Press®, an imprint of The Haworth Press, Inc., 10 Alice Street, Binghamton, NY 13904-1580

Excerpts from this novel previously appeared in different form in *Harrington Gay Men's Fiction Quarterly* and *Rebel Yell* (Southern Tier Editions/Harrington Park Press, 2001).

PUBLISHER'S NOTE
This is a work of fiction. Names, characters, places, and incidents either are the products of the author's imagination or are used fictitiously, and any resemblance to actual persons, living or dead, business establishments, events, or locales is entirely coincidental.

The lines from "Yom Kippur 1984," from YOUR NATIVE LAND, YOUR LIFE: Poems by Adrienne Rich. Copyright © 1986 by Adrienne Rich. Used by permission of the author and W. W. Norton & Company, Inc.

Cover design by Marylouise E. Doyle.

Cover photograph by Leo F. Cabranes-Grant.

Library of Congress Cataloging-in-Publication Data

Jaffe, Daniel M.
    The limits of pleasure / Daniel M. Jaffe.
        p. cm.
    ISBN 1-56023-372-9 (alk. paper)—ISBN 1-56023-373-7 (akl. paper)
    1. Gay men—Fiction. 2. Jewish men—Fiction. 3. Parents—Death—Fiction. 4. Amsterdam (Netherlands)—Fiction. 5. Americans—Netherlands—Fiction. 6. Grandchildren of Holocaust survivors—Fiction. I. Title.

PS3610.A36 L56 2002
813'.6—dc21

                                                                        2001039105

For Leo

Acknowledgments

Deep thanks to my mentors from the MFA in Writing Program at Vermont College: Sydney Lea, who showed me how to dive beneath the surface of myself to create the novel's early scenes; Diane Lefer and Sena Jeter Naslund, who offered continuous guidance and support; and Ellen Lesser, who nurtured several of the novel's chapters, lending me her courage when my own faltered. Thanks as well to Ron Mohring, Nadine Sarreal, Ann Shultz, Linda Legters, Robin Lippincott, Mark Apelman, and my other friends from Vermont College who also read, heard, commented upon, encouraged, and inspired various parts of this manuscript. I am also grateful for the many insights and suggestions offered by Linda Woolford, Kim Davis, and Andrea Williams.

Thanks as well to Melody Stevenson, Will McMillan, Jane Katims, and Leo F. Cabranes-Grant, who arranged opportunities for me to read publicly from the manuscript-in-progress, thereby helping me gauge audience response.

To my generous friends and hosts in Amsterdam—Irina Grivnina, Masha Neplechovitsj, Jeroen Janssen, Volodja Neplechovitsj, Jana Neplechovitsj, Lee Delahanty, and the nameless men: eternal gratitude. Special thanks to Masha for reading the manuscript and suggesting appropriate tweaks in my rendering of Dutch life.

Deep deep gratitude to my editor, Jay Quinn, a wellspring of support and compassion for people both real and fictional.

And boundless thanks to my family for the enduring embrace that has meant everything.

To Leo F. Cabranes-Grant, who for years enthusiastically welcomed Dave into our conversations and our bed, who generously shared in the imagining of this novel from the beginning, who lovingly shares in the imagining of myself every day: *Poesía ... eres tú.*

What is a Jew in solitude?
What would it mean not to feel lonely or afraid
far from your own or those you have called your own?
What is a woman in solitude: a queer woman or man?
In the empty street, on the empty beach, in the desert
what in this world as it is can solitude mean?

From "Yom Kippur 1984"
by Adrienne Rich

"By all the codes which I am acquainted with, I am a devil-ishly wicked specimen of the sex. But some way I can't con-vince myself that I am. I must think about it."

From *The Awakening*
by Kate Chopin

"Khrot khrofadder khrkhrbleeft."

Dave focuses. They're coming up from the hold . . . hmmm . . . Not able to get the whole thing in his sights, so . . . alright . . . just get the first guy, with part of the flag . . . that's it . . . yeah, the light's perfect. Looks like a real body under there. Okay . . . ready . . . aaand—click!

They all come to attention. *"Blahboomblahboomblahbooom Jan Jacobsen."*

Finally, something Dave understands, a name. Okay . . . now get the whole plank with that flag-draped lump. Yep . . . focus aaand—click!

If you want a complete photo record of the city, Davey Boy, you really should shoot the Anne Frank House, you know.

But that's touristy shit.

And this isn't?

They tilt the plank up, the lump slides and—splash into the water. Man overboard! The crew, dressed à la eighteenth century in baggy black knickers, gray shirts, and red bandannas, bow their heads. The local tourists bow their heads. We all fucking bow our heads. Listen to those bells mark time, the poor sucker's life reduced to a couple of chimes and a permanent saltwater bath. Ultimate purification. God's Final Solution.

Hey—did Jan Jacobsen ever really exist? Who was this goddamn sailor who died? Who's supposed to have died. Who the actors are pretending died. The lump of straw or sawdust or newspaper we're all pretending once breathed and now died and slid off into the harbor. Artificial death. Because it's two o'clock and the Maritime Museum's Summer 1997 schedule promises: "at two o'clock there shall be a burial at sea aboard the *Amsterdam,* a reconstruction of the ill-fated Dutch East Indiaman, wrecked on her maiden voyage to the Far East in 1749."

Silence on deck, then: clap clap clap. It's Dave.

Everybody glares, including an Asian—Chinese, maybe . . . no, there's something un-Chinesey about his face, not Japanese . . . looks sort of like the waiters in that Thai restaurant back home, even has the same boring white shirt and black pants, but he looks different. He glares at clapping Dave, then turns on his heels and swishes away. Hey, a prissy queen!

Some old lady with a fan—period actress in lace blouse, or fucked-up tourist?—scowls. Don't want me to ruin your little fantasy? "Sorry," Dave says to the actors, and he stops clapping. To the dozen junior tourists staring at him: "Don't mind me, kids, you're lucky bas—" The old lady scowls again; these fucking Dutch all understand English. "—lucky babies, all of you. Living in history. Clean, isn't it?" No plague, no pock marks, no scurvied toothless mouths, no unwashed sailors stinking of vomit and sweat; just the mild stink of one day's sweat beneath the sun—one day's, not three months', you wouldn't even know the difference because you never smelled a person gone three months without a bath, have you? Or three years. None of us have.

Dave leans over the ship's side. No dead body in sight. Nothing in sight. What do they do, drag the river bottom for the lump so they can use it again for the six o'clock show?

Lots of muttering in Dutch behind him. At him. Who gives a fuck what these cheese-eaters think? Europeans living through old history, sanitizing it as they go. For them everything is sunshine and lace.

One crewman plays the violin, another folds the flag, the mourning group disbands. Dave climbs from starboard to aft (aft to starboard?) pokes his head into a brick room with a grill, looks at dishes soaking in a wooden tub. Authentic re-creation of history. He turns, pauses, lifts camera to eye aaand—click! Wonder if they re-create anything at the Anne Frank House: a little dark-haired girl writing in her diary (forever writing in her diary, and by candlelight, probably, because of course she couldn't go out and write in the finger-pointing sunshine) and she hears church bells as usual, but then—a noise, a strange noise from the bookcase-entrance, and . . . Actor-soldiers storm in with fake bayonets to scare the tourists? Like that's exactly what happened in '44 or '45. Will we ever know for sure? Grandma thought she knew. Grandma in the camps.

Damn, what a hard time Dave gave Grandma all last year, after she died. Blaming her for his own shit. Hers too, sure, but so much for his own. He sees that now. And Chanukah—what a freak you are, Davey Boy, taking dead Grandma cruising with you around Boston. Look what it led to, you almost . . . Shit, forget it. Well, you're here now, that's all that counts. She always wanted to get you here. Although not just to the city.

Enough.

She wanted to get you to—

Enough!

A crewman Dave just photographed eases into a hammock and munches sunflower seeds, spits out mangled husks. Another actor, in clean white blouse and black velvet knickers—gotta be an officer—saunters over, talks to the sailor in the hammock. Come on, guys. Show us what life on the open seas was really like. You—yeah, you, officer—just look at that bulge in his crotch; he wants it, can't you tell? Ah, get out of the way, matey, let a real sailor show you how it's done. Sailor Dave, head wrapped in a black-and-white striped bandanna like some Russian babushka, a gold hoop through his pierced right ear (macho swabby or sissy fag?), green hula-girl tattooed on his left bicep, black eyepatch over left eye or right, depending on which half of the world he wants to hide from that day. Peg-leg Dave limping about, a long-tailed parrot perched on his shoulder, squawking, "Beware! Beware!" Captain Dave brandishing his cod-piece and bellowing, "Who wants some of this buried treasure? Aaaargh!" Dave as macho sailor. No, Dave as macho pirate terrorizing all men into submission. Yeah, Dave as pirate. As outlaw. Outlawed Pirate Dave.

He climbs below deck. Crew's quarters. Bunk beds. Damn ceiling's so low, you gotta bend over just to walk—"Hey, I bet that gave 'em lots of ideas after a couple months at sea." He says this out loud, not even realizing. The milling Dutch ignore him now. No other Americans here, none that he can tell.

Down one level lower, the cargo hold. High ceilings. A cavern.

Dave spots the Asian guy who glared at him up on deck; narrow eyes meet Dave's, then dart away. Ahah! So gaydar works here, too.

Dave saunters over to him, this slim man with dark skin and a cute, biteable ass, stands at his side, looks with him into a glass-covered crate full of Chinese porcelain nesting in straw. "A specimen of the cargo they would transport to Europe from China," the Asian says in British-accented English. "Then there were the spices. From Indonesia, naturally."

"Naturally." Ah, Indonesia. That's gotta be it . . . Hmm . . . Never fucked an Indonesian before.

They face each other. Dave takes one step closer so the Indonesian can feel his heat. "And what did the Dutch sailors take to Asia *for trade?*" Will the guy know this slang for macho men who "let" fags blow them?

"Silver and gold coins." The Indonesian clears his throat. "Textiles from Haarlem and Leiden."

Nah, he didn't get it. Or if he did, he's slapped on a perfect blank mask. Inscrutable.

"American, are you not?" the Indonesian asks.

"How'd you know?"

"Your accent, for one thing; clearly not British." The Indonesian's eyebrows lift in pride, "One has studied in London."

"Well bully for One." Dave applauds. "And you're Indonesian . . . are you not?"

A flinch. "One is *Dutch*." A swallow. "Those white sneakers give you away as American. And another clue as to your origin was your applause . . . upstairs, during the funeral service."

"Fake funeral."

"Quite, but even so . . . " The Indonesian sighs, and then, almost to himself and with a slight shake of his head, says, "American . . . " He extends his hand. "One is called Alexander."

"Dave." He shakes the light brown hand, holds it tight even after he feels Alexander trying to tug free, feels sweat on Alexander's palm, slick and warm. Then Dave lets the hand drop, turns away, saunters around the hold. A casual glance up at wooden beams lining the hull's inside, horizontal erections supporting this ship of men. Will the guy follow?

In a moment, Alexander's footsteps approach from behind. Not looking back, Dave climbs up on deck, squints at the sun. Alexander follows. Of course: no good boy can resist a bad one.

Dave spins around so as to catch Alexander off guard: "Wanna go somewhere and fuck?"

* * *

You must not say that naughty word . . .
You must not say that naughty word . . .
Amster-Amster- DAM! DAM! DAM!
Amster-Amster- DAM! DAM! DAM!
You must not say that naughty word.

* * *

a damn how they react. Fuck 'em they can't take a joke, the shmucks. Bunch of putzes. Dave takes another swig of his imported Heineken.

Just goes to show. Just goes to show.

He swivels on the bar stool, looks at the empty stools on either side, at the men leaning against the opposite wall, other men in T-shirts, but in black leather jackets with shiny metal zippers and snaps and studs designed to lend the jackets and the men who wear them an aura of danger and threat. But it's not real danger because this is Boston and here leather's just a twinkie-boy costume shed before bed. Dave's not wearing a leather jacket.

Each man in turn looks at Dave's left arm, then up at his burning eyes and away. Bunch of Jews. He clamps one eye shut, glares his open one at each of the men against the wall. The Evil Eye. Don't wanna look at me? If you look away you must be a Jew.

Ah, not really. They're not really all Jews. Not the blond ones with their cute upturned noses and bubble butts to match. It isn't only the Jewish men with their hairy chests—God, but Dave loves hairy chests!—who're looking at him strangely tonight. Gentiles are, too.

Dave loves that word, repeats it in his mind while swiveling on his bar stool: Gentile Gentile Gentile. Genteel. Refined and genteel. Oh so pinky-in-the-air genteel. Middle finger in the air genteel. Fuck-finger genteel. Fist-fucking genteel. He laughs. The uptight ones wanna be loosened the most. But gently. Yes, be gentle, Davey boy. "Be yentl," a blond, Norwegian trick once said to him. "Be Yentl." Dave laughs again, bounces up and down on the bar stool like a little boy at a soda fountain. "Hey, Yentl," he calls to the blond bartender, a small man with the tattoo of a snake's rattle curling around his neck, ending by the jugular. "What I wanna know, Yentl," Dave says, raising his voice to carry over the bass of the music, "is if the rattle's up by your throat, where the fuck's the snake's mouth?"

The bartender—Yentl—forces a tight smile. "Another, Dave?"

"You got it, Yentl. Shmentl, Bentl, Bonanafanafofentl—Yentl!" The non-Jewish men look at him because they don't understand. But the Jews understand. That's why they freak all to Hell. They nearly wish we all were Catholic so we'd have a Hell they could tell me to burn in, right guys? WE JEWS DON'T GOT NO HELL BUT WHAT'S HERE ON EARTH. Faggots. Dave would burn them all at the stake if only he could find his cigarette lighter. Not that he usually smokes; ever smokes; ever smoked before tonight; ever will again, he's sworn it, but tonight he needs to create smoke and flame. A pillar of smoke by day leading the ancient Hebrews through desert, a pillar of flame by night. One if by land, two if by—"Where the hell's my cigarette lighter?" Dave pats himself down, lingers over his nipples, pointy and sensitive beneath his T-shirt. He traces the flat, black leather straps around his left arm in case he stuck the lighter in there and forgot, then his pockets. "Yentl! My lighter!"

"Behind your beer bottle." Yentl moves the bottle aside, exposing the red plastic lighter that looks like an excited dick with a shiny tip about to spurt the wrath of God.

"Snake eyes!" Dave says, grabbing the lighter, pulling a half-crumpled cigarette from his back pocket and lighting up. "Ah. *Mechaieh*, as Grandma would say." Grandma with her face like a rubber mask, burst blood vessels spidering her nose. And the oversweet rose-scented perfume she'd wear as though always trying to camouflage a stench that wouldn't fade. Dead Grandma. "You know *mechaieh*, Yentl?" Yentl's busy with another customer. So fucking what? Dave'll listen to himself. "*Mechaieh's* an ice cold glass of milk on a hot July night on the fire escape of Grandma's Amsterdam Avenue fourth floor walk-up, Washington Heights, New York City, US of A, a few blocks from Yeshiva fucking University. Beautiful building. Looks Turkish with its minarets and domes but it's Jewish." Of course, the beautiful part wasn't for Grandma and Dave. She wouldn't take him to the big auditorium on Shabbos, no way, but to the small sanctuary with its old wooden tables and hard metal folding chairs and scruffy, bearded old men. Dave draws on the cigarette, coughs lightly. "Lots of tattoos there, Yentl. Ugliest fucking tattoos I ever saw." Or didn't see. Tattoos hidden under long shirtsleeves and suit jackets even in the hottest summer. Hidden, like Grandma's sparse hair, only sprigs of white fringe sticking out from beneath her curly red wig. Prayer shawl fringe. "*Tallis* fringe, Yentl. What a holy Grandma I had."

Noticing a stack of square white napkins on the bar, Dave knocks them over with the back of his hand. Yentl didn't see. Staring at the white napkins all over the black floor, Dave laughs. A Shabbos when he was eight years old or nine: standing in the small sanctuary, right in front of the curtained partition, the *mechitsah*, that separated the men's section from the women's; flipping pages in the *siddur* to amuse himself. "Old Mr. Katz sticks his wrinkled lightbulb nose into my business," Dave mumbles to his beer bottle. "Licks his crooked index finger with its cracked, yellowing nail and turns the pages of my prayer book—*my* prayer book—to put me in synch with everybody else. Only I don't wanna be in synch; I'm just flipping around for the hell of it. I look up and growl at him. Damn straight." Draw on the cigarette. "I fucking growl like a guard dog, a pissed German shepherd. Grrrrr. The man jumps back and I wanna laugh. Grandma sticks her hand through the curtain and yanks my hair. 'Ow!' I yell, and she yanks even harder. In front of all those old men with long beards, 'Mr. Katz has a tattoo!' "

"Hey, Yentl," Dave says, again raising his voice over the music. "You think Mr. Katz would let me lick away his tattoo now? Or how about you, Yentl? Let me lick your tattoo!"

"In your dreams," Yentl says, his smile friendly until he notices the napkins on the floor. Hah! He comes around the bar, stoops to pick them up, and Dave swivels so his crotch is right beside Yentl's bent head. Stroke that blond hair, Davey Boy, stroke it, stroke it good. Yentl swats Dave's hand away, returns to his position behind the bar.

"Grandma Hannah's dead, Yentl." An entire fucking month Dave's been putting on *tefillin,* wearing it in public. You're not supposed to wear it in public except in synagogue, every decent Jew knows that, but Dave is wearing it. IN YOUR FACE. Grandma Hannah wore short-sleeved dresses even in winter, revealing her tattoo to the world. Nothing made her happier than a fucking stranger in the subway asking about those seven digits on her left arm. Lectures in local Hebrew schools, at synagogue Sisterhood meetings. They even flew her over to goddamn Israel once to get an award for her work in never letting anyone forget.

Sticky Friday nights in summer, snack time on the fire escape; Dave's T-shirt and briefs—soaking wet. No air-conditioning because, according to Grandma, "we weren't meant for too much pleasure. We survived and that's enough. Alright, I lost your grandfather after the War, but at least we both survived the nightmare. Survival carries a price. We owe. Look up," she said between mouthfuls of banana cake. "Six million new stars in the sky. Six million new stars this century. Otherwise nothing makes sense."

"Have some milk, Grandma," Dave said in order to change the subject, that goddamn fucking every-single-night-of-the-week subject.

"Ah, the milk is cold, a *mechaieh*. Did I ever tell you . . ." Grandma reminisced for the millionth time about life in her *Fiddler-on-the-Roof* Belorussian *shtetl* before the War. Dave strained to catch glimpses of neighbors' televisions through their fire escape windows, to see sitcoms about families having fun. "Six million new stars, Daveleh-my-Adam." She always added "my Adam" to his name. "We need a new Adam more than a new king. Drink more milk. Eat more cake. Grow strong. Make Jewish babies. Did I ever tell you it's written that a woman who sees her great-grandchildren is guaranteed a place in Paradise?"

Dave looks up across the bar at one of the jockstraps dangling from the ceiling for decoration.

Her funeral was simple. A few old friends. At the cemetery, Mr. Katz fell to his knees. Something going on between them? A few shovels of dirt from the handful of mourners and it was over. Dave stayed to watch the workmen fill in the hole. Then he looked at his parents' headstones beside Grandma's plot. What would they think of him if they'd lived? Would they have wished to have more children? A different one instead of him?

Dave brings his smoldering cigarette butt to the leather wrapped around his left hand. Let the fucking butt slip, Davey Boy, and stub it out on your own skin. Dare you . . . double dare you. Singe the dark macho hairs poking between those bands of leather, smell the hairs burn, feel your skin sear.

But he holds the cigarette steady on the leather. Fucking coward. Takes a drag on the butt—"Khe, khe," he coughs. "Shit." Stubs it out on the beer bottle.

Standing, he leans against the bar. Sea legs before even leaving dry dock. A weave past the pool table, past wimpy fags in designer jeans and cute leather baseball caps, and he enters the back room—dark, but not pitch-black, shadowy—where the real men will be. Not an anything-goes back room, a cruising back room. Heavy cruising with pants-on fun. No back rooms like this in the *shtetl*. Dave's work boots scuff against the black floor. Vibrations of heels against concrete. The loud beat of the bass.

Shirtless men. Shirtless Dave. Smell of sex.

He leans against one of the black metal oil drums set up for atmosphere, stares at the black-painted cinder block wall opposite. No, he thinks to a fat man with a black mat of hair on his low-hanging paunch; I'm not looking at you, Grizzly Belly. And I'm not looking at you either, Big Tits—this to the hunk with a pumped up chest—although Dave does look at him, a thickly muscular man with a hooked Jewish nose. Dave rubs his hand along the leather circling his left arm like barber pole stripes. They should be looking at Dave. At Dave. At the anemic leather snake slithering around his left arm.

The morning after Dave's bar mitzvah, Grandma supervised his laying of *tefillin* for the first time. Sure he'd practiced with the synagogue cantor, but this was the first time that counted. Forever in your debt, Grandma. The *tefillin,* black leather cubes affixed to black leather straps, are holy, alright, contain the most important biblical quotations there are about God, including a reminder that God saved us from Egypt (Egypt, so why the hell not Germany?), and that He rewards the pious, punishes the wicked. The *tefillin* are so holy you aren't allowed to talk while wearing them, you can only pray. And if you drop them on the floor—whattaya think of this, Yentl? Yentl? Where the hell are ya, Yentl?—you gotta fast a whole day or donate money to charity.

That morning after his bar mitzvah, Dave slipped the hand *tefillin* over his left bicep, beside his heart, said the blessing while bending his left forearm and coiling the rest of the leather strap tightly around, seven times. Then he took the head *tefillin,* a black leather cube suspended on a black leather loop, said a blessing while centering the box over his forehead and placing the loop on his crown like the Geronimo headdress he'd worn as a child. He tightened it. Two long, black leather straps dangled down from behind his head; Grandma brought them forward to hang on his chest like braids. Back to the hand *tefillin,* winding the ends of the leather strap around his hand and middle finger in a pattern that spelled the Hebrew word "Almighty." Grandma inspected the fingers of his left hand to be sure they were properly bent, that his arm was bent, bound and uncomfortable, that he was bound to God, uncomfortable. "Now, finally, you're a good Jewish man—*Es iz mir arop a shteyn fun hartsn.*" It's a stone off my heart.

She left the room so he could pray. And in addition to saying the shema, the *shemoneh esreh* and the other prayers in the *siddur,* Dave prayed for God to make him just like other good Jewish boys. The same goddamn ritual for years, until college when Dave found himself still horny just for men—fuck the *tefillin!*

"So after Grandma's funeral," Dave mutters to no one in particular, "I start laying *tefillin* again." Every morning for a whole month, although without any goddamn prayers. "Maybe I should get a *tefillin* tattoo winding all around my arm?" Nah, Dave doesn't deserve a tattoo.

Big Tits, with his hooked Jewish nose and pumped up chest, saunters over to Dave in the shadowy dark. He doesn't say a word, just trails his finger along the black leather *tefillin* coils on Dave's left arm, kneels in front of Dave, rubs his nose on the black leather of Dave's hand, sniffs, licks the leather, licks Dave's hairy forearm.

Dave smiles down at the Jewish man, rubs the *tefillin*-wrapped fingers on top of the Jewish man's black-haired head, over the Jewish man's eyes and Jewish nose. Dave shoves his *tefillin*-wrapped fingers into the Jewish man's mouth. "You like that, Big Tits? Like that holy Jewish hand?"

The Jewish man looks up into Dave's eyes, sucks on Dave's *tefillin*-wrapped fingers until Dave pulls them out.

Dave unwinds the end of the *tefillin,* erases "Almighty" from his hand. He bends the man's head down to look away from him, to face the floor. Then Dave flicks the *tefillin* strap to whip the naked shoulders of the kneeling Jewish man. Then Dave flicks the *tefillin* strap to whip himself.

2

Alexander sips a koffie verkeerd, looks around April's, absolutely the most popular of the Reguliersdwarsstraat bars. Tasteful posters on the doors advertising this upcoming community event and that. Men dressing with self-respect, unlike elsewhere in Amsterdam. Rarely in leather here, not playing identity games, secure in their masculinities. A place to chitchat. No sleazy darkroom in back. Not, thinks Alexander, that one is averse to a little naughtiness now and then since all boys foray into seediness on occasion. Hormones demand attention, after all. Nature's call. (Although one has not responded to the call of the wild for some time now. Regrettably?) However. There are places and there are places. Human beings are creatures of intellect and rationality.

Oh look, it's Marcel—my, how he's firmed up that chest since . . . how long has it been? Chatting up some Nubian demigod with lips like a puckering fish. Imagine them around one's . . . *Bravo, mon cher—bon chance!* Sip sip sip. Now that's a handsome number over there—light brown hair, scruffy beard, big chest. Must be rather new here. Yummm. With his hand on—is that Hans? The dirty little tramp. Haven't seen him for ages. A bit plumper about the middle, are we? No longer able to earn what you used to for a night of fun, one imagines. Letting that hunk fondle your bum here, of all places. (Raised eyebrow of mock outrage—mock outrage!)

Jeroen never liked April's, preferred the more traditional, straight Dutch "bruin" bars with their brown wood wainscoting and cramped neighborhood feel. How easily he became bored here; did not at all share one's fascination with observing the rabble's flirtations. Whereas oneself, on the other hand . . . on more than one occasion, one ordered a beer for a stranger and instructed the bartender to say it had come from someone else entirely. "I just love being a catalyst for mischief!" he'd whisper and Jeroen would shake his head. And Alexander loved to catch as many glances as he could—"collecting them like shiny pebbles," Jeroen would say. Precisely! Jeroen wasn't as dumb as he appeared.

Alexander stretches at his small round table, smiles thinking of the modest collection of evening pebbles now in his pocket. That's all one wants this evening.

No, not as dumb as he appeared at all. Jeroen. Every neighbor's confidant, forever dispensing advisory solutions the way one now prescribes mild cough syrups—with ease and the certainty that one is, at least, doing no harm, and is, perhaps, actually helping. Tea in the morning for Jeroen, never coffee. Cheese with breakfast toast, but not ham. Supper—beer, never wine . . . Hours at the gym—"I do it for you." Cycling, weight lifting (Lord knows), swimming . . . Blue shirts and green. No rings on his fingers. Nor bells on his toes. Fungus on his toes. Deformed nails all cracked, brittle and yellow, pressing against one's calf or foot during the night, scraping . . . one could hardly bear it . . . How shameful a disgust. And here one's even a medical student! But one bore up later, did one not? Yes. Rallied one's resources and bore up admirably. Brought a degree of professionalism into one's home. Stiff upper lip and all that . . . Stop . . . Stop . . . One promised oneself not to. One promised! One must return to the spirit of the evening regardless of the effort required. One must. Post-haste! *Immédiatement!*

Where is that Dave? Sip sip sip.

How lovely in summer when April's outer, glass wall is moved aside, the boundary between in and out eliminated. One dislikes boundaries. Limitations that reduce choice, create a unifaceted life. Everyone knows the most valuable diamonds to be the multifaceted. Hmmm. That's quite a clever thought. One must remember it.

Ah, here he is; flushed and somewhat sweaty-faced. Probably a salty-tasting brow to be sure—oh, Alexander, you scamp, behave yourself! Should one stand and go greet him? No, let him make the approach.

"Sorry I'm late," says Dave, standing on the opposite side of Alexander's small round table. "Got a little lost on Rembrandt Square."

"Rembrandtplein." Dave's crotch is at Alexander's eye-level.

"God, this city's something else. I mean everybody's spilling outside. From here and from bars up and down the street. Like the whole block is one big gay bar."

"Do order yourself a beer at the bar, then come sit."

How totally amusing, this American. Product of a culture with no roots of its own, a hodgepodge of bits from this nation, smatterings from that. No wonder he's somewhat vulgar. But, truth to tell, there is a sexy air about him. He certainly does not strike one as the affectionate sort, so no need to worry about that. And he's only here a couple of weeks—no likelihood of entanglements. Perhaps one should have taken up his rather grossly phrased invitation of yesterday? Hmmm. Boorishness can be a source of fornicatory pleasure. However, one has limits.

Lusciously chunky buttocks, though—just look how his left gluteus maximus lifts and protrudes as he leans on his right leg at the bar . . . vice versa as he shifts. Now lift your beer . . . yes . . . commence your return . . . yes, a lovely soft bulge through the T-shirt. A chest formerly not unmuscular—a thin layer of fatty tissue suspended over muscle. Retention of a squarish shape. Echoes of a chest that was. Absolutely inviting nipple nibbles. With sharp incisors. Nyarrrrhhh. Fun!

But dangerous for a variety of reasons. "Have a seat. Comfortable?"

"Yeah, it's fine," says Dave.

"Shall I tell you a wicked joke?"

Dave grins in expectation.

"Why is American beer like screwing a whore on a houseboat?"

"I'm game. Tell me."

"They're both fucking close to water!"

Dave stares for a moment. Then he smiles. "Hey that's good. Didn't think you had it in you."

One loves entertaining rough-edged boys, so capable as one is of bringing out the civilization in them while they, in turn, bring out the . . . ahem . . . An entire . . . what?—ten minutes since one has thought of Jeroen? . . . boat ride tours of the canals as if we were tourists . . . how Jeroen loved water . . . visits to the Maritime Museum . . . Odd to have met Dave there, of all places . . .

Conversation. One must have conversation. "One is uncertain whether one is doing the right thing becoming a doctor." Hmm. Rather a private subject for mere chitchat. Oh well, the plank has been walked and the plunge taken.

"What?" says Dave, unlocking his eyes from those of a husky man across the street.

"Are you cruising or simply perusing?"

Dave flashes Alexander a mysterious sort of smile.

"While you're out with *moi?*" Alexander asks. "Is that polite?"

"Depends. Is this a date? I don't know how to tell with you people."

Alexander's skin feels suddenly hot; he narrows his eyes, knows that Dave would describe them as almonds. "And by that you mean exactly what, pray tell?"

"I don't know what's normal for gays here. I mean, you and I meet on that dumb boat and I ask if you wanna go fuck—"

"A Prince Charming if ever one was."

"—you turn me down, so I think okay, that's it, but then you say let's have a drink tomorrow at this April's place and you'll take me to some gay belly dance thing. Is this a date? I don't know how to read you."

"So it's either a date with implications for immediate gratification or . . . what? A platonic waste of time?"

"What else could it be?"

Alexander smiles to project his own air of mystery; actually, he does not know the question's answer.

"You being a cock tease?" Dave asks.

"As one was saying, one has been questioning the wisdom of attending medical school."

"Yeah, I think you're being a cock tease."

"In case you haven't noticed, the subject of conversation has been changed." What is it with this American? No sense of propriety or social grace. "Spending afternoons with the lower echelons of society."

"Like me?"

"The reference was to oneself as physician in hospital."

"Never fucked in the mud, Alexander? It's fun."

"As a matter of fact, after a particular rainstorm—no, never mind . . ." There. He thinks he's so very much a man of experience and that one is totally *ingenu.* "The rich know preventive medicine. But the poor? One finds oneself treating the poor hour after hour. Immigrants mostly. And one cannot really change their lives. A few pills, that's all."

"You pissed because you can't fix them or because you gotta deal with them in the first place?"

"What a nasty little question." Alexander sets his white coffee cup down on its saucer with a harsh clack. "You've an odd way of being friendly."

"I'm nicer when I know it's a date."

"When you think you're going to get something carnal." Alexander sneers.

"I always think I'm gonna get something carnal."

"You must be frequently disappointed."

Dave chuckles. "You're such a little fucker."

"Don't you just hope? . . . So tell me, Dave, what is it that *you* do?"

"Used to live off my dead parents' life insurance."

"Oh." How awkward.

"But for the last year, I've been living off Grandma's."

"Oh." Does that make him unemployed lower class or playboy upper class?

"Any other questions?"

"No. None at all." Terribly awkward. And his smirk suggests he's enjoying the awkwardness. Alexander lifts his coffee cup, holds it over the table in a motion of toasting: "So, cheers or whatever it is you Americans say."

"Over the lips and through the gums, get ready to gag—here Dave cums!"

Gross, indeed. "Well come then, Dave; a brief trolley ride and we'll be there."

Ten minutes of relative silence with Dave seated on one side of the trolley aisle, Alexander on the other. Enough time to compose oneself. Ready. A brief walk, then in past the bouncer at the COC's front door, down a hallway displaying community posters and brochures, into the dance room.

"This music is wild!" Dave yells.

"One adores the woodwind trills." Alexander points toward the center of the crowd, at a short Moroccan man pivoting in circles and, with arched back, wiggling his hips. "Modernized belly dance."

"How can he move his ass so fast?" Dave asks.

"Practice, one supposes."

"Must be a great fuck."

Alexander sighs. "Can't you think of *anything* else?"

"What's the point?"

Some coquetry and devilish banter are amusing, but one has one's limits. "May one suggest the balcony?" Alexander gestures above the bar. "It's in shadows, but might offer a different perspective. Pardon, but time for one to mingle." Rude, perhaps to abandon him. Not perhaps—definitely. However, Alexander was gracious enough to bring him here. And it's not as though one would leave the community center without him. "Is it a date?"—how rude a question. Must one decide in advance? It's only a date in retrospect; if one has felt that nearly forgotten twinge.

Dave certainly is not behaving as if this were a date. Brazenly cruising other men. Looking is one thing, but cruising is quite another. Any self-respecting gay boy recognizes the difference. And realizes it only polite to invite one's host to dance. But, obviously, one has no reason to expect politeness from Dave. So what? One does not need politeness from him, anyway. Although the mix of polite and piggish might bear certain appeal. Perhaps Dave does not even know how to dance.

There's Ali on the dance floor—wave wave—shimmying those luscious shoulders of his. Has he lost some weight? Oh dear, one hopes not. Absolutely horrendous Dutch accent, that Ali, but one must give credit for effort. Yummy Turks. Look at those two, Ali and his friend, bum to crotch under the strobe lights, twisting left together and right. Their sexy prominent noses! To die for, absolutely to die for. One must not stay away so long again. Dark-haired, swarthy-skinned sex machines, "whores of the Middle East," as everyone calls them, with wives at home. Ali's a dear . . . that blush-inspiring invitation some months ago . . . six months ago? . . . no, no—a year ago, right after . . . a proposition one now regrets not having accepted . . . but no, one behaved quite correctly . . . not in the community center's toilet. There are places and there are places. One comes here to dance, to forget the outside world's games and manipulations. To forget a good many things . . . until one has regained the strength to remember . . . To socialize, yes. To mix interculturally. Yes, one should attend with greater frequency so as to make these Mediterranean immigrants feel welcome in broader Dutch society; that's the least a native-born Dutchman can do. But no provision of service in toilets. One has one's limits.

Yet—how one detests limits while respecting them all the same. Where would society be without limits? Imagine if all humans were to indulge their impulses like beasts. Murder and mayhem. Sex on street corners. No one would accomplish a thing. Limits on behavior are necessary. However. Limits on definition? By no means. Why, for example, should one be entitled to define these Turks? Their accents define them. It's not for another to say who they are: more Dutch, now that they're living here, or more Turkish because that's just obviously who they are? Not for one to say . . . My, how terribly difficult to construct a consistent worldview. Yet one needs infrastructure, girders to clutch when in the midst of free fall.

Alexander inhales deeply the room's cologne *au naturel* of cigarette smoke and sweat. Ahhhhh. There go the Algerians again, in one of those sexy line dances. Muscular arms on muscular shoulders. Oh my, enough to make one—my heavens, what is that Dave doing?

An Arab man in khaki fatigues is leading Dave onto the dance floor. Leaner than Dave and with a sweet smile, yes, but gaps between his teeth, a too-wide, almost frog-like mouth. So why does Dave go with him? Especially when one is much cuter. A different sort of cute, of course, but even so. Well, fancy that! Dave is belly dancing. Hah! How right one was. His attempt to weave his hips in a figure eight . . . he appears nearly spastic . . . My word, what's this? The Arab tugging up Dave's T-shirt, lifting it off over his head? And Dave allowing him? No resistance whatsoever! Base. Common . . . Look how Dave lets that frog-mouthed Arab rub his hands all along his sides . . . hairy, sweaty sides . . . Up and down. Arab palms. Up and down. Palms flat against Dave's chest now, and against his mature ring of belly. Look how this American loves to have his nipples pinched; tilting his head back. Oblivious that all eyes are upon him. Just like the time Jeroen coaxed one to drop one's pants in that abandoned Zaanse Schans windmill: moments of lustful joy, then a mix of screams and scoldings from rather matronly onlookers. Oglers. Perverted voyeurs. How mortifying! No shame whatsoever. None. For God's sake! This is not some darkroom or Jack-Off Night at the Stablemaster Bar! If that's what you want, Mr. Dave, go to the Warmoestraat leather bars! There are places and there are places!

One refuses to watch this, absolutely refuses. A quick spin, a march to the bar, a shot of Oban Malt Scotch Whiskey in one gulp. Enough. One's evening has been irreparably sullied. Time to leave. One will be gentleman enough to wait for the American and show him which night bus to take from Dam Square to his hotel. But that will be the extent of it. Americans. "Whores of North America." (One's own new appellation, and highly apt.)

So where is that Dave? The Algerians are still at it . . . and Ali . . . the pivoter . . . an assortment of Iranians . . . a sprinkling of Dutch—

that is, of native-born Dutch . . . But no Dave . . . Movement over the bar, on the balcony.

"One does not believe it. One just does not believe it." True, in the shadows and against the back wall, but still—on the balcony. Completely visible to any who might look up. The frog-mouthed Arab's face is buried in Dave's crotch!

How dare he. How dare he! Vulgar and nothing less than pig-like, rutting in the mud. No sense of decorum. The toilet's more acceptable than this public display!

As Dave shudders, Alexander cannot break his unilateral stare.

The Arab lingers there on his knees, nuzzles nose against crotch, then pulls his head back, allows Dave's softness to pop from his mouth; he tucks Dave back into his jeans, stands, leans in for a kiss. Dave dodges the lips, but gives the Arab a hug. Down the stairs, Arab first. Off he goes to the bar. And Dave, spotting Alexander, heads straight for him. "Now this is what I call a gay community center!"

"One cannot believe you did that. One simply cannot believe it."

"Hey. Don't wrinkle your petticoats, girlfriend. An Arab wants to blow me—you think I'm gonna stop him? Loved the feel of his hot desert mouth on my Jewish dick."

"There are places and there are places!"

"And every place is the right one for sex."

"Not at all. The opportunity for Jewish domination of an Arab notwithstanding."

Dave jabs an index finger into the air at Alexander's wide, flat nose. "Who the fuck you think you are telling me what to do, you little gook?"

Alexander's eyes burn, his cheeks, the juncture of esophagus and stomach. How dare this American speak this way? How dare he! "Goodbye!" Alexander turns away.

"You're jealous. I get it—you're jealous."

Alexander turns back. "What?!"

Dave's face appears suddenly lighter. "You're jealous because I had sex with somebody other than you. So this was a date, after all."

"Do not make one laugh."

"Hey, if you'd told me it was a date, I wouldn't have screwed around on you. I did ask, you know."

"You Mediterranean types might all be motivated by your passions and jealousies, but we Nordic types are more civilized."

"Nordic type?" Dave's eyes stretch as wide as two 2½-guilder coins. "You?"

"One was born in Amsterdam." Alexander's voice lowers in volume. "So one is as Dutch as anyone in this room."

Dave looks around at Ali, at the Algerians, the Iranians, at the frog-mouthed Arab. He purses his lips as if to keep from laughing, but a guffaw spurts out.

Alexander continues to feel offended, wants to hold onto his rage and humiliation, to hide behind them as behind an earthen dike in the face of a tidal wave, yet . . . he must admit: a stupid analogy to have made. A counteranalogy. He gives a modest chuckle, a face-saving one containing the teensiest relief at the discovery that his reasoning, and therefore his rigidity, is imperfect. "You're disgusting," Alexander says, meaning it, but sounding as though he doesn't. "You're awful. Absolutely awful."

"Yeah, I am," says Dave, his laugh now gone. "Absolutely awful. But I'm learning to live with me." Dave's face blanks for a moment, then a smile returns a bit too quickly, as if remembered at the last moment. Dave places a hand on Alexander's waist, moves in close. "So, Alexander, I still have some energy if you wanna go fuck."

* * *

Humpty Dumpty sat on a wall.
He sucked and he fucked and had a real ball.
All the King's horses and all the King's men
Took turns screwing Humpty again and again.

Little Jack Horner sat in a corner, jerking his dick with his hand.
Along came a spider, slid—lubed—like a glider:
The tightest damn fuck in the land.

* * *

Seated on his cloth sofa beside the brown leather oxfords, Dave scratches himself—his crotch through his green jogging shorts, his bare, hairy paunch. He twirls a pinky in his dry belly button, leans forward to the coffee table, presses the remote control mute button so he can hear himself think. Shhhh to the Olympics, the 1996 Centennial Games. Shhhh to the muscular gymnasts. Hunky men swinging their legs over pommel horses, toes pointed way into the air. Hunky men on the high bar—they shoot their legs into the air, but where they land they know not where. None of them can stick a fucking landing. "What's the matter, assholes, you blind?" Doesn't matter: after the men's routines, their gray-haired, grinning coaches hug 'em tight anyway, hug the musclemen. Older men grabbing the Olympic youths. Recapturing their own youths. Rejuvenating through the gymnasts, those lucky gymnasts, hugged by their gray-haired coaches with sagging bellies and fleshy tits.

Dave lifts the shoes from the sofa to his lap, his father's brown leather wing-tipped oxfords with plastic-tipped laces; hard, thin laces Dave has already pulled loose from the eyelets into loops, hoops through which he now pokes his fingers, in and out. Rank-smelling, bitter-smelling brown leather oxfords. Loose loops. Loose hoops. In and out. The cracked rubber heels scratch the skin of his thighs. Dave rubs the lace-covered, leather tongues against his still-soft crotch.

The acrid pungency fills his nostrils. He smells it, stares at the *yahrtzeit* candle on top of the black TV, the off-white wax in a glass. Such a tiny flicker all the way across the room, across the years, but it carries the acrid burning smell as of the brown autumn leaves Dad would rake from the front yard into the gutter and set ablaze. The *yahrtzeit* candle in a glass.

No, not the real anniversary of his father's death—exactly six months away, as far away from the true date as possible. Still, today feels like Dad's real death day, even though it's not, feels like it is in the burn behind Dave's eyes, the medicine ball filling his stomach.

Yahrtzeit candle in a glass.

Fucking looks like a specimen glass.

Shut up, Davey Boy, show respect.

Off-white wax that will burn twenty-four hours, wax the sallow color of a dead man's face, dead skin melting in heat, dripping. An anniversary-of-death candle. "Happy Anniversary, Dad!" Dave slaps himself across the face, hard. "Don't be an idiot." He shoves the shoes off his lap, back onto the sofa.

Another gulp from his half-drunk glass of Heineken, then— SLAM!—glass onto table. His fifth glass. Sixth glass? Seventh glass? How many times has he gone to piss during tonight's Olympics? Another handful of peanuts from the bowl beside the shoes on the sofa.

Dave chews and swallows all but one, which he spits into the beer. Hear the plop. "Yeah, plop. Plop plop fizz fizz. Drink your beer then take a whiz." Dave laughs and, with his bare left foot, kicks the remote control off the coffee table—it lands on the green cotton area rug without the crash Dave was listening for.

Gotta piss. Starts for the bathroom then stops, turns. Dave wants God to watch him piss. Back to the living room, to the glass doors. Slides them open. A woosh of August humidity slaps Dave in the face. Out to the balcony, the acrid smell following on a billow of conditioned air. At the balcony's edge, the very edge, on tiptoe over the guard rail, Dave pulls down his green jogging shorts, aims at a patch of dry August dirt beside the steamy parking lot tar. He lets loose with a grunt, looks up, "Take that, God," he says now.

"Bye, pee," he used to say at age three when learning to stand at the toilet, learning to hold his penis like Dad. How to pee like a man— one of the few things Dad had time to teach him. "Bye, pee," and Davey would wave bye-bye. Dad always waving at Davey from the elementary school's basketball court, Dad playing with other suburban dads while all the little boys watched. One of Dave's strongest memories. Narrow-hipped Daddy leaping high in his white sneakers. Daddy in sweat-stained T-shirt, dribbling the basketball. Broadshouldered Daddy all sweaty under his arms, sweaty on the center of his chest, the center of his back. Sweat pasting Daddy's curly brown bangs to forehead. Dribble dribble: a steady rhythm as other men hovered round, trying to reach below Daddy's small-pot-bellied waist, to reach Daddy's ball, to get their hands on Daddy's big orange ball. Steady bounce. Dribble dribble, pivot in sneakers, side to the men, back and ass to the men, dribble dribble. Daddy moving his big orange ball from left hand to right hand, protecting it. Then the big leap, a leap so high that Daddy's big white sneakers soar a thousand feet into the air, a million feet above every other dad's head, those amazing athletic Daddy feet—Shoot, Daddy, shoot! Get it in! Big orange ball sails right through the hoop. Score! Davey clapping at Daddy's basket. Thumbs up from Davey, thumbs up from Daddy. Daddy's heaving chest. Daddy's tired grin at Davey, "My Number One Fan." Daddy giving Davey a hug. Daddy sweaty and smelling like a dad. Victory beer for Daddy, victory soda pop for Davey. Daddy and Davey. Davey and Daddy. Davey's last memory before his birthday. Daddy and Mommy in a car wreck and fire. Daddy dead.

Mommy covered with burns, in the hospital for two weeks. Mommy dead. Mommy and Daddy gone to God.

"Who the hell is God to take them?" Dave asked Grandma when he was fourteen and angry on his birthday. Grandma answered with a slap across Dave's cheek, a slap that brought blood to the corner of Dave's mouth, which he then opened wide, bearing his teeth at Grandma, vampire-like. Slap number two. *"Du farkirtst mir di yorn!"* You'll be the death of me! Strict Grandma, religious Grandma, well-meaning Grandma who never tried to make Davey feel guilty about his parents' death. Oh, no. Not Grandma. "Me? I should make you feel guilty? What satisfaction would such an old woman as me get from blaming a six-year-old boy for the death of his father-my-only-son? My grandson, I should blame? From the camps I crawled out on bloody knees so I could be accused of such things? Shame on you, shame on you." And then, turning her head and lowering her voice: "My homemade banana cake wasn't good enough for him; had to have a chocolate birthday cake from Goldman's Bakery."

Hey, who's that? Dave hadn't noticed him down in the parking lot before he pissed. A little kid, six or so in a red and white striped T-shirt, like Dave's childhood favorite. Brown hair and freckles, an upturned nose and scabby chin, scraped, probably during a fall over wrongly tied laces, a fall of the naïve, the innocent. Shit, might have sprayed him by accident. "Hey kid!" Dave yells down.

The boy looks up, stares at Dave, brings hand to open mouth—in shock, Dave thinks, in wonder, in admiration, perhaps, in glee at watching a grown man up on a balcony with his pee-pee showing. Then the boy darts away.

Where'd that little fucker go? One palm still wrapped around his dick, Dave lifts the other one, splays the fingers out over his eyes, as though the glare were shining from above instead of from the wind-shields below. Dave spots him crouching in the waves of heat radiating up from a green car; the boy is a wave of heat, hazy, an unclear face surrounded by a rainbow halo. Dave, encountering an angel in the desert, an innocent to watch over him, a sign of approval from God; but after Dave squints, the halo disappears and all he sees is a child in Dave's favorite little-boy T-shirt. "Hey, give me back my shirt!" and he lets loose another stream of yellow, away from the kid, onto the dirt Dave has already muddied. The little boy bubbles and squeaks like Irish sausage in a pan.

Daniel M. Jaffe 23

"This time, Miller, you've gone too far!"

It's Les, the superintendent. Where did he come from? "Les is more! Or is it 'More is Less?' " Dave yells down at the red-faced, fist-hurling man, yells and shakes his dick, hoping the final drops will land smack on the superintendent's head; but in the shimmers of heat, Dave can't tell. Maybe they evaporate—Dave's sacrifice to God?

The thin man mutters to the boy—Dave hears "mother" and "trustees"—hustles him inside the building. Big fucking deal. So the trustees won't let him piss from his balcony again. "Big fucking Goddamn deal."

Dave pulls up his green jogging shorts just as Les rushes out of the building. Behind him strides a pudgy, red-headed woman in pink shorts and yellow T-shirt, a white towel in one hand, the scabby-chinned little boy in tow in the other. "There he is!" Les shouts.

"Did that man show you his pee-pee?" the woman demands from the child.

The boy looks up at Dave; Dave blows him a kiss. The boy's face is blank.

"Answer me!" says the mother, her voice rising, the panic on her face rising.

"Calm down, lady, you'll bust a gut," Dave calls down.

Again she asks her son: "Did that man show you his pee-pee? Answer me!"

The little boy picks at the scab on his chin, looks at the muddy puddle, up at Dave, shakes his head, "No."

Dave wants to take the little boy in his arms and rock him and cuddle him and protect him from every grown-up danger in the world. He wants to peel the scab off the little boy's chin, to scrape it off with his teeth, to chew it, munch it, taste the boy's innocent blood, to heal him. To be him.

"But I saw him!" Les says.

"Are you sure?" the woman asks both him and the boy.

Both nod.

She wipes the white towel across her forehead, under her arms, sets a hand on the boy's shoulder. "My son doesn't lie," she says to Les. "I don't know what your problem is, making up a thing like that."

"Then how do you explain this?" Les points at the muddy puddle.

The mother's hand slips off her son's shoulder and Dave sees the question on her face.

The boy looks up at Dave, back to the puddle, says, "I did it." The little boy says this.

"You?" says Les.

"You?" says the mother.

You? thinks Dave.

"No, it's not true," Les says. "He's ly—"

Her glare shuts him up. To her son: "But, honey, why? We're right inside. The toilet's right inside."

The boy shrugs and in that shrug, that honest inability to explain his actions even to himself—his lie to himself—Dave sees his own reflection.

"Your father won't like this. Not one little bit." And, to Les: "Neither will the Trustees."

"But—!"

Up at Dave, she says, "Sorry, mister." Poking a thumb at Les, "This one's been out in the sun too long."

"Go easy on him," Dave says, first meaning Les, then meaning the boy. "Boys will be boys." The greatest compliment Dave can give.

"Inside, young man. We'll just see later what your father has to say about this."

Dave hates himself.

Les shakes his fist at Dave, then follows the woman and child inside.

Back into his apartment, cool air, sliding glass door closed and locked, back onto the sofa. Dave wonders if the little guy will suffer punishment because of him. Hell, he thinks, it's just water. What can a father do to a little boy for water? He'll probably laugh it off, tussle the kid's hair for being such a little macho pisser. The boy'll be okay. Sure he will.

He pictures the little boy smiling up, happy that Dave showed him adults can be free and have fun, that men can be free, that pee-pees can be displayed in sunlight, that grown-ups can do naughty things. But then the little boy frowns at Dave, grimaces in fear, tells a lie, not to protect Dave, but to protect himself from vengeance by such a crazy, dangerous grown-up neighbor who pisses from rooftops in daylight, who causes good little boys to be belt-whipped by righteous fathers. What evil has Dave done now?

You fucker. You goddamn fucker.

Dave sticks a single peanut into his mouth, sucks the salt off it, spits it into his beer and listens to the sound. This time, he thinks, it's more "pop" than "plop." Pop goes the peanut. Pop goes the weasle. The weasle goes pop. Pop? Dave looks at the TV screen, at the coaches, squints to see more clearly. Weightlifters. Popeye. Bulging-muscled, spinach-eating Popeye. Pop in the eye of the beholder. Pop's in the eye of the beholder. "Hug those coaches, boys," Dave mutters to the TV.

Dave hated team sports in high school. Didn't mind letting himself down but hated disappointing the other guys on the team, and Mr. Billings, the gym teacher. Dave dropped fly balls, Dave struck out, Dave served volleyballs into the net, Dave fumbled, Dave fouled. Dave could tumble well on the mats, both forward and backward, but that was all and who the hell cared? When adjusting the height of the parallel bars, he caught his pinky finger between metal tube and wooden casing—six stitches; nearly castrated himself on the pommel horse; couldn't hold a position for a millisecond on the rings; felt too scared to do more than hang on the high bar.

He tried the rope once. Hadn't planned to, feared the rope, knew he lacked the upper body strength to haul himself, with his wide hips and baby-fat heavy ass, up that rope. But the school's tubby principal had shown up, and this was Dave's chance to inspire pride in Mr. Billings, a husky ex-football player with a muscular-turned-soft chest Dave licked and bit and squeezed in his jerk-off fantasies. So. Dave, in regulation white T-shirt, regulation white shorts, white socks and sneakers, grabbed hold of the rope as he'd watched other boys do, right hand over left; he jumped up, snaked right leg around the rope, pressed left sneaker against the rope against right sneaker, and pulled. To Dave's surprise, he moved upward. "Good boy," said Mr. Billings, suddenly proud Mr. Billings. "That a boy." Tingling warmth rushed from Dave's crotch to the top of his head. Dave again pushed with feet and pulled with hands, felt the hard rope thick in his hands, the rough, coarse, ribbed, French-ticklered dangling prick he was determined to master for Mr. Billings. Grab. Look up. Pull. Push. Hand over hand, fist over fist clenching that thick hard rope, that long rope rubbing against Dave's crotch. Grab and yank that hard rope. Grab and . . . Just before reaching the top, Dave felt a burst of weariness, a sudden realization of what he was doing, exhaustion. "Don't push," Mr. Billings called up. "You did great. Don't need to go all the way. Come on down."

In bed that night, unable to masturbate at thoughts of Mr. Billings, Dave wondered at his own stupidity. Why hadn't he thought just to reverse the motion, to push the rope with his hands, to move his hands one beneath the other, to clamp the thick rope with his feet for balance? He'd seen other boys do it. "Come on down." No, Davey wasn't so stupid as to jump down from so many feet (ten feet? fifteen feet? twenty feet? how many feet?) in the air, but he was stupid enough— he screamed as he slid down the thick hard rope, as he burned palms and right thigh raw.

Now Dave looks at the shoes. *Yahrtzeit.* Respects to Dad. "Don't be an idiot."

On every death anniversary, Grandma would take Davey to synagogue to recite *kaddish.* Every year, year after year, *yahrtzeit* candle for Dad, and *kaddish.* Two weeks later, *yahrtzeit* candle for Mom, and *kaddish.* Candles and *kaddish.* "Candles and *kaddish,*" Dave sings on the sofa, "candles and *kaddish*—go together like a horse and carriage!" Dave slaps himself again.

No *kaddish* after Grandma died two months ago, no more ancient Aramaic glorification of a God Dave has never been sure he believes in, maybe fears, but does not like. Yet here it was, the half-year-away-from-Dad's-real-*yahrtzeit,* the real *yahrtzeit* that was also Dave's birthday, here was Dad's brand-spanking-new *yahrtzeit,* Dad's new deathday as declared by Dave. Dave had to do something. Something special for Dad. So—Dad's shoes, the only Dad-clothes Davey was able to sneak out of the cartons before Grandma gave them all away to charity, Dad's shoes out from the back of Dave's closet, polished now with Dave's very own T-shirt and spit. And the *yahrtzeit* candle and the Centennial Games.

Dave sees, against the flames of Dad's candle, old shadows of him and his Dad, shadows which never were except in his mind. Dave drinks and sees the shadows form into clear, interlocking silhouettes. "Don't be an idiot!" He hurls the beer bottle across the room, crashes it against the wall behind the TV. "Shit! Shit! Shit!"

Beer drips down the wall behind athletes and Dad's candle and Dave thinks of the idea that has been evolving over time, nudging him at night when he turns away from the shadows in bed, an idea that feels right, but has always struck him as frighteningly strange, more an impulse than a thought, a thought shaped by impulse, an impulse and idea rising like gray smoke from char.

Sniffing the shoes deeply, he smells their bitterness, the candle's acrid pungency, looks around to reassure himself that nothing's on fire. The *yahrtzeit* candle. Would Dad like the idea?

What idea?

You know.

"Don't be an idiot."

Doesn't matter; the shoes are just here to watch TV, that's all.

Like shoes can really watch TV.

Maybe not, but they can watch you. They can see that you've become a big strong man. That you know how to take aim, to sink a basket for Dad.

Dave puts down the Heineken, lifts his father's brown leather wing-tipped oxfords with loosened laces looped over their tongues, sets them on the floor. Dave's chest heaves as he stares down at them. Dad and Davey. Davey and Dad. He raises hands to face, presses thumbs hard against eyes, hard until he sees colors, sees red, smells fire. "Don't be a fucking idiot!"

Eyes closed, he pictures himself slipping off his green jogging shorts, kneeling over the open mouths of Dad's shoes, kneeling and stroking himself hard.

Eyes still closed, he watches himself stroke and stroke, thinks of muscles and bald spots and toes pointed in the air, of soft-bellied coaches and Olympic hugs, of soft-titted Mr. Billings and cocky young gymnasts, of proud proud Dads. Dave thinks of afterward, of how he'll slip his naked feet into Dad's brown leather shoes, how he'll feel his own cold semen on the inner soles of Dad's brown oxfords, on the balls of Dave's feet and the undersides of his toes: Dave's semen seeping and soaking into the soles of Dad's brown leather wing-tipped oxfords, Dave's semen mixing with Dad's ancient sweat—sweat from heat and walking and working and brown nylon socks. Two men's fluids mixing in bitter-smelling leather, merging in cracked soles, leather and sweat and cum. Two men's fluids. Two men's bodies; two men's souls. Half the same body; half the same soul. Sweat and cum. Father's and son's. Dave's and his Da—

3

Following on Alexander's heels down Kinkerstraat, Dave is surprised and excited at the invitation to have sex. Finally. Sure, the invitation was indirect, but hey, maybe it just wasn't in Alexander to come right out and beg. Finally realized that his hanging-out-but-not-putting-out was making Dave lose interest; there's only so much energy a guy can channel into conquest before the prize stops feeling worth the trouble.

Not that Alexander's really a prize. Too skinny. Never fucked an Indonesian before, that's all. No Thais, no Vietnamese. Dave heard that during the Vietnam War, Vietcong whores would hide razor blades up their cunts so when American GI's fucked them—sliced deli thin. Danger and risk make sex fun. Not that fucking Alexander would be particularly dangerous, he was sort of a prissy wimp. Pretty though. A tight ass, probably. Worth it just for the novelty. Another notch, Dave thinks, on his prodigal bedpost—proverbial.

Alexander turns a corner, out of the sunlight. Dave follows into the shade and, smacked in the face by buzzing hubbub, he stops. An outdoor market. And that smell? Cumin, cinnamon, God knows what else.

They walk past melon stands and pepper stands—green, red, yellow—with as many colors, Dave thinks, as the faces in the crowd. Alexander lives here?

As they wind their way through, Dave stops to watch women in gray robes and headdresses shake purple eggplants beside their ears, thump them, sift through mounds of brown lentils and pink ones. "Arabs?"

"Turks mostly," Alexander says. "Some Moroccans and Algerians."

"Look like tanned nuns in . . . whattaya call it . . . wimples."

"Trust me, they're not."

"And those over there—"

"Kindly refrain from pointing; one lives here."

"—those blacks behind the brown dildo pile. African?"

"Surinamese. With sticks of yucca, if you please—a Caribbean root vegetable."

"Their bananas don't look ripe." Wink.

"Plantains. They're supposed to be green."

Distracted by a jangle, Dave turns and looks. "What's that thing?"

"One of our *pierementen*," Alexander says with a proud smile. "Street organs."

About seven feet high, ten feet long; pale green front with gold curlicues; yellow and red roses painted on; a window curved like a grin of tin pipes; the whole thing on covered-wagon wheels. "Out of a cartoon," Dave says. A man in a white smock wheels the overgrown toy slowly through the crowd while it plays piccolos, cymbals, drums; another guy, unshaven and with several teeth missing, jiggles a metal cup, collecting coins. "Belongs in a circus or Disneyland."

"Not at all. A traditional feature of Dutch marketplaces. You Puritan Americans are forever separating fantasy and reality; no ability to blur boundaries."

"Wanna bet?" Another wink.

"Here we are."

Behind a stall of T-shirts hawked by a white woman, Dave watches Alexander fumble with keys in a front door—nervous, maybe, about the sex? That's good, that's real good; Dave likes to be the one in control. Then up a steep, winding, narrow staircase to the third floor. All the while, he watches the wiggle of Alexander's small ass. Mmmmmmmmm, probably a tight fuck. Dave wants to grab or slap or pinch, but controls himself—if he embarrasses Alexander in public, the priss'll get mad and change his mind.

As soon as they're inside and Alexander shuts the apartment door, Dave shoots out his right arm and, like a frog tongue wrapping around a fly, encircles Alexander's waist. He presses crotch to ass, bites the dark neck.

Alexander jabs an elbow into Dave's ribs and pulls harshly away. "Just what do you think you're doing?"

"Getting started, you little fuck." Dave massages his ribs—is this guy into rough stuff? Hmmmm . . . who'd o' thought? He reaches out again, but Alexander steps back, stumbles, bangs into a high, dark wood wardrobe.

"How dare you grab me that way!"

"What?"

"Keep away from me!"

"What the fuck is it with you and your mixed signals?"

"What mixed signals? Are you insane?"

"Last night I say I still have energy if you wanna fuck and you give one of your mystery smiles then say no thanks—AGAIN—but how's about I come to your place tomorrow afternoon for tea."

"So?" says Alexander.

"So?" says Dave.

"The invitation was for tea."

"Oh sure, you said 'tea,' but that's a code-word—you know, 't-room?' "

"What are you talking about!"

"T-room sex. Toilet sex."

"One did *not* invite you here to have sex in one's toilet!"

"Duhhh! But you did invite me over for 'tea,' and who the hell drinks tea in the middle of the afternoon? This isn't England."

"One said 'tea' and one meant 'tea.' "

Dave stares at Alexander's flared nostrils, heaving chest, clenched fists. Whatever the punk meant before, he's serious now. Doesn't want it. At least not from Dave. What a weird little shithead. Dave'd never turn anyone down. If you don't like the guy then shut the lights or stick a paper bag over his head or flip him face down onto the bed, but don't ever miss a chance to fuck.

Miss Priss, alright. Maybe he really meant "tea." Or maybe he's just a cock tease. Fuck it. "You want I should go?"

A moment's hesitation, then, "One invited you, a foreigner, into one's home. For a libation. You're a guest and you're welcome to stay. For *tea,* T-E-A—"

And what if Dave doesn't feel like staying? Shit!

"—and if you behave yourself like a gentleman, and if we find ourselves able to engage in civilized conversation, perhaps, just perhaps—"

Dave should leave. He should just walk out and let this wacko spend the day jerking off with Madam Rose and her five daughters. Dave doesn't need him or his uptight shit.

"—one might fix you supper, as intended."

Supper? What is it with this guy? Now he wants to cook for Dave? Hey, Davey Boy, maybe the guy gets off doing kitchen stuff. Dave pictures Alexander naked in front of a stove, stirring a sauce pot with one hand, jerking off with the other. Supper. Hey, if it turns him on, why not?

Maybe Dave made his move too soon. Maybe the little guy wants it, but needs to go snail slow?

One of Alexander's clenched fists turns into a scolding finger. "Supper, *if* you behave yourself."

Dave could go slow. Not that this twinkie's particularly worth it, but . . . hey—beats eating dinner alone again in some overpriced tourist restaurant on Leideseplein. "Supper. You never said anything about supper. Sure I can behave myself for a good meal." Dave'll be a proper English gent, he will; pinky in the air and all that sort of snot. Yeah, right. "Just like a puppy dog. I'll even wag my tail for you."

"We can forgo that pleasure."

Not waiting to be asked, Dave steps past Alexander, out of the entry hall and into the small living room. Plops onto a green sofa beneath a broad, lace-curtained window. Is he gonna follow? Yeah, he follows. That's it, if you can't lead the water to a dog, lead the dog to the water. Okay, it's not too serious; his breathing's back to normal already. "Have a seat, why don't you?" Dave says, pointing to a green armchair catty-corner to the sofa. "Over there, not next to me— wouldn't want to give you the wrong signal or anything."

"How droll." Alexander leans against the living room door post, as if uncertain whether to enter the room.

"So tell me," says Dave. "Is it just me, or you don't want it from anybody?"

Alexander's eyebrows rise so high they nearly hit his hairline. "Unbelievable. Thoroughly. No sense of tact or discretion."

"Part of my charm." Yeah, flash that grin, Davey Boy. "No hard feelings?"

Again, Alexander hesitates. "One is uncertain how you mean that."

"I know."

"You're absolutely wicked."

"I know. No hard feelings?"

Alexander rolls his eyes. "No. None. Regardless of how one interprets your question."

"So, is it just me?"

"Irish Breakfast or Earl Grey?"

"Or is it that you don't fuck Jews?"

"Ho-ho, how terribly clever. Accuse one of anti-Semitism, so that in an effort to prove one's moral purity, one will feel obligated to succumb to your caveman charms."

"Worth a try."

"Anti-American—perhaps. But not at all anti-Semitic. How dare you! One did not even realize you were Jewish when we first met."

"Now that you know . . . ?"

"Makes no difference at all."

"We whites all look alike to you, right?"

"Fresh out of Irish Breakfast, come to think. We shall be forced to settle for Earl Grey."

"I don't give a shit about his title as long as he's hot."

Alexander shakes his head and turns to leave.

"Makes us kind of alike, you know. Both minorities."

Turning to face Dave full front: "The Dutch are not minorities in the Netherlands." Melodramatic stare, then swish swish swish down the hall to the kitchen, creaking over the wooden floors, pitted and nicked.

Dave's shoes off, feet up on the long glass coffee table. "Nice flowers!" He yells across the apartment while looking at the velvety purple trumpets in a pot. "What are they?"

Silence, broken only by the clang of kettle on range top, cups on saucers.

Shrug.

Little bitch got his nose out of joint. Who the hell cares? Persian area rug under the coffee table. Couple dozen CD's in a rack next to the player. A shelf with a pewter-framed photo of Oscar Wilde, two Buckingham Palace guard dolls, a miniature Tower of London—Anglo shlock.

No chopsticks lying around, no kimonos, no pointy straw hats or pictures of rickshaws. Not even a grain of rice.

Alexander carries in a tray with milk-white teapot and cups, sets it down on the table by Dave's feet. "One is unfamiliar with American custom, but in this home, the practice is to keep one's feet on the floor."

"You'd have more fun lifting them in the air."

Come on, play nice, Davey Boy. Play nice. You're a guest, after all. Feet off the table.

Alexander sits in the green armchair.

"Great old dresser," Dave says, pointing his nose at a mahogany chest with brass handles.

"Why yes, one adores that tallboy! Only 200 guilders!"

"A hundred dollars? That's all?"

"From a neighbor. On Queen's Day all Amsterdam turns into one big used everything sale: furniture, dishes, pots, clothes, books, toys. The entire populace absolutely floods the streets selling their pasts. We Dutch are fastidiously tidy, you know."

"What past did you sell? On *Queen's* Day?"

Alexander pours the tea. "Forgot to ask—sugar?"

"Nah, I'm man enough to drink it straight up."

"How absolutely macho."

"So what did you sell?"

Alexander lets loose a sigh, then catches himself, like he realizes he nearly let an honest emotion escape. "Picture frames." And then forcing a smile, "Merely picture frames. Wooden ones, metal ones, paper and cardboard ones."

"Used picture frames?"

"Yes."

"And the pictures?"

Quietly: "Into a dresser drawer."

"You sold the frames, kept the pictures, and bought a fancy dresser to keep them in."

Alexander slaps his knees. "Time to prepare supper!"

"Pictures of who?"

"Family. Parents and . . . others. Yes, a simple supper. I was thinking *Stamppot van boerenkool met worst*—hotpot with kale, potato, and sausage. Traditional Dutch peasant food."

Like Dave doesn't notice the change of subject. Like Alexander could possibly think Dave doesn't notice.

"Easy to make," Alexander continues, then takes a long sip of tea. "But it will require a bit of time. One should commence *immédiatement*. Would you care for some cheese and biscuits meanwhile?"

Dave leans forward and asks in a challenging tone—not I'm-gonna-beat-your-ass challenging, but this-pitbull-won't-let-loose-til-you-spill-it challenging. "You're hiding something about those pictures."

Alexander's lips pout first out, then in, lower lip slips behind upper teeth, all while his eyes move in a circle around Dave to floor, window, ceiling, window, floor.

The mystery of it, that's the thing. Not that Dave really gives a goddamn. "I'm just like a stranger on a bus," he says.

Their eyes lock.

Dave continues, slowly, "Just like a hole in the ground you can talk to."

"Do you disclose your deepest secrets to strangers on buses?" Alexander looks serious.

"Grandma always taught me never to talk to strangers."

"Or to holes in the ground like me?"

"I don't have any secrets," Dave says. Okay, let him give his best shot. "Whattaya wanna know?"

"Do you truly regard me as you would a mere stranger on a bus? Not as . . . someone just a mite closer than a stranger?"

Heavy shit all of a sudden. What is it with this guy? We just met a couple days ago. Sure we've spent some time, but still. Haven't even kissed yet.

Dave gets up from the sofa, turns, pulls the curtains aside, leans forward, looks down at the market below. "Still going strong down there."

"You have not provided an answer," says Alexander.

"What's your question?"

"Is one truly just like a stranger to you?"

"One what?" Stall stall stall.

"You truly do not understand?"

Dave makes a fist, taps it against the window. What can he say? Dave may be kinda rough sometimes, but he's not out to hurt anybody's feelings on purpose. Not unless he really has to. "No," Dave says to the glass. "Not like a stranger on a bus."

"But like a hole in the ground. Or just a hole."

Oh, to hell with this shit. All this for an exotic fuck? Not worth it. Not worth it at all. Dave turns, drops back down onto the sofa, crosses his feet beneath himself on the cushions, notices a grimace flash on Alexander's face. "You're right, Alexander. Better I don't know anything about you—if you get to know somebody too well, the 'sexcitement' gets lost."

"And, of course there's no such thing as an intimacy that supersedes fucking."

What the hell kind of revolving door is this? Heading inside, heading outside, inside, outside. . . . He tugs at the toe of his white socks. A hole. He rubs the big toe's callous, scrapes thumbnail against it. Into it. Hard. Feels a twinge, looks up. "What is it you want from me?" There.

"Now that's an honest question," Alexander says.

"How's about an honest answer?" This is new. So new for Dave that his heart is pounding faster than normal.

Dave listens as Alexander sets his teacup and saucer onto the table, but can't hear even the slightest clink of porcelain against glass. Hands fold together on Alexander's lap, and he addresses his remarks to his fingers. "In all candor—one does not know what one wishes from you. From you or anyone."

"But you're sure it's not my dick?" Heart pounding eases a bit. Dick. Cock. Prick. Familiar words, safe.

The edges of Alexander's lips lift slightly—Dave said something funny? "Your boorishness," says Alexander, "is refreshing in a lower-class sort of way."

Quietly, Dave answers, looking right at him, "You think I don't know you just insulted me. But I know. I don't care, is all. Otherwise your face'd be a bloody pulp."

"Goodness, how charming!" Alexander stands. "If one does not start the potatoes now, supper will not be ready until breakfast time." And as he moves toward the hallway, "No—that is not an oblique in-vitation to spend the night!"

"Like I don't know that." Fool me once, shame on you; fool me twice, shame on me.

* * *

How much ass would a woodchuck fuck
If a woodchuck could fuck fast?

If Peter Piper picked a peck of pickled pricks,
How many pickled pricks did Peter Piper pick?

* * *

"Sam did what?" Sam's dad says.

"He peed outside," Sam's mom says. "Near the parking lot. On a patch of dirt."

Sam hears them through his bedroom door, even though it's closed and he knows he shouldn't be listening.

"Shit, is this the start of something?" Sam's dad says. "Another psychological thing? I thought we were done with all that."

"I don't know."

It's Dumbo's big elephant ear pasted on Sam's door—that's why Sam hears everything even from the living room far away at the apartment's other end. Because Sam's ear is pressed against Dumbo's. It's Dumbo's fault, not Sam's.

"Anybody see him?" That's Dad again.

"Les said the nutcase did it. From 26A. From his balcony."

That man's tippy-toe on his balcony. Superman? Spiderman? No—Nutman. "Nutcase," Mom always calls him. "That crazy neighbor" who comes in "drunk at all hours of the night. Doesn't say hello in the laundry room . . . stares at his underwear whirling around in the dryer . . ."

"So why you blaming Sam?" Dad's angry. "Just because he . . . it was only a few months, it doesn't mean—"

"Sam admitted it."

"Then why does Les blame the guy in 26A?"

"Les hates the nutcase and loves Sam. You figure it out."

"Still . . ."

Mom says, "A grown man's not gonna pee from his balcony, especially not in front of people. Not even a nutcase. You've gotta do something. Nip this in the bud."

Green shorts down, up there on that balcony. Pee-pee showing . . . Pee-pee showing? . . . Pee-pee showing! . . . Hee hee hee! . . . Mumbling something and shaking his pee-pee. Holy ravioli—Nutman's peeing from the roof! Real pee! The sky is falling the sky is falling! Run for your life! It's raining it's pouring the old man is snoring! Eeeeeee! Whew—protected by the green car. The poor dirt getting wet with pee. Mud. Here comes the super. Uh-oh uh-oh . . . somebody's gon-na get it! You're not allowed to pee from a balcony, mister. Gotta pee in the toilet. Everybody knows that. Not allowed to pee outside, not in your bed.

Creak creak creak. Dad's pacing up and down the hall, to Sam's door and back to the living room. "What the hell was that guy doing on his balcony, anyway? For the view? Nobody uses their balconies. A view of the parking lot?"

"Fishing, maybe. I don't know. Sunning, I guess."

"He could go out by the pool for that."

The pool. Uh-oh uh-oh.

"Sorry," Dad says to Mom.

"Like I know what he was doing on his balcony?" Sam can't see his mom, but he knows her pudgy cheeks are turning as pink as her shorts and she's picking her thumbnails. The pool. Nobody's allowed to talk about the pool anymore. Can't go to it, can't talk about it. Mom continues, "Go talk to Sam."

Sam picks at the scab on his chin, tears it completely off, winces, feels the red wetness with his finger, tastes red metal, presses his whole palm against his chin so a new scab will form. All he did was fall on the sidewalk day before yesterday; hardly even hurt. "What a lucky boy you are!" said Les, the super, lifting Sam to his feet. "Just a little scrape on the chin. Nothing that'll upset your poor mom, God love her." Hardly even hurt, doesn't even deserve a scab.

Dad asks, "What have you said to him?"

"That he should wait in his room until you get home."

"Good thinking." That's what Dad says, but it doesn't sound like that's what he really means.

"How should I know what to do?" Mom's voice is hard the way it gets when her green eyes narrow and she tries not to cry. "I used to know what to do. I don't anymore, alright? I admit it."

"And I'm just bursting with great ideas." Dad's pressing his fingers against his temples where big veins throb in and out, Sam just knows that he is. And then Dad's voice softens, "Ann, it wasn't your f—"

"Shut up about that," Mom snaps. "I've told you. Just shut up about that."

"Fine. I'll go talk to him."

Sam yanks his ear away from Dumbo's. He rushes to the bunk bed. He grabs Jimmy's Bluedog from the pile of stuffed animals that covers the lower bunk these days. Sam quickly climbs the ladder to the upper bunk, lies with Bluedog on his chest.

Creak creak creak down the hall. Knock, and the door opens. "Hello, Sam."

Sam stares into Bluedog's empty glass eyes.

Dad pets Bluedog. "How's he doing?"

"Fine."

"Been behaving?"

Shrug.

"Been peeing where he's supposed to?"

What should Sam say? "Dogs are supposed to pee outside."

Dad sighs. "Got me there, partner. But you know what I mean, don't you?"

What to say?

"Why'd you do it, pal?"

What to say?

"I know you miss . . . we all do. But that's no reason—"

"I didn't do it!" Stupidhead, why are you saying that?

"Your mother says you did it, says you said you did it."

Tattletale, tattletale, snitch and you'll become a snail.

"Maybe," says Dad, "Bluedog did it?" Dad slaps Bluedog on the snout and shakes a finger, "Bad dog. Bad dog. Dogs are supposed to pee in the toilet."

Sam thinks, 'What?' but doesn't say that, doesn't say anything. Dad looks away, up at the colored border where wall meets ceiling. Sam watches Dad's eyes travel from a blue fish to a yellow to a red one, Dad's empty eyes.

Fish under water, making bubbles.

Dad presses his temple.

Sam whimpers.

Dad kisses Sam on the cheek, lifts him from the upper bunk, lies with him down on the lower one, on top of the stuffed pandas and lions and dolphins. Dad cuddles Sam, who cuddles Bluedog.

Sam sniffles, "Did it hurt him?"

"You mean Jimmy?"

Sam nods against Dad's chest, and Dad hugs him tighter. Sam feels Dad shake and breathe in that funny new way. Dad clears his throat. "Nope, he just fell asleep under the water, that's all. Didn't hurt a bit. So don't pee outside anymore, okay?"

"Okay."

As Dad sits up on the lower bunk, Sam notices how careful Dad is not to bang his head. Sniffle sniffle. "Okeedokee, pal. Whattaya say we wash up and get some grub? You first."

Sam hands Bluedog to Dad, scampers to the bathroom, washes his hands under cold water. He wonders why he no longer wets his bed at night the way he did for a while "out of missing Jimmy," as Mom used to explain. Sam still misses Jimmy—he does he does he does.

Sam fills a paper Dixie cup with water, carries it back to his room. Dad's gone, the stuffed animals are all over Jimmy's bed. Sam offers Bluedog a sip from the cup, then climbs to his top bunk. He thinks of Nutman. Sam pulls back the blanket, pours the water onto the center of his bed. Who does Nutman miss?

4

Sitting in the medical school library, at a table by the window, looking out as clouds transform themselves in the breeze from plump to wispy, Alexander taps his pediatrics text lightly, as if keeping time to his thoughts. No particular event transpired last night at dinner, but that conversation . . .

"So whattaya call this again?"

"*Boerenkool.* How surprising that you enjoy it."

Dave looked up with the obvious question in his eyes—if one did not think Dave would enjoy the dish, why prepare it in the first place?

Because it had been ages since one prepared the dish, simple as it was. Because one felt an irrepressible urge to prepare it last night. Not because Dave might like it, but because Jeroen always did. Yes, that's the truth. Jeroen. *Boerenkool* with beer. *Speculaas* for dessert, followed by a sofa snuggle.

The past, Alexander. What's past is past. Trite. True.

Rather surprising that this American chewed with mouth closed, did not shovel food in like . . . An enigma. A boor with a modicum of refinement. A mere modicum, yet still. That's very much the point. A devastatingly charming combination. If one were in the frame of mind to be devastated. Again. Which one is not. Although one might indeed have been were this American a trifle less argumentative and challenging in the manner of an old friend expressing honest criticism. Yes, that was it: in the manner of an old friend, rather than of a new potential *amour.* Perhaps Dave was right in his crass wisdom— "sexcitement" tends to dwindle, the better two . . . friends . . . become acquainted?

How, then, to explain the deepening of love over time in a romantic relationship? One has known such a deepening, felt it within one's very marrow.

"Hello?" Dave asked, tracing his finger in the remains of mashed potato on his plate.

"Beg pardon?" Ah, finger in potato. Now that's what one would have expected. The comfort of predictability.

"You here?"

One was wondering then: does passion, in a relationship, diminish in indirect proportion to the deepening of love? To the extent that, over time, two become one, lovemaking together becomes solo sex, after all, somewhat akin to masturbation: when one knows precisely which touches elicit which responses from which of one's partner's erogenous zone nerve endings . . . knows the other's anatomy as intimately as one's own . . . produces orgasm in one's other half as only one can produce them in oneself . . . yet without the novelty. Longing for those familiar caresses, sacrificing the excitement of the new for the deeper pleasure of the familiar. The familiar which, because of its ever-growing intensity, feels new upon each encounter. No, not a sacrifice.

"Hey!"

"Terribly sorry. Daydreaming."

"About sex with me? You don't have to daydream." Dave rubbed hand over crotch.

One came to oneself at that point—oh, please, not another misunderstanding—sat up straighter in the chair, set plate of half-eaten supper back onto the coffee table. "Haven't we become rather bold?" He *was* merely teasing, was he not?

"Well," Dave continued, "I figure you cook somebody dinner, you expect a thank you."

"An oral thank you will suffice."

"Now you're talking—I love oral."

"A *verbal* thank you." How exasperating.

"Don't you have that expression over here—'The way to a man's dick is through his stomach'?"

"A rather circuitous surgical route, is it not? And, one would suspect, quite messy."

"Party pooper. Bathroom?"

Ah, yes. Mere banter for its own sake. Relief. "Bathroom? You mean you wish to take a bath?"

"The toilet."

Toilet again. Not, one hoped, another reference to lowly sex practices. "Ah, yes. One has heard about your uncivilized American habit of placing toilet and bathtub in the very same room. Down the hall, on your right. You can find it very well on your own."

"Of course, on my own. Unless you want to hold my dick for me while I piss."

A dismissive wave of one's hand and Dave left the room with a swagger. Now one realizes. Yes. It was not the potential novelty of sex with Dave that had initially sparked one's interest. Quite the opposite. It was precisely his boorishness that prompted reconsideration of the possibility . . . experiencing reminiscent touches, familiar ones.

Flush. Sink faucet. Door click. Footsteps. "You sure know how to show a tourist a good time."

A tourist, yes, who would be here for another . . . what? . . . week? Insufficient time to develop the necessary familiarity. A brief affair would not suit one's current needs. A man here today and gone tomorrow: very much akin to the original source of distress, was it not?

Loneliness could turn even the most clear-headed into a fool. Trite. True.

Returning to his seat, Dave actually picked up his plate, brought it to his face, licked it clean. "I'm a pig, aren't I?"

Ah . . . one understood . . . yes. He knew precisely what he was doing. For effect. À la Madonna, that most American of icons, wearing silver-cone breastplates or rubbing her crotch in San Juan with the Puerto Rican flag. Dave was, indeed, a product of his culture.

"You didn't answer my question," Dave said.

"Yes, you are a pig."

"And my question from before?" Dave asked.

"Which was . . . ?"

"What is it you want from me?"

Not a flinch, not a blink, not a hesitation. Bravo, Alexander: "Would you believe that all one wanted was some companionship?" (Should one believe oneself?)

"From me?" The lift of Dave's eyebrows registered genuine surprise, revealed his entire self-image in one contraction of facial muscle. How intimate a revelation. This . . . yes: perhaps self-revelation was what one sought from him . . . From someone . . . "Perhaps," Alexander asked, "we should conduct an experiment?"

"I'm game."

"What if we were to set aside sexual innuendo and double entendre, just for the remainder of the evening, and see if we could engage in sincere conversation?"

"My sexual innuendoes are always sincere."

"Undeniably. But grant this modest request?"

"Whatever revs your engine."

"Thank you. Make yourself comfortable while one attends to the dishes."

"Need help?"

"The kitchen is much too small for two."

"We could squeeze in together."

Exit to clear one's head. Dishwashing as a reprieve. Repeated physical activity. How well one has grown to know the routine: Washing. Scrubbing. Dusting. Vacuuming. Polishing. Anything to numb the mind. After this past year, one's apartment has come to absolutely glisten.

So quiet there at the back of the building. Rolls and clangs of trolleys in the distance. Faint echoes of neighbor parents scolding children in various languages and—gongs? What on earth—? Not from outside, but from . . . Little did one realize the mischief Dave could get himself into if left alone for even a minute.

Alexander rushed into the living room, glared. "Who granted you permission to play music?"

"You said to make myself comfortable. Found a CD you didn't even open yet. Never heard anything like it. What is this shit?"

"Javanese gamelan. You have no right—"

"Weird. Gongs and xylophones."

"Turn it off, please."

"It's wild. Your people's music?"

"The CD was a birthday gift from my parents, yes."

"That's not what I meant," Dave says.

"One is quite aware what you meant."

"If I got a birthday present from my folks, I'd play it day and night."

"Well, it is not from your 'folks,' and is not yours to play." Push of the CD "off" button. Silence. "There. Let's maintain the quiet, shall we?"

"Don't you like your own people's music?"

"Of all the CD's before you, dozens, this is the one you choose? One that had not even been opened? You don't play Bach, you don't play Chopin, not Handel, but this. The nerve! Opening another person's CD. Turning on his CD player without authorization."

"Didn't realize I was in sacred space. Want I should leave?"

"Perhaps that would be best."

"Fine. Thanks for dinner. See you around sometime."

Alexander watched Dave stomp to the front door. Stop. Do not permit him to leave like this. Not on this note. He's the first man you've entertained in a year. "Dave—"

"Yeah?" He turned.

Such a sour look; if his face were citrus, he'd be too tart to kiss. Heavens, one was beginning to think like him. To be rude like him. For the sake of holy isolation? Some abstract notion of duty and respect. Foolish. After all, one was not some wizened Sicilian Catholic widow! "Listen—"

"Yeah?" Dave asked.

"I . . . I . . ."

"You're in a snit for reasons I don't get."

"Yes. Understood. One should explain. But sometimes life is difficult."

"Tell me about it."

"Another time, perhaps? One needs to think. Then, perhaps, one would be prepared to share."

"You saying you wanna get together again?"

A nod of the head with penitent eyes looking first at the floor, then up at him. Ah, he sighed: an indication of understanding, or at least, tolerance. "Perhaps one could show you some Jewish sites? We've a marvelous Jewish museum, so one is told. And the Anne Frank House is, of course—"

"Not interested. I don't feel like visiting the Jewish Victim Memorial."

"Not a memorial to victimization," said Alexander, "but to survival. The fact that it's a museum demonstrates that good won over evil."

"Yeah, right."

"Like the Homomonument."

"The what?"

"You don't know?"

"What?"

"Really? One just assumed. The Homomonument. A memorial to all gay people who've suffered, especially those killed by Hitler."

"A *homo* monument? What'll you Dutch think of next? Gays killed by Hitler. Whattaya know? . . . A couple months ago a group of rabbis picketed some Holocaust museum in New York because it showed that Hitler killed abominable fags as well as holy Jews."

"I can check when the Anne Frank House is open," Alexander said.

"Forget it. If I don't see it, it isn't real."

"How terribly Australian of you. But an ostrich *sans plumage* is nothing more than an oversized ugly duckling."

"Drop it, for God's sake! All my life I heard about Grandma's pilgrimages to that 'Secret Annex' where they all hid like cockroaches in a wall waiting to get gassed."

"Come now, that's not—"

"I don't want to see Grandma's pain, alright? Just drop it."

"Your grandmother was in hiding with Anne Frank?"

"No, goddamit. But for her it was all the same thing. Her suffering, theirs. A child's. She'd look at me as a kid, sometimes, touch my left forearm with her finger, the spot where a number . . . a tattoo would have . . . and she'd bawl her eyes out. Shit. Shit! Change the fucking subject."

"Fine, fine, fine." Good heavens, how the man is clenching his fists. "It's not in one's nature to push." Goodness, can he pronounce, "exposed nerve"?

"Maybe we should take a couple days to chill."

"Apart, you mean?" Heavens, he really has taken offense.

"Exactly."

"If you wish. Yes, one should catch up on one's medical studies. One has been neglectful. Well. The weekend, then? View the parade together?"

"The what?"

"You've been in so many of our gay venues and still have not become aware from the posters and fliers?"

"I don't go to clubs to read."

"This weekend's Gay Pride."

* * *

Online chat room sex (fast fingers sex)—Dave as image, his creation or theirs: fat bald hairy bearded big-bellied bear Dave ("Woof!"), smooth lean swimmer's build BarelyLegalManForOlderMan Dave ("Wanna get fucked, Daddy?"), OlderMForYounger ("Been a bad boy?"), DungeonMasterMuscleStudCop Dave ("Lick 'em, BootDog, lick 'em good!"), SizeMattrsM4M, BlkM4BlkM, WhtM4WhtM—sometimes white Dave, sometimes black Dave—DomBlkM4Sub

WhtM—sometimes Top Dave, sometimes—NO NO NO! ALWAYS TOP DAVE!—LatinoM4M, AsianM4M, NCarolinaM4M ("Howdy, y'all!"), WVirgM4M, NHM4M, TulsaM4M, SanFranM4M (of course), CleveM4M, MinnplsM4M, RchstrM4M, GaydaytonaM4M, Atlnta BiMarriedM4BiMM, DallasBiMM4BiMM, BaltMDGay4Str8, Str8 SnglM4M, NWChicBurbs2SvcMM, Str8M4Str8MPhllyBurbsNOW, UnusualM4M (what the hell's "unusual"?).

Men in every room IM'ing Dave—ping-ping—with an Instant Message here, and an Instant Message there, here an IM, there an IM, everywhere an IM-IM . . . with a "Wanna cyber?" here and a "Gotta pic?" there, here a "Rimmer," there a "Sucker," everywhere a "Big-Dicked Fucker" . . . with a "you got a place?" here and "lookin' to travel" there, here some head, there some ass, everywhere it's cold as glass . . . Old McDavey's computer baths . . . eeyi . . . eeyi . . . ooooooo.

* * *

Dave looks over to the pastry counter, at the husky guy who just walked in, his straw-colored, rubber-banded ponytail bouncing off his shoulder. 6'2". Nah, too tall. The little one next to him? 5'6" or so, blondish also, in black-and-white striped tank top, white cutoffs (circumcised shorts), its white threads dangling on his thighs like thick strands of fresh cum. Tempting, but the guy's too short. So, Goldilocks, where the hell's the one that's just right? And what'll Dave say when he thinks he's found him? "Hey, are you the one I'm supposed to meet?" Sounds like some romantic pie-in-the-sky come on.

Should be a little shorter than Dave from what he said—5'9"—and chunkier, 190 hot pounds. Dirty blond hair, which could mean nearly anything from white to light brown. Shit. Can't believe he forgot to ask the guy's name.

Dave'll give him another fifteen minutes and that's it.

A new possibility walks through the door: couple inches shorter than Dave, trimmed brown hair. *Boston Globe* folded under his arm—did they arrange a signal? . . . No . . . Muscular calves sticking out of his khaki shorts (it's September—what is it with these faggots wearing shorts now?), sprigs of hair through the collar of his green and white checked shirt. The white socks in sandals are a turnoff, but hey—it's not Dave gonna be the one licking feet. Yeah, Dave could get into this guy. White Socks gives the place a once-over, a look on his face like the room stinks. (Dave sniffs, smells only coffee.) Is that a smile? A smile for Dave?

Dave's about to give a yeah-it's-me-so-you-finally-made-it grin, but before the corners of his lips can even lift, the guy's eyes dart away. So he's not the one. Then why does he walk over to the square-topped marble table next to Dave's and sit?

Dave wants to flat out ask—are you Srvce4u? But if the guy isn't, Dave's question would sound fucking weird.

Shit. White Socks isn't exactly sitting with his back to Dave, but he's not facing him, either. Sideways, so he can either look at Dave or ignore him. A game player, no matter who the fuck he is. Dave likes games.

Dave brings paper cup to lips, sips coffee, observes.

Not looking at Dave? Not at all? Nah, he's waiting for Dave to make the first move. Yeah, nobody makes the first move in icy cold Boston. Ice beer, anyone? Everybody nuts for the Bruins. Everybody wants an icy smooth muscle boy—he couldn't fucking believe those ads in *Bay Windows* for laser hair removal "treating all anatomical locations." Dave's chest is muscular, kinda, but still soft enough so he's a real person, and hairy. He's no First Night ice sculpture. He read in the *Boston Phoenix* that Harvard Square has more ice cream stores than any other neighborhood in the country; Starbucks makes a fucking mint around town with its iced lattes and frappacinos; frozen daiquiris and margaritas in all Back Bay's hip, yuppy guppy restaurants. So we can all be as numb on the inside as we are on the outside. Glacier City. Icicleville. Oh sure, everybody's up for some hump hump hump, but then you cum a few dozen times on this iceberg chest here, or inside that frozen slush ass there, and eventually your dick turns into a Good Humor popsicle, always hard and sweet, and numb forever after. This town needs a meltdown!

"I know the ice rink of your soul!" Dave mutters, sort of to White Socks, or not to him exactly, but in his general direction. "And I'm gonna strap on my skates to glide right across it, digging in sharp grooves wherever I can." White Socks shifts in his v-backed wooden chair, but doesn't lift his eyes from the paper. "Yeah, I might slip and bruise my ass, but it'll be all over you, and you'll lick it for me! Just don't let your tongue stick, 'cause once I cum, you're outta here." Dave's still muttering—loud enough for White Socks to hear, soft enough for White Socks to pretend not to.

The waiter—dyed-black buzz cut and goatee, countless ear piercings, like he's aping to be one of Satan's point men—brings White Socks his coffee in a white cup and saucer. A couple white napkins. Hey, thinks Dave, White Socks didn't even order. Ah, a regular. White Socks and the waiter shoot the shit about leaves beginning to change already and you should get up to New Hampshire next week for the golds and reds and would you like the usual honey ham on focaccia yeah you bet bud, thanks: there—White Socks is glancing at Dave. Not like he's really looking, more like he's trying to survey the watercolor of flowers on the wall behind Dave's head, but hey—the guy's a regular so he's seen the watercolors before so he must really be trying to get an eyeful of Dave.

Maybe he is the one, after all. Or maybe he isn't the one, but trying to decide if he's interested, or maybe he already knows he's not interested, but he's so horny that he's double-double checking isn't there some way he can put up with Dave long enough to get hard and cum today with the bonus of a breathing body at his side.

Dave keeps staring at him, but White Socks looks away—of course: nobody wants to be observed while checking out the merchandise, especially not by the merchandise itself. White Socks brings the steaming coffee cup to his lips, slurps and flinches, sticks out his tongue to soothe the burned lower lip.

Nice tongue, Dave thinks. Now's his chance to throw out one of his oh-so-hot icebreakers: "I like to cool my coffee by spitting in it."

White Socks angles his head in Dave's direction, looks at him for a second, gives a sort of nod like, "Did I hear you right?" blinks, then turns back to his reading. Or pretend reading. From watching his eyeballs, Dave can tell the guy isn't really focused on the page, keeps shifting his eyeballs in Dave's direction, but without moving his head. So . . . is the shmuck gonna make conversation or what?

"What you reading?" Dave asks, giving White Socks—and himself—one last chance.

White Socks, forced to shit or get off the pot, squeezes his eyes tight. Dave asks again, louder, "What you reading?"

"A newspaper." White Socks squeezes this out slowly, softly, like he knows he should say it but doesn't want to, or knows he shouldn't but does want to.

Goddamn wise-ass! "You don't know what you're missing, pal. I got fifteen inches."

"Yeah, right." White Socks smirks now, with a grin that says he figured Dave right, after all.

"Take me to your place and I'll prove it."

"Dream on, girlfriend."

"Elephants love my dick," Dave says.

The guy smiles despite himself. "Really?"

Got him! Forget the net and straightjacket, Dave: you can catch anybody just by fucking with his head. Online, offline—doesn't matter, guys just wanna have fun! "Not that I go around looking for elephants," Dave continues. "I mean, I'm not some freakazoid. But a shlong like mine's handy in the zoo when I run out of peanuts."

White Socks scrunches his face and shakes his head like "What the hell am I doing talking to this one?"

Has Dave read him wrong? "Peanuts—penis, pretty much the same thing as far as elephants are concerned." Guys love Dave's wildness, so this one will too. "They'll wrap their trunks around anything and shove it into their mouths. I just unzip, stick it through the bars, and we have a jerk off party."

"Yeah, sure."

One last-ditch try: "I heard this on the radio—there's a kind of leech that mates only inside a hippo's ass. Isn't that a hoot?"

"Yeah, well, I've got to get back to my paper."

"So your name isn't Svce4u, is it?"

White Socks looks, thinks for a moment, then says, "Not 4 u."

The waiter brings White Socks his sandwich, asks in low tones, pretending he doesn't want Dave to hear, but of course he's loud enough for Dave to hear, "He bothering you?"

"Kind of a freak show," White Socks says. "Meal and a show. Not a problem. Yet."

"You want I should leave?" Dave asks the waiter, who does a phony double take like "You talkin' to me?" The waiter shuffles over to Dave's table. "Can I get you something to go with the take-out coffee you ordered at the counter half an hour ago?"

"Waiting for a friend." Friend, yeah, right. A fuck. Waiting for a fuck. A goddamn fuckity fuck who was supposed to be here half an hour ago but didn't show and Dave's still sitting here like a shmuck pretending he hasn't been stood up. He *said* he lived at Tremont and Berkeley, he *said* he was really *hot for you man, so hot. Wanna suck your dick, lick your ass, your feet, suck your balls, be your pig.*

And Dave typed *Really?*

And the guy typed back, *Wanna lick your hairy sweaty pits. Call me a pig!*

You're a pig.

Yeah, man. You're so hot. Gonna fuck me with your big dick?

Gonna fuck you hard, Dave typed.

I'll take it bareback for you, Sir.

NO BAREBACKING, ASSHOLE.

No, Sir. Of course not, Sir.

Is that what turned the kid off? Dave insisting on condoms? What is it with these young punks? Dave may be crazy but he doesn't have a death wish. Does he?

Whatever you want, Sir.

I want you on your knees, Dave typed, *begging for my cock.*

Feed me, Sir. Please feed me.

So where the hell is that twerp!

"Would you like a proper coffee in a cup?" asks the waiter, fidgeting with his wire-rimmed glasses.

"Granny glasses," Dave thinks, wondering what Gen X calls them these days.

"A proper cup of coffee," the waiter continues, "instead of in that paper, take-out cup. Since you're staying here anyway . . . "

"You mean so you can get a tip this time?"

The waiter maintains a frozen daiquiri smile.

Dave grabs his own crotch. "I'll give you a tip."

The waiter takes a step back—not in shock, like this has happened to him here before, and says, "There are other cafés along Tremont Street you might like."

"Yeah, but I'm in this one, sweetheart, so bring me my 'proper' coffee here, okay? And wiggle that ass for me."

Now the waiter's smile melts. He slinks away.

Oh, everyone's a buddy in the chatrooms, alright, and the more outrageous you are, the better. *How fat is it, Fatpipe34? . . . Hey, I got a big one for you, SckItAllNite . . . I'm starving here, EatMeNow.* They always answer Dave with a *fuck yeah!* or *where are you?*–as if they'll ever actually set up a meeting or type anything more than, *we should get together sometime,* or *look for me online next week so we can hook up.* Bored and horny cockteases, jerking off at the keyboard. Dave especially loves to click into the chat room for Boston bi married guys, to talk sex with these horny men who can't sneak away from home. He has a riot giving them hard-ons and a hard time both. They love it. Like this morning:

Fatpipe34: Where does a Str8 man get some?

DaveDuzItGood: Get some what?

Fatpipe34: Cock

DaveDuzItGood: What does a Str8 man want with cock?

Fatpipe34: Str8 acting

Azzman: Home Depot for marr guys

DaveDuzItGood: How do you pick up a married guy at Home Depot?

Fatpipe34: Which one, Azz?

Azzman: Play with wedd ring. Somerville

Svce4u: Oh yea, just walk up to a guy in Home Depot and say hi I am bi wanna blow?

DaveDuzItGood: LAUGHING OUT LOUD!!!!!!!!

Azzman: Don't LOL Dave, it works

Fatpipe34: Seriously, Azz. How?

Azzman: Twist wedd ring. No one else suspects

Fatpipe34: That's a signal?

DaveDuzItGood: What if a guy just has an itchy finger?

God it's fun to be a ball-breaker!

Fatpipe34: Cuz I really wanna know how a str8 guy can find cock

DaveDuzItGood: Like you're so str8

Azzman: Home Depots only place marr guys can cruise w/o people suspectng anythng

Fatpipe34: What does twisting ring mean? I told you, str8 acting

Azzman: Means your bi marr

Fatpipe34: What direction do I twist it in?

DaveDuzItGood: To the right if you're bottom, to the left if you're top

Azzman: Doesn't mattr, just twist it

Svce4u: Azz, you just walk up to a guy and start twisting?

Azzman: I'm subtle

DaveDuzItGood: You reach over and twist some other guy you never met's ring? Doesn't sound subtle to me

Azzman: U twist your OWN ring!

DaveDuzItGood: Oh, I see

Playing dumb suckers them in every time.

Azzman: If he twists back, start convsation

DaveDuzItGood: He'll reach over and twist my ring?

Azzman: You shittin me, Dave?

DaveDuzItGood: I'm not as smart as I look.

Fatpipe34: That's the truth

EatMeNow: Now now, boys, behave

Azzman: Start convsation about where u find pipes and caulk

Azzman: :):)

Svce4u: LOL

EatMeNow: Will be crowded in caulk aisle

Azzman: Its like gay bar for str8 guys

DaveDuzItGood: For str8 guys who suck cock

Fatpipe34: Give it a rest

DaveDuzItGood: In your mouth

Fatpipe34: You wish

Azzman: Sum guys go to men's room <evil grin>

Azzman: One guy workin there's hot & flirts

DaveDuzItGood: What does he look like?

Azzman: Blond, stache

EatMeNow: Just be careful you don't get arrested

Azzman: Nobody gets arrested at Home Depot

DaveDuzItGood: And don't whip it out in the tool department

Azzman: LOL

DaveDuzItGood: And be careful which pipes you fondle in public

Svce4u: Or those toilet ballcocks . . .

Azzman: Anyone ever cruise guys at work?

DaveDuzItGood: Yeah, in my law office . . . I was eating cherries at my desk and this young accountant walks i

Damn! Why the limit on how long a message I can send at once?!

DaveDuzItGood: in and I offer him some cherries and he says he prefers big hard bananas!

DaveDuzItGood: I act like I don't know what he's talking about, but he got me hot!

Azzman: WOW. He str8?

DaveDuzItGood: He got married a few months later.

EatMeNow: Don't lose your job over dick!

DaveDuzItGood: I had a boss once, asked me to close office door and then he sits there scratching

DaveDuzItGood: his balls

Svce4u: What u do?

DaveDuzItGood: When I looked at his crotch he just smiled. Asked me how I liked my job. I said I licked it—

DaveDuzItGood: I mean liked it . . .

Fatpipe34: Asked if you want to keep it

Svce4u: LOL

DaveDuzItGood: He laughed . . . said if I ever want a promotion, we could talk about it over dinner

Fatpipe34: Did you talk about it?

DaveDuzItGood: Mom taught me never to talk with my mouth full.

Fatpipe34: For real?????

DaveDuzItGood: Yeah, she really did

Fatpipe34: No, I mean . . . you blew him? Really?

DaveDuzItGood: Well . . . I'm CEO now

Svce4u: You slept your way to the top. My fantasy

DaveDuzItGood: My boss loved the blow jobs, so he told VP.
   Then I had to blow him. And then

DaveDuzItGood: the treasurer . . .

Fatpipe34: ur lying?????????

DaveDuzItGood: And then we had this big Board Meeting gang
   bang . . . boy was I tired

Azzman: LOLOLOLOLOLOLOLOLOLOLOLOLOLOL

Yeah, Dave knows how to be popular, alright . . . Svce4u sent Dave
an Instant Message after that conversation: *You sound so hot. Wife's
at work. I want to service you.*

Dave'd never met anybody from the chat rooms before. Never in
real time. And from the looks of things, he never would. This proves
his theory—the cyber world's a dream space that dissolves if you try
to make it real, if the other guy gets close enough to really look into
your eyes and penetrate your ice soul, if he can see you're not 100
percent what he's imagining. Yeah, when it comes to fantasy, 99 percent just isn't good enough.

*Much as you want. No limits, Sir. Anything. I want to service some
stud regular when my wife's at work.*

Hmmm. Now that's one hell of an offer. Someone regular. Hmmm.
Someone to do him over and over. So Dave'd know where his next
suck's coming from. Someone who'd know exactly where on his
balls Dave likes to get licked while jerking off over a chest, to make
Dave's cum shoot really thick and far and his shudders really intense,
or who knows exactly how to tighten his ass around Dave's cock at
just the right instant—that all takes practice and repeat service.
Maybe even somebody to joke around with a little between fucks.

There's a café on Tremont, opposite the BCA.

The what? Fuck, Dave's only been living in this city twenty years.

Boston Center for the Arts.

And what's the café called? Dave typed.

Can't remember the name, Sir. But you'll find it. We can meet there. At 11:30 this morning? Then we can go to my place around the corner.

Couldn't remember the café's name? Shit! Fucking shit! The clue and you missed it. Every scam has a give-away clue; you just gotta look sharp for it. Bet the asshole doesn't even really live in the South End. Maybe not even married. Whole conversation was one big cyber fantasy scam. And you fell for it, Davey Boy.

Dave would never treat anyone that badly. He may be a home-wrecking slut, but he's a home-wrecking slut with principles.

The waiter brings Dave a "proper" cup of coffee, sets it down and gives a forced smile. Dave says, "Really hurts your cheeks, doesn't it?"

Nose in the air, the waiter turns and leaves.

Should Dave stay? Goddamit, he came all the way downtown, might as well make the best of it. Maybe . . . never picked up a guy in a café before, but hey—this is the fucking South End, Boston's gay ghetto; the whole neighborhood's one big gay bar. And White Socks has been giving Dave mixed signals, so maybe—

White Socks sets his coffee cup down, folds his paper, pays the check and leaves without even glancing in Dave's direction.

Who the hell wants a wimp in white socks, anyway?

The only other customer left is a guy in a lavender shirt, sitting two tables away. Not much to look at, sort of a pimply faced Pillsbury Doughboy, but might be company while Dave drinks his coffee. And sometimes the ones too ugly to get some are so grateful for dick they turn out unbelievably hot. Yeah, why the hell not? Dave lifts his cup and saucer, shoves back his chair—

Two other guys walk in, both with shaved heads, gray T-shirts and jeans, walk over to Doughboy and all three hug with pseudo-macho back-slap hellos, sit down together. Dave clanks his cup and saucer back onto the marble table top, spills a little coffee, sees the waiter glare. Dave sticks out his tongue; the waiter sticks out his own, shoves hooked pinkies into the corners of his lips, stretches his mouth wide and wiggles his tongue at Dave. "If you want me," Dave calls out, "then come over here and plop down your Granny ass on my lap!"

The waiter makes a "V" with his right index and middle fingers, taps it against his lips as if puffing a cigarette, then barks in a not-so-bad Bette Davis imitation: "Your lap? Hah! Only to take a dump!" and off he swishes into the kitchen.

"Not into scat, girly girl!" Dave yells after him. Forget it; Dave wasn't even thinking about him. Too femme, anyway. `

Those other three guys—Doughboy and his friends—look at Dave and laugh, wink, give a thumbs up, then return to their conversation about last night's sitcom, about a condo for rent around the corner on Union Park, a new play by some local Puerto Rican gay writer, Cabranes Somebody. Dave should still go over and say, "Any you guys up for a good suck today?" or, "Lemme pull up your face, Doughboy, so's I can have a seat." Intro lines that'd produce LOL's online.

But this is real time. Goddamn fuck piss.

Real time.

Ah, doesn't matter. Doesn't matter doesn't matter doesn't matter. Doesn't matter shit. There are a million ways to get company in this town, and Dave knows them all. He could go for a blowjob at Blue Hills Reservation . . . but the cops have put up barriers so you can't park anymore. And there's always a cop car now during rush hour at Recreation Road off Rte. 128—no more desperate married guys on their way home. Same old mouths at the Bird Sanctuary by the Charles River. Hasn't been to the Fens in ages—tough to get it up late at night when most of the action's going on there, but maybe he should give them another shot. Dave's done the t-rooms at Harvard, like the Science Center basement men's toilet, and Northeastern University's Ell Student Center men's room—although with the new school year, a whole new crop of horny college kids has shown up in town for Dave to try. There's always the third floor toilet in Macy's downtown right after work, the second floor t-room at Lord and Taylor's off Rte. 9 in Natick on Saturday afternoons and a dozen others; but Dave doesn't feel like rushing anymore and you gotta rush in those places to avoid getting caught. And nobody kisses.

From the next table, Dave grabs a white napkin that White Socks left behind. Dave crumples it tight in his fist, stuffs it into his cup, watches it soak up coffee, turn brown and hot wet. Let the waiter have fun with that!

Dave shoves his chair back hard so the legs screech, he stands, tosses a quarter onto the cold marble tabletop, leaves the café without looking at anybody. Too bad he doesn't have a wedding ring, or he could do Home Depot.

5

Dave leans over the concrete balustrade, lifts a hand to shield his eyes from the mid-afternoon sun. He looks out at rows of flat, narrow gray and black and brown buildings lining the Amstel Canal, at the various, curlicued seventeenth-, eighteenth-, nineteenth-century gables and pediments and cornices, gazes at the surface of history, feels part of it, far from it. These were wealthy merchants' homes, Alexander said, many of them renovated into modern apartments.

No signs yet of the parade, except for the crowd all along the canal and the bridge. He'd have missed it completely if not for Alexander. At least Alexander's good for something. "Companionship," he said. Whatever. The dinner he fixed the other night was good. Maybe Dave should just forget about getting into his pants? Not likely. But he's decided to ease off for a while, to wait and let the little guy come to him. Dave'd behave. He's said that before, but this time he means it. He's here to enjoy the parade and that's exactly what he's going to do.

"Here, Dave, pass along your camera," says Alexander, reaching for it.

His back to the canal, Dave stands, arms hanging at his side, a smirk on his face.

Alexander focuses and clicks.

"Thanks for bringing me," Dave says.

"A pleasure."

Dave looks past Alexander, to the city's new opera house—red brick, marble, glass. A monster. "In order to build it," Alexander explains, "the government destroyed dozens of medieval houses, all that was left of the old Jewish quarter. Tragic."

"Just decrepit old buildings, right? I get it. Rubble that didn't mean shit to anyone except, maybe, to Jews. Even here. Even here." Dave takes the camera, photographs the opera house, the Jewish Quarter that was.

The crowd's grown. Men with men, women with women, men with women, parents with children, old folks—click—"A lot of them must be straight."

"Of course."

A redheaded woman, in her fifties maybe, stops her walk along the bridge, turns her head at their conversation, leans to them, says in Dutch-accented English with t's and d's substituting th's, "So what do you tink of our tolerant city? Everyone here for de Gay Pride Parade. We love our homosexuals."

"Like you loved your J—"

Alexander interrupts and points, "Goodness, the beginnings of the parade?"

Dave looks—no parade. He says to Alexander, "You know me already."

"Quite."

Patronizing bitch. *Somebody in Amsterdam snitched on Anne Frank and turned her in.* The woman would pale if Dave said that, might confess to having been the stool pigeon at all of two years old and, from guilt and anguish, would dive off the balustrade into the canal. Surprised at his own nationalism—would Grandma be proud?— Dave spits over the bridge, at the water, watches his mucous splat onto the canal's shiny surface, mix with it, drift away.

"No parade yet," says the redhead, and she moves on.

Shit. Dave climbs onto the balustrade, edges around one of the concrete columns, sits on the ledge at its base, dangles his feet over the water.

"Be careful," mutters Alexander.

"Yeah." Dave's always thought Gay Pride Parades stupid back home. What does cock-sucking have to do with pride? Being a faggot just is. Like being Jewish.

Who the hell are you, Dave? You used to know.

I used to know who I wasn't.

And you weren't . . . ?

The goddamn Messiah, Grandma's *Mashiach.*

"Maybe one day, Daveleh-my-Adam—you'll turn out to be the *Mashiach?* Blasphemy, I know, may the King of the Universe forgive me. But who better than the grandson of a survivor? Maybe that's the reason—a test for us: not one Jewish boy only, who suffered for humanity like those Christians think, but an entire generation. It would give meaning. Honor you'd do my soul. All our souls. Promise me, Daveleh-my-Adam, if you're the *Mashiach,* you'll go back to the old neighborhood and tell Esther Mintz with her fancy shmancy wallpaper and two-tiered china dessert server, that the *Mashiach*—it's *my* grandson. I should only live to see the look on her face." Grandma winked when she said that; she and Davey shared a rare smile.

How do you know you're not the Messiah?

A faggot?

Where is it written the Messiah's straight?

Dave spies the first boat in the distance—one, then another and another. An entire flotilla sailing down the Amstel Canal toward the bridge: a couple of skiffs spiked with rainbow flags; others draped in strands of multicolored balloons; in a glass-windowed tourist boat, shirtless men gyrate to music Dave can hear long before they approach; a launch filled with pink balloons resembling bubble-bath foam sails beneath the bridge and Dave's legs; rowers in undecorated canoes whoop and wave at the onlookers. Dave snaps a couple of photos—now this is faggot history if ever there was, an entire town out to honor its queers, the true meaning of "gay"—PARTY! At the prow of a small motorboat, two women in white wedding gowns each wave like the Queen. A guy on a yacht lifts his foot to show off wooden shoes, gives his white Dutch cap a tug, hikes up his black skirt to reveal a strap-on dildo; the English sign on his boat—"Chicks with Dicks!" On a canoe, men in white shirts surround someone stuffed inside a pink, human-sized rubber. And then, ahhh, here's what Dave's been waiting for even though he didn't know it, a black barge flying a leather bar's banner—The Cockring.

"Fuckin' eh!" Dave hoots, and nearly drops the camera from his lap. Men in leather harnesses dance in the sunlight and one, at the very prow, in nothing but black leather jockstrap, shoots a water rifle at the crowd. A muscle man. On steroids for sure. Huge, boulder-like muscles on arms, chest, thighs. Bulked up, yet graceful. Blond. An Aryan Samson making his slow approach. Dave's breath quickens, he wants him. "Hey, Muscle Dick!" Dave cries. The man spots him, braces the butt of his water rifle against the leather pouch of his jock, aims up at Dave's face. "Yeah, Muscle Dick, do me! Shoot it quick!" The man does, drenches Dave's face in cold water. Dave laughs, shivers, feels clean while thinking he should feel dirty, likes the sensation. His lashes blur with drops of Muscle Dick's water reflecting the sun, and he knows it's unbelievably faggy to take a photo now, but Dave has got to capture this prideful afterglow with the most gorgeous hunk he's ever seen, so he lifts the camera, focuses on crotch, on chest, on grin—that goddamn grin meant for Dave—leans forward aaaand . . . wait, the barge is passing below Dave's legs—below the bridge! . . . no! Dave leans and clicks and feels his ass lift from the ledge and his thighs start to slip and—Alexander grabs Dave's arm from behind, jolting the camera from his hand. Plunk, it falls into the canal.

Dave spins about on the ledge. "What the hell did you do that for?"

"You were about to fall."

"So I'd fucking fall. It's only water. You made me lose the camera!"

"It's only a camera."

"It's me in Amsterdam. Now I don't have proof."

"You're here," says Alexander. "With or without proof."

"That stud—"

"Memory's better than photos; much easier to touch up."

"He wanted me."

Alexander puckers his lips in thought, then, "One was saving this as a surprise: there's a Mister Leather Holland contest tomorrow night. And one rather suspects your muscle man to be a contestant. Shall we attend together?"

Dave's cheeks nearly split from his broad grin. "Fanfuckingtastic!"

"On one condition."

* * *

White T-shirt, red T-shirt, green T-shirt, blue.
   Gray T-shirt, beige T-shirt—what's the right hue?
Thin socks, thick socks, striped socks, white?
   Low socks, high socks to hunt in the night.
Full shave? Partial shave? Scruffy beard? Clean?
   Doesn't really matter—just gotta look mean.

Steppin' out . . . in your leathers—vest or chaps to snare the boys?
   Hide that flab but strut those feathers, with your macho peacock poise.

* * *

I have a little penis,
All stiff like hardened clay,
And when it's good and ready,

So gaily I shall play,
Ohhhh . . . penis penis penis,
All stiff like hardened clay . . .

* * *

"Why'd you run away from home?" she used to ask Dave. "Away from New York? From me, from your world, all the way to Boston? You want to crush my heart like grapes?" Grandma would ask this during every single holiday visit, whipping her old-world tongue with the witch-like wart on its tip, the tongue that knew better than any other how to spit barbs that snagged the skin and tore. "Barbs my tongue got from wires around the camps," she'd say with a smug grin, then flick the wart against her upper teeth, pink against yellowing-white, soft against hard. How defensively smug Grandma was, defensively proud, forever defensively easing her conscience for having, defenselessly, survived. Warrior Grandma.

"Runaway." As though Dave had moved to Boston for reasons other than to attend college. As though he'd settled in Boston after college—shit, nearly twenty years ago—other than to . . . to . . . Dave spits at the hard ground. Runaway to get sucked. To suck or not to suck, that is the question. He smirks.

Chag Sameach. Dave looks up at the sky. Happy Chanukah. So, where are you exactly, I mean *exactly*—pacing around your flat, potato pancake moon? Or hiding behind the flickering stars? Twinkle twinkle little star, how I wonder what you are; up above the world so high, hiding Granny in the sky?

Dave turns his gaze from the sky to The Fens, leaves the sidewalk and traffic behind, enters Boston's after-hours, outdoor playground for boys. Hasn't been there for ages. The Fens, the victory gardens, World War I individual plots for growing veggies and flowers in short supply, so that civilians could think they were contributing to the war effort. "Like cucumbers and daffodils really scared off the Germans," Dave mumbles.

Beside a tangle of sticker bushes, he nudges the toe of his boot against an empty poppers bottle, sees a used condom beneath a leafless apple tree, and softly sings, "Don't suck under the apple tree on any old cock but mine, any old dick but mine, any old prick but mine—no no no . . ." The Andrews Sisters, Grandma's favorite group.

Down a bumpy dirt path, past wire-fenced patches of shriveled flower gardens; tended in summer when alive, abandoned in winter when dead. The last night of Chanukah, holiday of rebellion and light. Such a good grandson, so respectful and loving and dear and devoted to the memory of the recently departed. Bringing Grandma along to celebrate the holiday.

Dave passes a tall man in black sweatshirt, a short man with more wrinkles in the moonlight than were noticeable in the semi-lit Ramrod down the road, and a fat man who groped Dave there not half an hour ago; so many men who didn't get what they'd been seeking before last call and 2 a.m. closing, men now out on the prowl, wandering like Dave, leaning here against a wooden fence post, there against a tree trunk, hands thrust in jeans pockets, shoulders slouched, men struggling not to let others see them shiver like wusses in the cold—warm for December, but still chilly—see them shiver like fags in the cold night because they're all fags, but none of them want to look it.

You should wear a *tallis*, Dave thinks to himself—a white *tallis* with fringe. Wrap it around your hunched shoulders so everyone can know you're a Jewish fag with a cut cock—for them that goes for *Bris* Boys. "*Bris* Boys," he says aloud, rolling the phrase in the hollow of his mouth above his tongue, popping it off his lips—*Bris* Boys, who sacrificed the tips of their pricks for that civilizing mono-god. His Covenant. The People of the Cut Dick. *Bris* Boys, all chosen by God. "Who the hell wants to suck a cock chosen by God? . . . Holy suck, Batman!" Dave laughs as nearby reeds and dead gardens muffle the echo. Dave loves to suck cut cock, Jewish or otherwise, to feel the spongy round head slip between his lips. It's like starting a bag of fucking potato chips . . . more more more! Only not unkosher cock—yuck: the first time he took one in his mouth, he gave the foreskin a little nip to see if it carried feeling—he'd always wondered—and the guy slugged him.

All the men are out like Dave, but none, Dave is certain, are here to celebrate like he is. Sitting at home a couple of hours ago, staring at the menorah on his coffee table, he was preparing to light the eight candles, to chant his own Chanukah blessing: "Go on, boychik, light those fires." He even struck the match, but then shook it out, guffawed, looked up at the ceiling. Yes! Is that the hidden meaning of the holiday? Menorah. Men-orah. Men oral? Who'd o' thunk it—Chanukah's meant to be a suck festival. Don't squint in disgust. A mystical meaning skipped over by medieval Talmudic scholars, discovered by a modern American homo-Jew. The true meaning of Chanukah. That's it, Davey boy, go out and give Chanukah head; after all, 'tis better to give than to receive. Nah, wait a minute—that's the Christmas motto. What to do? What's a good Jewish boy to do? Go on, boychik, light those fires. Come on boychik, light my . . . yeah, that's it! A clear solution—to be sucked, to become the candles—eight lighted Chanukah candles, all in a row. Dave shucked his bathrobe, tugged on jeans, T-shirt, leather jacket. Dressed for success—"for suck-cess," he smirked—he drove off, first to get relaxed at the bar, then to get sucked in the Fens by eight men, one for each holiday night, for each night he'd gone without, each night he'd sat at home, alone, and lit the colored candles on his silver menorah, Grandma's old candelabra fashioned somewhere in Belorussia. ("How lucky it survived the War, Grandma! Just like you!" "Luck—*shmuck!* The Holy One, blessed be He, works in mysterious ways. Chanukah is, after all, a holiday of miracles." Then she mumbled to herself, "Survived the War, but pregnant and with no husband. Some miracle.") The silver menorah, Grandma's only memento-souvenir-relic from the abandoned village she returned to after the War, the nine-branched menorah she and little Davey would light together every Chanukah from as far back as he could remember. He'd always choose the candles—blue the first night and a white one as *shames* to stand higher than the rest, to stand guard, "the candles' conscience, so they shouldn't forget to burn the way they're supposed to," Grandma would say, a quirky explanation Dave would repeat, a nonsense explanation that caused Dave's Hebrew School teachers to shake their heads and shrug in embarrassment, but how could you contradict a concentration camp survivor?

That was a question Dave understood well: How could you contradict a concentration camp survivor? How could you tell her that no, you did not want to go to *shul* every Shabbos and pray among the old men with their scary, creased faces, their stinky breaths and clacking false teeth, that you'd rather fumble around playing touch football with the guys outside? How could you tell a concentration camp survivor that no, she shouldn't barge into the bathroom to check on why you've been in there so long because sometimes a boy needs time for reasons having nothing at all to do with constipation or diarrhea? How could you tell a concentration camp survivor that no, you didn't want to attend NYU in the City, but Boston University, so far away, in a land where a boy could escape from Shabbos mornings, could play touch with the guys all he wants, could play in bathrooms to his dick's content? How could you convince a concentration camp survivor that your "no" was not a withdrawal of love, not a betrayal, not a negation of lullabies and washcloth baths; was not, as she would accuse, a Hitlerite erasure of Sholom Aleichem bedtime stories and sweet lamb *tzimmes* and forehead-kiss murmurs of "May the Lord bless you and keep you and shine His countenance down upon you"; was not an obliteration of lessons she drilled into him: "be a good Jew grow strong and proud be a worthy Jew make me proud before God and all Jews I survived so you could live"? How could you tell her "no," when every utterance of that little word, of those two innocent little letters, every mere whisper of them transformed, on their journey between the spittle of your lips and the wrinkles of her ears, into a rifle butt to the head, a boot stomp smack in the middle of the pregnant gut? How many times could you tell such a person that no, you don't want to marry the cantor's daughter down the block, the butcher's niece around the corner, your teacher's younger sister . . . but that you'd gladly screw the rabbi's hunky son? How do you say "no"? Dave never found a way.

On the second night of Chanukah, little Davey always picked yellow and red candles and a green one as *shames;* and other candles for the third night and so on and so on until the last night of eight candles plus the *shames:* an entire beautiful "rainbow from heaven, a gift from God to our very own living room," Grandma would say, and she'd light the *shames,* would use it to light the others, Davey and Grandma chanting the blessings together, just the two of them, Grandma's strong hand gripping Davey's shoulder, lifting to caress his *"shayna punim,* such a pretty face that defeats Hitler's wicked plans with every smile." Grandma smiling for Davey, Davey smiling for her, each pretending not to miss Davey's dead parents. He and Grandma would sing *"Maoz tsur yeshuasi,"* "Rock of ages praise to thee . . ." and would eat greasy, fried *latkes* made from hand-grated potatoes, "like in Belorussia we used to make when I was a girl," pancakes with sour cream that smeared all over their cheeks and Davey would giggle and Grandma, too. Then she'd make *punchkas,* deep-fried doughnuts yummier than any others Dave has ever tasted since. Chanukah, the holiday of oil and light, when one night's oil burned for eight in the ancient Temple. A miracle. Chanukah, the holiday of rebellion against foreign oppressors, a routing of the invaders. Eight men to suck him, so that Dave would be—once, twice, eight times a candle, a menorah blazing up at heaven in commemoration of the ancient victory, liberation. And Grandma: company to enjoy the holiday moment, a witness, his *shames,* the candle who keeps watch and makes certain he doesn't fail to ignite the way he should.

Dave, ready now in the Fens, saunters over to the wooden fence post, rubs the back of his hand against a belly, the fat groper's belly, and the man does what fat gropers do, reaches out to Dave's crotch, fondles the soft, denim covered basket, looks up into Dave's face with eyes awaiting permission or command. Dave lifts his hand to the man's shoulder, shoves him to his knees. He unzips Dave and in a moment: "I'm blue," Dave murmurs up at the stars, his fists on his hips, not caressing the greasy hair, not yanking the man's head closer, just letting the man enjoy while Dave does. When Dave's really hard, really really, he pulls out from the wet lips and slick tongue. Eight men to suck him, sure, but no way Dave can spill his melted candle wax seed eight times in a row; miracles, after all, ceased in ancient days, although maybe, if Dave were twenty years younger . . . He pats the head—"Thanks." (Grandma always taught him to be polite.)

Zip up, wander into a grassy clearing edged by twenty-foot-high reeds on water. Two blond men, tall and short, walking together. Late thirties, maybe? Early forties like Dave? Ogle ogle ogle and Dave holds their gazes; they walk, look back, he stares. They look at each other and one nods. Into the tall reeds, the two men and Dave, along a narrow path created nights before, weeks before, months before by other men at night. Three Tarzans in the jungle, Dave thinks, or two Tarzans and one Jane, or one Tarzan and two Janes. Three Janes? Dave winks into the empty night. The ground by the pond is soft and muddy. Darkness, but not pitch black; their eyes catch moonlight while checking out his crotch bulge, step closer. Dead reeds crunch on the ground; the munch of Grandma's fried potato *latkes.* Dave reaches beneath the men's leather jackets, pinches, through flannel shirts, right tit with right hand, left tit with left hand. Perfect balance. Both men drop to their knees. Ha ha! thinks Dave, triumphant. Easier than he expected. One unzips him while the other undoes Dave's black leather belt; one licks his balls while the other sucks his cock. Dave knows he won't stop them short. They lick and suck and switch positions and lick and suck and "I'm gonna shoot!" Dave hears himself spurt lightly onto dried, broken reeds. "I'm green," he mutters, "I'm red." The blonds stand, support him for a moment as his strength drains at their doing. One Delilah, two Delilahs, three Delilahs, four. Five Delilahs, six Delilahs, seven Delilahs, more! Feeling generous in his Chanukah victory, Dave kisses each of the men on the cheek, says, "*Chag sameach.*" The two squint, hurry away.

Dave sighs in the hollow of reeds, feels the cold December breeze blow on his soft cock, still wet with saliva, wet and dangling and out in the night air, beneath the stars and the moon and Grandma, the *shames*. He shakes his head to blur the vision of Grandma's clucking, wart-tipped tongue. He crouches to peer at the broken reeds and the mud, speckled with small white drops of Dave shining now in the moonlight, proto-Jews out among the bulrushes, shivering and dying in the cold on the last night of Chanukah. He thinks to plant the sole of his right leather boot firmly on this whiteness, on his purity, his liquid soul, to mash it into the mud—his manhood, his faggot genes. But he doesn't. It's Chanukah and he's the menorah.

He walks into the clearing, walks and strolls and regains his strength, sheared Samson somehow receiving God's undeserved favor. "Time to be Candle Number Four," Dave whispers.

Now, Grandma, thinks Dave the tour guide, on your left you have guys sizing each other up. Known as "cruising." Off they goooo, into the wild reeds yonder, sucking off under the sky . . . Good old American homo boys. Patriots every last one of them. On your right is my favorite Fens spot, a circle of maple trees. Look at all the studs, Grandma, a dozen at least, in a tight little circle. Ever see a circle suck before, Grandma? We'll saunter over, real casually, as if we've no interest at all in what's going on although of course this is the reason we're here. I'm here. You're here because I'm here, and you just can't leave me alone for a second. Even though you don't really want to be here, do you Grandma? . . . Or do you? Could you maybe want to be here—just for a minute? To share the holiday like we always did, to make sure I'm having fun? . . . Nah, that's bullshit. You puking up there?

Dave looks at all the hungry cocksuckers milling about, wants them to worship his cock that made a covenant with God when Davey was only eight days old. The *bris*. At eight days old. Eight days of Chanukah. Eight candles, eight suckers. One little, two little, three little cocksuckers. Four little, five little, six little cocksuckers. Seven little, eight little—gotta stop there, Davey Boy. Eight's your limit, your Jewish limit. It's the Christians got twelve days. Lucky Christians.

Dave approaches the closed circle of men, hears slurps and grunts, looks over shoulders and sees a man on his knees, bent over and burying his face in first one open fly, then another. The suckees stand impassively, like stone, enjoying but not revealing their pleasure. Without turning his head, the short man in front of Dave reaches behind and rubs Dave's crotch. The man rubs and rubs and Dave's body begins to respond. The hand unzips, skillfully, reaches in and squeezes Dave in his white briefs, maneuvers the elastic waistband down and tangles his fingers in Dave's hairs, pulls out Dave's cock, strokes. Dave loves the feel, thinks "Candle Number Four—white" but then realizes that stroking doesn't count. Sure, maybe it's a prelude to the suck, but still. Dave moves closer, rubs himself against the man's jeans-covered ass, reaches around and feels the man's soft, uncircumcised dick dangling out of his pants. Dave plays with it and at Dave's squeeze, the man drops Dave's dick, leaves the circle and walks away. Oh, the guy's a total bottom. Too bad, Dave thinks, missed a chance.

Dave takes the short man's place on the circle, watches the sucker nurse on one guy's dick, take it so deep into his mouth that Dave can no longer see it. Poppers pass from hand to hand, Dave takes his turn, feels the rush, smells the melting Chanukah wax he'd notice every time he entered the living room where the lit menorah stood on the coffee table, in front of wide open curtains, for all to see. "Be proud," Grandma would say, "let the world see who you are." My cut dick's out under the stars, Grandma, is that proud enough for you, dear? He leans forward, tussles the sucker's hair—no response; tugs on the hair—no response; yanks on the hair—but the guy won't give up the dick from his mouth. Shit. Come on, it's Dave's turn! He beats his hard cock on the side of the circle sucker's head, rubs his cock in the sucker's brown hair. At this, the sucker responds, turns— yes! Dave is Number Four—white.

He gives the guy a few seconds to make the lighting fully count, then pulls out of the mouth. Dave is about to move away when two other men drop to their knees to service the circle. Since Dave's gun is already out of the holster, why the hell not? He moves closer to them and the two each look at his cock, up at his face; they turn away, clamp their mouths on two other guys. Hey! Why them first and not Dave? He examines the suckees' square-jawed faces—their late teen-age faces?—is that it? A shit-eating reason like that? But this isn't about age; it's about dick. And Dave's is as hard as any of these youn-ger guys'. Well, it was just a minute ago. It was! Dave's pissed, waits his turn. Eventually, after his hand tires at making himself hard again, he gets to be the yellow candle and the pink one—Five, Six, suck those dicks—but he doesn't shoot because he still needs to become Seven and Eight and because these two suckers weren't joyful matchsticks. It's suppose to be a goddamn holiday, a glorious holiday, a celebration!

He zips up, wanders across a stretch of grass. Tough night.

Over there . . . what's going on by the willow? A group of young guys with buzz cuts like soldiers. A cluster of service-men? Hah! Dave goes over, peeks above a high shoulder at the circle jerk, begins to nudge his way among them, hoping that here he'll get to be Num-ber Seven.

"Go away, old man." A muscled arm shoves Dave aside.

What? What is this bullshit! Dave's only forty. No one's com-plained before tonight—not at the bars, the baths. A little gray at the temples, sure, and a few gray pubes—but how would this twenty-five-year-old punk know that? Can he see, in the dark, the wrinkles by Dave's eyes? The booze-puffiness beneath them? The two-inch roll of fat around Dave's middle? Dave's pants are still on, so how could this young son-of-a-bitch—?

Dave's about to force his way into the circle when he feels the wind against his face, hears Grandma laugh at him. He stops, feels sud-denly tired and ancient. As old as Chanukah. Dumb-ass idea—Dave as menorah. Dumb-ass idea—Dave as Jew.

He rubs a palm across his greasy forehead, stomps away from the circle, heads to leave the Fens, to return to his hand-me-down meno-rah at home. He walks past one garden and another, spits onto a roseless bush, then sees a trim-bearded, long-nosed, Jewish-looking man, the first Jewish-looking man he's noticed under the Chanukah moon. Their eyes meet and they stare. Dave thinks to avoid this young competitor who might reject Dave as old, might understand and mock Dave-as-menorah. Yet Dave is drawn to him.

Could this maybe—could this possibly be the next match to light his candle? If not Grandma's hand caressing his *shayna punim,* if not wooden *dreidels* spinning across the kitchen linoleum, if not chocolate Chanukah coins melting on his fingers, if no holiday laughter, then at least, at the very least, Dave can get sucked by another Jew. A young Jew. What luck!

Dave's Jew walks down a narrow path between garden fences, turns his face back from time to time as if to check on Dave—yes! Yes! He wants it!—moves across the clearing into the reeds, but before Dave can step in, a redhead does. ShitFuckPiss! Dave crunches through anyway, sees the redhead on his knees sucking Dave's Jew, the Jew who looks at Dave and smiles. Not waiting a historical millennium, a century, a second in which youth and joy might again slip away, Dave leans over the kneeling, sucking redhead, leans in and kisses the Jewish mouth, slips between the Jewish lips, feels the soft, thick, wet, wartless Jewish tongue slide along his own. The redhead pivots, unzips Dave. Candle Number Seven, and Dave sees himself as orange. But it's not over.

Dave and his Jew kiss above the sucker and undo shirt buttons and reach hands in, cold hands in the cold Chanukah night, Dave's cold fingers on a muscular, hairy chest, across a rippled belly, and Dave sighs in pleasure, soul pleasure, the deepest pleasure of the night, of the holiday, of the season, of the year, reaches his cold fingers down in order to feel the cut cock of his hot Jew and—*un*circumcised? Dave pulls away from the kiss, looks down, feels and sees and goes soft in the redhead's mouth. The redhead pulls away, spits, stands, and leaves. Dave holds his Jew's uncircumcised cock, stares into the other's eyes. "Jewish?" Dave whispers. His Jew nods but avoids Dave's eyes. Dave looks up at the stars and thinks and it dawns on him: here, too, is someone raised by survivors of the camps, born to survivors of the camps or their children, to new Marranos fearful of pee-pee betrayal to whichever Inquisitor might one day seize power, Jews who did not permit fulfillment of the Jewish covenant with God, who broke it in order to remain alive and without fear and still Jewish in their hidden hearts, but not in their visible dicks. Dave's Jew leans forward to kiss Dave again, reaches down for Dave's cock, and Dave thinks that he's about to become blue Candle Number Eight and how perfect to have a Jew be the one to set Dave finally ablaze, to be the *shames* lighting the last candle and watching and guarding and shining warm holy countenances. But no. Here's an uncut Jewish boy, a Jew circumcised from Jewish history, and this, Dave decides, is the man who deserves to be the last candle of the holiday night. So Dave pushes the hand aside, drops to his knees, draws in, between his lips, the Jewish foreskin, wets the thin Jewish hood, feels the silky, *tallis*-like skin glide along his tongue, thinks to bite so as to taste Jewish blood, to circumcise this Jewish cock and connect the man to Jewish history. But Dave does not bite because, for the moment, he cares less about binding this man to history than about binding him to himself, wants this Jewish man to feel good, to like Dave on Chanukah, to love him, to think Dave the best little Jewish boy in the world.

6

"I can't believe I'm letting you drag me here," Dave says. They turn the corner.

"And one is not even a drag queen."

"Bad pun. You know English too well."

"If not the Anne Frank House, then . . . here. You should see at least one of them. You do not realize how admirable you Jewish people are—preserving your identity throughout history no matter how dispersed around the globe."

Should Dave feel proud at his people's knack for holding onto a dead past? He doesn't know.

Ah, he's alright, this Alexander. Taking Dave to the synagogue because he thinks it's good for Dave. Not that it is. Or maybe it is, who the fuck knows? But because he thinks it's important for Dave. A good little guy.

They cross the street. Dave slows as they reach the brick building.

"One has always wanted to see this place," says Alexander, "but has always felt strange at the thought of coming alone."

"Yeah, I don't like cumming alone, either."

"Terrible pun. And blasphemous *here* of all places. Go ahead, ring the doorbell."

"There really is a Mister Leather Holland contest tomorrow night? You promise you'll take me?"

"On one's own Hippocrytical Oath. Now ring the doorbell."

Dave doesn't want to, does want to, doesn't want to, but he definitely does want Alexander to take him to the Mister Leather Holland contest and Muscle Dick, although he probably could find it without Alexander, but that wouldn't be as much fun. "I haven't been to a synagogue in God knows how many years."

"Do you think He keeps track?"

"If He does, I'm fucked."

Alexander claps his hands. "I just love being a catalyst for mischief. Now ring the bell."

Dave does. In a moment—*buzzzzzzz*, then the door lock clicks open. Dave nods to himself: security. Makes sense. This is Europe, where everyone's just a tank roll away from Germany.

He steps inside: *yarmulkes,* Israeli CDs, *mezzuzot,* books about the Portuguese Synagogue, Dutch Jewry, the Holocaust. "It's a goddamn gift shop."

Alexander steps around him, ogles the display of menorahs. "Dave, these are all so pretty!"

"Yeah. We can look at this sh—at this stuff afterward. Let's get it over with. Where's the entrance to the synagogue?"

In Dutch, Alexander asks the *yarmulke*-wearing salesman behind the counter, the middle-aged man Dave won't look straight in the eye for fear the man will see who Dave is, will know him, will say that although Alexander, this gay Dutch Indonesian is permitted entry, Dave is not. The salesman, a dull expression on his face, points to the gift shop's back door. Alexander goes out; Dave follows.

A courtyard. Dave looks around and understands—the gift shop is part of a fortress of low buildings surrounding the synagogue itself. Security. "Everyone's always after us Jews."

"Not everyone," Alexander says with a hip wiggle.

Dave looks up at the high, brick synagogue built by Jews fleeing the Inquisition.

Dave can't believe he's here, about to enter a famous synagogue, any synagogue: old men constantly readjusting their body-wrapping *tallesim,* like huge white shrouds, so the tassles—no, you asshole, not "tassles," this isn't some stripper show—so the *tzitzit,* the fringes, won't hit the floor, old men shuffling a few steps forward, mumbling in Hebrew, shuffling a few steps backward, muttering the *shemoneh esreh,* the prayer of eighteen benedictions to the God Dave is convinced died long ago, or never existed in the first place, or who abandoned Earth once He saw the evils men were capable of, or who hangs around just to laugh His white cloud head off at the prank that was Creation; Grandma's God, who, she always said, rescued her from the camps—who, Dave always thought, stuck her there in the first place.

He follows Alexander inside. No other people. Lots of light from huge windows. And wood everywhere. Dark wood. Walnut? Mahogany? Shiny brass chandeliers like he's never seen, with candles. So beautiful. A three- or four-story high, barrel-vaulted ceiling of wood. A gigantic open space, the grandest open space anywhere, a plaza, half of Jerusalem beneath one Jewish ceiling. Not some dumpy room like Grandma's cramped auditorium at Yeshiva University. Dave points out to Alexander that the *bimah,* the stage where the rabbi and cantor stand during services, is across the room from the *aron kodesh,* the holy ark holding the Torahs; this is the Sephardic way, different from Grandma's Ashkenazic tradition.

"But still Jewish," Alexander says.

"Of course, still Jewish." And there, hanging before the *aron,* burns the eternal flame which, Grandma taught him, symbolizes the eternal nature of God. "The *ner tamid."* Dave still knows these words.

He rubs his fingertips along nicked wooden benches, walks on worn, planked wooden floors, hears the creak, imagines scampering about as a little boy, catching his *yarmulke* before it falls off, seeing old men's pseudo-scolding fingershakes at their little Jewish future, the very reason they struggled to survive. And their "what a *mensch"* shoulder pats after he steps down from the *bimah,* having chanted *maftir* from the Torah's *Mishpatim,* and the *haftorah* of Jeremiah as well—Dave's having become bar mitzvah at age thirteen. . . . And they tell Dave's Dad, Dave's *kvell*ing Dad they're envious of the *nachas,* the soulful pride, that this son with a *Yiddishe kup* must give him every day—Dad? Mom and Dad died years before Dave's bar mitzvah. But it's Dad there on one of the wooden benches, in gym shorts and T-shirt, shifting a basketball from hand to hand, beaming a smile at Dave brighter than any eternal light, then winking up at the women's balcony to Mom in her yellow, daisy-trimmed pillbox hat, she waving and throwing kisses down to her boy in the huge *tallis,* her good Jewish boy.

Dave squeezes his eyes shut, looks up again to the women's balcony.

Nobody there.

Off-limits to tourists now.

And during services it's always off-limits to men.

Yeah, keep women separate so the men won't be distracted during prayer . . . like the panels and curtains of separation, the *mechitsah* in Grandma's synagogue, ever kept Dave's mind from wandering to sex, kept him from getting a hard-on during prayer, from watching some of the almost old, but not too old men around him, so many men cramped together in that small room . . . the scent of soap on their skin every summer Shabbos morning . . . Dave would imagine them showering, lathering hairy chests and asses and cocks, washing for God, for Dave who'd slip into the shower stall with them and substitute his slippery hands for theirs and rub his face against their bellies while they caressed him and—they're taking the Torah out of the *aron* so you've got to stand, and—quick!—fold your hands in front of your crotch so no one can detect your forbidden thoughts, you wicked little boy.

Off-limits. So much is off Jewish limits. Dave is.

"What a beautiful place to get married," Alexander says.

Dave pictures it, he and—Alexander? . . . no, not Alexander; Alexander as best man, maybe—pictures Dave and a faceless other groom standing beneath the *chupah,* the wedding canopy, saying "I do" and then dropping their tux trousers so they can exchange cockrings. "Yes, that's it—gently," says the rabbi, "first slip his left ball through since that one hangs lower, and now the right ball and now pull the soft dick through—come on boys, don't get hard—some decorum, please!"

Like they'd ever accept Dave. Even here in homosexual-loving Amsterdam.

Fuck!

Dave grabs Alexander, backs him against a concrete pillar facing the *aron,* kisses him beneath the light of the *ner tamid,* sticks tongue into mouth, tastes Alexander's lemony saliva, wills blood to flow to his own crotch so he can at the very least rub his cock against another man here right here right fucking here in God's scowling face.

A moment of stillness, then Alexander shoves Dave away. "Are you insane?"

Blood has not flowed to Dave's crotch. "Don't get any ideas," he says. "This isn't about you."

Dave stomps along the decrepit wooden floor, kicks a ratty bench, flings open the synagogue door, runs into the courtyard. He rushes through the gift shop, pulls the front doorknob—it won't twist. Pulls again, pushes—the door doesn't open. Dave yanks and yanks. Still, the door won't open. He twists, yells at the *yarmulke*-wearing salesman, "Let me out!"

* * *

There once was a Jewboy named Jesus,
Who liked to eat burgers with cheeses.
"That's unkosher," said Dad.

"Pop, you make me so mad."
Said Mom, "Let God do as he pleases!"

* * *

Larry looks at the worn dollar bill creased and wrinkled with age, the way one should be with age, a lucky old dollar bill on Larry's young pink firm-fleshed palm. He traces a finger along his sleek-lined "wave" telephone, all black, envies its repose on the brown carton where the teak night table used to be—one of two teak night tables he gave away only a year ago, soon after conscious denial finally faded. Should have given away the fancy telephone, too, but Larry needed some remembrance of things past, of futures once thought yet to be.

Maybe they would be yet? So much has changed, keeps changing month to month that Larry sometimes fancies himself a polished boomerang zinging back and forth between hope and despair. Maybe he should move down under? No, he thinks, he already is down under, any deeper and he'd surely drown. What a lovely title for a book, *My Life As Australia*. Exotic. Escapist. Would probably sell. Not that Larry would ever write it. Not that he would ever write anything, in disgrace with fortune as he is, although not yet with men's eyes—no lesions, no emaciation, no hair loss. But that outcast day will come. No time to write, he tells himself, told himself, no time. Bull. No ability. Once, perhaps. But no longer.

He reads the telephone number the guy—Dave, was it?—scribbled on the dollar bill's dirty, cream-colored border. What irony for Larry to have had a pen in his back pocket that night, in the Fens of all places. Must have stuck it there automatically; he generally functions automatically these days, like a television commercial toy rabbit operated by battery . . . going and going and going until one day the battery finally wears out. Will wear out. Old habit, old hopes. Larry's no writer. He proved that. Seven years. Seven wasted years learning little, spending a lot. Money he didn't have. Should never have bought those teak night tables in the first place after non-graduation, or the rest of the teak bed set, which he was also to give away later, keeping only mattress and box spring. Or the ever-so-soft, gray tweed, L-shaped sofa from Bloomingdale's, now replaced by frayed orange floor cushions scavenged from Tuesday morning garbage pickup on the street. Larry deserves no more. Or the Armani suits . . . well, he still needs—"needs" might be too strong a word—still uses the suits for work, assisting an accountant, working numbers but not words. Certainly he never should have *given* everything away and without claiming charitable deductions to boot, should have sold the furniture to help melt his snows of Kilimanjaro credit card debt. Could he do anything right?

One. 1.1.1.1. Solemn George. Larry turns the dollar bill over, and on the flip side sees the strong eagle and pyramid with an eye—what on earth does that mean? Had Larry majored in Near Eastern studies perhaps he'd be able to figure out the symbol now, but to what practical purpose were seven years of English? Who was the mystery man in some of Shakespeare's sonnets? So original an idea for a thesis . . . oh yes, so original. So original that Larry couldn't write it, even though thesis was a graduation requirement at Princeton, that Shangri-La campus just this side of paradise.

Three years sailing through—well, not sailing, perhaps, but tug boating through, canoeing through with charley horse arms, but managing course work despite weekends partying in New York. Not at first, for Larry was still closeted in the freshman autumn of his confused sexual discontent, but then one day after winter fencing lessons, the teacher initiated him to a different sort of parry and thrust, later brought him to the men of New York. Central Park bushes. Village bars. Chelsea private clubs. It had to have been one of the guys he met at the baths, but which? The one with the waxed mustache, or the man with the bird of prey tattooed on his back to ward off attackers, or the skinny blond with the unusually large endowment that left Larry bleeding yet smiling, unconcerned because they'd used protection, Larry always used protection, well almost always, he couldn't always remember after the beers, but usually protection—still all the same nevertheless anyway shit happens—or was it one of the fat or hairy or muscular or short ones or blacks or WASPS or Puerto Ricans or Jews or *Paisanos* like Larry? Which man was the one, the one man's meat which was another man's poison, Larry's, the one mistake, that one man among a thousand noted in Larry's book of memory, that one whom it makes absolutely no difference to recall.

Larry has no idea how this Dave will react, whether in panic or with calm understanding. To call or not to call: that is the question— whether it's wiser to suffer alone in the mind the outrageous arrows of misfortune or to speak, perchance to share the nightmare, to dream, to pour the poison from one's lips into another's ear, to dream of sharing truth and thereby ending, or at least moderating, the heartache and the thousand natural shocks that flesh is heir to, the decades trapped in one's mortal coil, to dream of escaping the inevitable whips and scorns of time . . . . Hmmm, perhaps Larry learned something in college after all.

In God We Trust. If only that were so and he could. Larry crosses himself. It took weeks for the medicinal cocktail to kick in, to effect its mere moderate improvement. How long does it take prayers? How many Hail Marys and Our Fathers finally to get out the damned spot of spots contaminating his blood? How many novenas and votive candles lit in Dorchester's St. Margaret's?

Every day for a year, that fourth year at Princeton after finding out, Larry would kneel in the nave of the neogothic campus chapel with its stained glass windows and concrete columns and would pray so long on bended knee that, when later sitting in Firestone Library before *Hamlet* or *Macbeth*, Larry would know the pain of supplication all afternoon, the ache in those knees that had dropped so often to leafy park dirt or hard bathroom tile in preparation for sucking his sweets. Supplication for succor, but not atonement: Larry'd done nothing wrong—nothing nothing nothing—clouds and eclipses stain both moon and sun, all men make faults, and what is Larry but a man as nature made him?

If only Larry could be saved by the God of altar boys and white-robed choirs, of Rubens altarpieces and Jesus descending from the cross, muscular Jesus, tender Jesus, a man for whom Larry might indeed have given his life had Jesus been corporeal and willing to caress him, kiss him, hold him, speak tender words of Godly love. Forgive if I blaspheme, Larry would think in the chapel while glancing furtively about to ensure his solitude, and then, on sore bruised knees he would crawl up one aisle and down another to show dear Jesus that he, Larry, would willingly follow the Lord's holy suffering path if only He'd sign that He was paying attention, that, as Larry had asserted at rallies on Gay Pride Day, Jesus loved him, too.

He'd sometimes lie awake in his dormitory single, in his narrow cot meant for one, and would slide close to the wall, press his body tight, his naked back against the hard white wall, would feel New Jersey's crusty mantle of wind and chill and rain bore through the castle's outer stone wall, through insulation and plaster to his body, God's chill touching his body, and he'd lie with his arm outstretched on the pillow imagining Jesus there, brought down from the cross and resting in Larry's bed, beside him for Larry to comfort and nurse, the hero of heroes whose bloody forehead thorn marks Larry would gently flick with the tip of his tongue. Larry would move slowly down, lap the hand- and foot- and spear-wounds clean, all the while tasting the Lord's blood, not as sweet purple wine, but as bitter red metal, the sacrifice of a newly shorn lamb. If only thus to have imbibed the plague, wouldn't Larry willingly die?

He'd drift, on those nights, to innocent sleep, the balm of his hurt mind; and he'd feel Jesus pressing close, Jesus, the grave where buried love lives, hung with trophies of lovers gone. Two men lying together, the Lord loving Larry, the Son himself a father transcending all fathers, beyond Larry's own who'd said, in the name of the Father, the Son, and the Holy Ghost get out of my fucking house you goddamn queer freak while Larry's mother stood in a cold white kitchen corner, kissing the silver cross from around her neck, looking up as though for a sign that she should, just once, contradict Dad, but how does Blessed Mary choose between her son and the father of her child when both are Lord? Loving Jesus holding him, a man who would never reject Larry, and Larry tasting the dying Lord's breath, the sweet frankincense and myrrh of His babyhood. But by morning the space beside Larry in bed would be empty, Jesus having ascended during the night, having abandoned him after all.

The inhibitors were not inhibiting enough in Larry, not this new cocktail, not that. Maybe all the Jesus blood that Larry drank in fantasy during those last years of college was interfering—not truly real blood, Larry knows, but real to him because he willed it, tasted it, masturbated to it night after night in silent whispered prayer to God to help him live at least until age thirty-three like Jesus himself and then to do with him what He will. God's placebo killing Larry as punishment for forbidden thoughts of divine love?

In God We Trust. Larry does, he still does, he does. Although at times he almost chides God for making him that countenance he is, so handsome to all men. Dave's eyes followed him from the start as Larry skulked among dozens of other sex-seekers in the dateless night, and then, after Dave reached down in the hollow of reeds and felt and saw Larry's foreskin, the man asked with a puzzled intonation, "Jewish?"

Larry had grown accustomed to the question in Jewish Brookline where he worked, when the occasional old woman also in line for a lunchtime bagel might chat a bit, then ask, "You want, maybe, to meet my granddaughter?" But never before had Dorchester Italian Larry heard the question posed by cruising men. Whereas Jewish Baby Jesus had sacrificed his ounce of flesh, Larry had not, so his nod at Dave's question was a total lie. This Dave, who looked Jewish the way Larry did, with gently curved long nose, narrow face, dark wavy hair, this Dave wanted Larry to be a fellow Jew, Larry sensed that he did and it had been so long since Larry'd been out cruising in Boston's Fens, so long since he'd allowed himself the comfort even of the safest sex, years since he'd learned his truth, discovered the finite nature of eternity. (Larry has grown to realize that although eternity is initially as vast as our conception, when one's capacity to think is later limited by the immediacy of death, when one suddenly feels death as more than the space beyond the flat earth's distant end, when one finally understands death to be a chasm merely steps ahead in the dark, when one's ability to conceive shrinks, then eternity shrinks to the paltry length of a foreshortened human life. How very much the Renaissance painters understood.)

So, in a moment of self-indulgence, Larry nodded that he was Jewish, he did it—yes—he did it for the relief. Relief! Relief! My kingdom for relief! Larry knew, for that briefest of instants, happiness—how little is needed to make a happy life. But then Larry realized what he'd done: he, who was never able to finish anything—not his thesis that he worked on for four consecutive senior years, not his degree, not a crossword puzzle, not a bowl of breakfast cereal; he, who for years had refused to finish anything because to finish one thing would be to invoke the start of the end of everything, his life; he, this pre-terminal man, had just spent himself in a stranger's mouth.

Before Larry could reach fingers in so as to scoop out the poison and redeem himself, Dave swallowed with a smile on his face, wished Larry a Happy Chanukah—well, it was December—stood, embraced him. Larry returned the embrace, so unusual in the reeds, in his life, the feel of another man against him, a real man holding him, resting head on shoulder, and Larry pretended Dave to be his savior at last, an angel if not the Lord, come to show that Larry was not past hope past cure past help, that Larry might not, as he'd for years assumed, necessarily die one day alone.

Larry waited for days after, waited past another New Year's Eve alone, until today, January 1, to start afresh and decide. He must telephone, at least to return the dollar bill if not to reveal that he is not, in fact, Jew, or that, unlikely as is the possibility—semen in the throat isn't the most notorious culprit, a mere petty criminal, a bumbler who rarely cracks the combination lock's code, yet . . . one who does, on rare occasion, find a way to break and enter—that he may have put Dave's life at premature risk and thereby have blown Larry's own chance to enter heaven and dwell there with the Lord forever. Not that he understands "forever." Or the Lord.

Larry lifts the sleek black wave telephone receiver.

No, don't speak either well or ill of yourself, not of yourself at all. For to speak is like to write; and to capture one's own form, whether on the page or in another's imagination, is to give in to devouring time, to aid its pen forever sketching antique lines on the brow of youth. No, disclose self neither to the page nor to another in the world, and thus stave off time, which may, perchance, refrain from stealing that which exists in no other form on earth but in one's own living self.

Larry sets the receiver down, stands, walks away from the telephone and out of the bedroom. Perhaps tomorrow. Or the day after. He will make that telephone call, he swears an oath to himself that he will do the honorable thing. But not tonight. Tonight Larry will sit quietly on a frayed orange cushion beneath his single halogen lamp and will read sonnets, will immerse himself in words from the past that have merged with his present, words which own the power to expand his present beyond itself in the only direction available, into a realm of hybrid time which, Larry hopes, might somehow actually exist in the eternal mind of God.

7

Stepping off Tram #1, Alexander smiles in a mix of pleasure and disappointment. It's noon precisely, on Koningsplein opposite the Albert Heijn supermarket. And here, so as to set a jocular tone to their adventure and to erase ignore blot out yesterday's biblical oppressiveness, one has been constructing quips to fling upon Dave's anticipated late arrival: "Lost track of time while cruising the public toilets, did we?" or "What kept you? Caught with your pants down in Vondelpark's rose garden?" or "You were just so popular last night at the 'Why Not?' brothel that all the escorts refused to let you go, right?"

Instead, the only jab coming to mind on the spur of the punctual moment is: "What's this? A tie?"

Dave's grin melts. "You said it was fancy, the place I'm gonna treat you to."

"A tie," says Alexander in a voice dripping with feigned condescension.

"I can take it off easy enough." Dave yanks at it and mumbles. "No 'Good morning;' no 'glad to see you.' First thing out of your fucking mouth is a crack about the tie."

Goodness, how sensitive. Again, one has underestimated him. Alexander leans in to give the traditional Dutch gay kiss hello—peck on right cheek, on left, then on lips—but stops himself, certain that Dave will misunderstand. "One apologizes," he says. "You're right, one was totally insensitive. A charming tie. Yellow and green diamonds suit you."

"Colorful for summer, you know?"

"A brilliant choice."

"Just wanted to thank you for dinner and for showing me around so much. And to apologize for being such a weird dickhead at the synagogue yesterday."

"*Très galant.* One adores the tie."

"You're not just shitting me?"

With lowered voice, "One is not into scat."

"Hah!"

Yes, to lift a child's mood, one must descend to the child's level rather than attempt to elevate the child to one's own. And Alexander hopes for a continuation of their developing camaraderie. They enjoyed themselves together at the parade, did they not, with voyeurism as a sexual tension relief for Dave . . . and maybe for oneself as well. The subsequent visit to the synagogue was . . . well . . . provocative in its own way, and certainly offered Alexander insight into a different aspect of Dave's personality. A sense of burden. But what to make of it all? Depth? Depth of pain? Grounds for further bonding, perhaps? That kiss in the apse (if one may call it such . . . mental note: check whether synagogues have "apses") was not one of romantic or even lustful passion. An expression of . . . what? Loneliness? Rage? Not actually a violation of one's person, if one takes motivation into account. Which one is uncertain whether or not to do in such circumstance. Had Alexander actually enjoyed that kiss? Truth to tell . . . no. Not the kiss. Rather shocking. Frightening even. Boorishness is one thing, but incipient violence is quite another. A boundary one is unwilling to cross. Perhaps best to keep this American at a certain distance. Too volatile for romantic involvement. Yet they've already gone too far simply to say *adieu*. Yes. Yes, it's true. Alexander senses an embryonic connection at a rather fundamental level.

And, one must admit, he's great fun to have around, this noble American savage. A wildman certainly gets one's blood to circulate. Even arguments are a welcome change to a routine of attending lectures, studying in the library, thumping bellies and dispensing pills in the clinic, supping alone on cheese and crackers, watching British comedies until boredom and fatigue conspire one to sleep. Not unpleasant to cook for another man, a friend.

Hmmm. An emotional response of uncertain etiology . . . Strangers on a bus, after all, but on an extended journey. Perhaps. Part of each other's world, yet not. Potential transatlantic confidants? One is not in the habit of bemoaning one's fate to another. Not to parents who reject one's relationship choice then send a bouquet of flowers to reingratiate themselves once the relationship no longer exists to threaten. Not to friends who urge one to "boogie and move on." Certainly not to Jeroen's family. Undignified. This Dave is just the sort to probe until he learns private details. Precisely a confidant's role. Perhaps one sensed this about him from the beginning.

. . . Unless he's the sort to lose interest entirely once realizing that sex is an unlikely option. Is that the actual reason Alexander arrived with an arsenal of quips about lateness? In determination to undercut, to undermine, to sabotage the budding . . . acquaintanceship? . . . friendship? Before one could be disappointed at its evaporation or worse, at its withdrawal?

"You've yanked your tie askew," Alexander says, "and it now resembles a hangman's noose. Not that this fails to suit you. Here, permit a bit of straightening." Heat against Alexander's fingers from Dave's neck. Stop. Pointless to indulge in even the most fleeting of such thoughts. Not with this emotionally erratic bohemian from across the sea.

"Like playing with my knot?" Dave asks.

"Yes, you dog." Banter, ever a gentleman's face-saver. And the foundation of our particular whatevership. "Let's be on our way, shall we? Not too far. A few blocks into the Jordaan." The tinkle of a bell behind them.

"Hey, what are you doing?" asks Dave.

"Grasping your elbow so as to guide you out of the path of oncoming cyclers. Don't get any ideas."

"If my elbow turns you on, go for it."

Not worth a rejoinder.

Over this canal bridge, down that narrow street. "With newly cobbled stones. To recreate an aura of glories past."

"Follow the yellow brick road."

"They're gray. Not in the least yellow."

"Forget it."

Yellow? A slight about one's ethnic origins? Alexander releases Dave's elbow. Enough. If the boor's to be run down by autos, so be it.

One can still enjoy the Jordaan. Artists' studios, galleries, cafés. No, one shan't point out the various chic boutiques.

"I bought the tie special, at De Buyin' Cough."

"De Bijnkorf."

"Whatever."

"Owned by a Jewish man, one has heard."

"Really?"

"The story goes that when the Nazis demanded a list of which employees were Jewish and which were not, the shop's owner refused to comply. Went into hiding."

"And?"

"No one knows what became of him."

Dave strokes the tie. "Glad I bought it there."

"There are cheaper places," Alexander says.

"Like that's the point. And like I know what the cheap places are."

"Forgive me. You know us Dutch, so frugal."

"*You* Dutch."

Another slur?

Dave continues, "Stingy."

"Be careful."

" 'Dutch treat,' 'Go Dutch,' " says Dave.

"Some call us Dutch 'the Jews of the North.' "

"Hey!"

"Ah, ethnic pride." And with a smirk, "How quaint."

" 'Dutch elm disease,' " Dave looks triumphant.

" 'Dutch process cocoa,' *'The Flying Dutchman,'* 'the Little Dutch Boy.' "

"Go stick your finger in a dyke, Little Dutch Boy. But don't be surprised if she screams."

"Beg pardon?"

"Yeah, beg."

"Aren't you in a mood?"

"I'm always in the mood."

"So one has noticed."

Stretching toward the sun, Dave's arm muscles accentuate themselves beneath the short sleeves of the white shirt. He possesses little else, goodness knows, but one cannot deny him his animal appeal.

"Got laid last night."

Swine. But what else would one expect? "Shall we ring the Westerkerk chimes in celebration?" Envious? Examine yourself, Alexander! Envious? . . . Hmm . . . more titilated than envious. Not envious that someone was with him. No. Curious at his sexual ways, but not envious. . . . Perhaps. Envious at the thought of successful carousal? . . . Hmmm . . . Nostalgia twinges.

"At the night baths on Kirk Street."

"Kerkstraat."

"I just lay back on a mat in the darkroom and before I could say 'Get it up,' they were on my dick like piranhas. Chompity chomp chomp."

"How romantic."

"One mouth after another."

"Did they leave scars?"

"Wanna see for yourself?"

"Your word will suffice." Any encouragement and he's just the one to unzip in public and fling his joystick about. "Mere vague curiosity," says Alexander, "about the state of that little morsel on which others chose to dine."

"Bitch, it isn't so little. And it's cut, you know."

"You're Jewish. Yes, one is quite aware."

"A silky circumcised cock. Looks better than the ones in little Dutch caps."

"Is that so?"

"Sure. Why else do you think Abraham let God cut his cock except to make it sexier? That's the Jewish covenant—give us the best-looking dicks in the world, God, and we'll follow you into whatever wasteland you want!"

"How unique a scriptural exegesis! And, one supposes, you wear skullcaps during prayer as a reminder of what you've sacrificed?"

"Hey—no fair—you're beginning to think like me!"

"Heaven forfend! So, pray tell, did you happen at least to glimpse the faces attached to those gluttonous mouths dining on your bare-headed, sacrificial member?"

"It was a darkroom. That's the whole point."

"There is such a thing as civilization, even in the night baths. There's a café downstairs, one recalls, for a thank you? A polite chat afterward while recuperating for another round of *liaisons?*"

"You don't have a clue about how to break loose, do you?"

"Oh no?" He thinks one such a prude. Time to defend the honor of one's worldliness. "How about this for breaking loose: lounging in a bathtub at The Web, waiting for some unknown collective to gather round, unzip, and urinate upon oneself?"

"Whoa!" Dave stops on a canal bridge, grabs Alexander by the arm. "You've gotten that down and dirty?"

"Yes." Now who's breached the bounds of polite society so as to experience the filthiest gutter, thank you very much? Admittedly a rather bizarre competition, but this is a question of masculine pride. One knew he'd find the admission to be of piquant interest. "No need to stop on the bridge and admire me; let's continue." But explanation is called for, lest the American think Alexander a closet pig. "There was a brief time. About a year ago. One was . . . for sundry reasons . . .

in a rather delirious state of mind, and undertook to engage in activities theretofore not experienced. For just a few weeks."

"Oh sure, just a few weeks," Dave says with a leer.

"Excessive debauchery tends to wear thin."

"So as long as the condom doesn't."

Sting. Barb. Jab. How dare he! "If you think—!" No. Dave could not possibly know. No, not possibly. Another pathetic attempt at humor, that's all. Must not dwell upon this. Move on, Alexander. Move on! "Just look about; enjoy the Jordaan." A scruffy, blond-bearded workman hoisting a replacement window frame up to a building's third floor; a dark-haired muscleman planing a windowsill before repainting it. Ah . . . summer. "Look here." A mother-of-pearl inlaid chest and candelabras in one storefront window, bright blue slacks and orange blouses in another. A secondhand art-book store—Bosch, Rembrandt, Breughel, Dalí, Monet, van Gogh, Meunier; a shop offering up an assortment of brightly colored plastic vases and pens, metal bookends and message pads; huge orange corals for sale, topazes, turquoises, each in antique, tarnished silver settings; a beige chaise longue draped in yards of various linens and silks.

"Neat," says Dave.

"Our unofficial museum of contemporary living. Here we are. *Regardes-toi à la vitrine.*"

"What?"

Alexander sighs. "Look at the display window."

Dark chocolates and light, truffles, brown cubes, rectangles, some wrapped in red foil, others in gold, others not wrapped at all; trays of marzipan morsels shaped and painted to resemble apples, pears, bananas and clusters of grapes, pyramids of chocolates topped with hazelnuts or pistachios or decorated with dribbles of white. And the pastries in true Belgian style: white or pink or brown ovals, wedges, slices layered, moussed, ganached, whipped-creamed.

"Man, I get a chocolate buzz just looking."

Inside, the fragrance—ah! Sodium pentathol cocoa fumes.

"Dag," comes from the lithe salesgirl with blond curls.

"Dag," to her. A glance at Dave, "Excuse me." Then a stream of Dutch conversation. Of course the salesgirl understands English, but this is a Dutch establishment and Americans need to be reminded that despite their macho assistance during the War, they no longer rule the world. A finger point at two slices of chocolate cake filled with mo-

cha mousse. "Come, Dave." Summoning him like pup or child. Following her up a few steps to the seating area.

Only one other table's occupied, by two women, one rather large, and the other extraordinarily thin. Do opposites forever attract? "Have a seat, Dave. I've taken the liberty of ordering."

"You wanna take liberties with me, that's okay."

How predictable a retort. "This is a favorite café in the Jordaan. Chocolate thrilling nose and palate, soft-cushioned chairs and marble-topped tables to soothe the skin, ornate beige woodwork on the walls to nourish the eyes. A veritable mixed bouquet of sensory pleasures."

Dave looks around, absorbing. "Nice, but a little pansy fay, don't you think?"

One half-expected as much. Refining a boor takes time. "Few men frequent the establishment, true, but that is not a detraction. One comes here to ogle only confections."

The waitress sets down first the coffees, then the pastries.

Alexander lifts his cup, extends it mid-way over the table toward Dave. "*À votre—à ta—santé.*"

"Say, what?"

Sigh again. "To your health. A toast. Should be over drinks. Forever inappropriate, isn't one." A bit of self-deprecation to reinforce the balance of egos. "*Très gauche. Le maladroit, c'est moi!*"

"Whatever. This looks great."

A sip of coffee to prepare the palate. Then a small mouthful of . . . mmmm . . . ecstasy. "Feel the bitter coffee on your tongue mix with the sweet vanilla lady fingers; press the thick chocolate mousse up against your palate . . . utterly orgasmic."

"If you want, I could dip my dick in Hershey's syrup for you."

"What! American chocolate! Never! Now, if we were talking Belgian . . . "

"Really? . . . Hey lady!" he actually calls out to the salesgirl. His gall knows no bounds! "Got any Belgian syrup?"

"Stop it!" Alexander can't help but laugh. "Never mind, *Juffrouw.* One's companion is *American.*"

"Yes," she says in English, too. "I understand." And she offers Dave a look of mocking compassion.

"Amazing how lovely the waitress's figure, given that she works here amidst temptation. Apparently she refrains from indulging."

"Wasting her time. But that one over there—"

"Lower your voice, please!"

"Didn't you notice that fat Christmas tree over there?"

"Must you be such a misogynist!"

"I like men."

"Don't we all? But even homocentrism has its limits."

"Oh, loosen up—I'm just playing. Look at her."

Alexander looks and, privately, acknowledges her resemblance to a veritable bauble museum: huge coral stones set in gold upon her fingers, Moroccan handworked copper bracelets, a double strand of pearls around her neck, half a dozen pendants on silver chains between her heavy, blue-chiffon-covered breasts.

"Bet she comes here every day," says Dave. "Twice a day. Pavarotti in drag."

"You know Pavarotti?"

"Hey, I watch TV."

"Indeed . . ." *Sotto voce:* "Perhaps a sluggish thyroid or some psychological compulsion in reaction against Hollywood images of female beauty. Extremely rare for Dutch women to grow quite so large. The occasional *derrière hollandaise,* as the French love to say—yes . . . but this exceeds the limits of our national taste."

"Maybe she's American." And Dave winks.

Alexander tosses his head back and laughs. "What a culturally self-hating thing to say. Even *I* wouldn't make such a statement."

Two sets of smiles across the table, but then gradually, ever so slowly, the smiles fade as illumination grows. On both faces. What has one just revealed? . . . Eyes hold for a moment. Goodness. Caught totally off guard. A self-inflicted blow to the solar plexus. Where to hide?

What's that? A nudge against one's foot. A nudge beneath the table. A nudge of the foot while Dave's eyes hold one's gaze like an infant in swaddling. Compassion? A gesture of understanding?

"Fuck—I'm gonna do it!"

"Beg pardon?"

"Just watch."

Heavens! Some lunacy to break the tension, to reapply his clownish greasepaint and restore order as we've come to know it. What now?

"Excuse me, *Jew*frow," he says to the heavyset neighbor.

Oh dear. "Dave, please—"

The lady hefts her girth in their direction.

"Did you know," Dave continues, "there's a species of leech that mates only inside a hippopotamus' rectum?"

"Dave!" Alexander exclaims.

"What? I didn't say 'ass.' This way we'll know for sure if she's American—if she has an accent or not when she answers."

The lady gazes momentarily at Dave's mouth, lingers with a look registering confirmation that the vomit has, indeed, spewed forth from that very orifice, then shifts her eyes to Alexander's, says: "You may communicate to dat ting wit you, dat he shall not, under any circumstances, ever have de opportunity to mate inside *my* rectum." With that she turns back to her thin blonde companion, who hasn't, for even a moment during the exchange, stopped nibbling her slice of walnut mousse cake. The two giggle like schoolgirls.

Dave, the stereotypical bully who respects only a left cross to his own jaw, makes a thumbs-up gesture at the lady's back. "You Dutch are a hoot!"

The lady turns, "Indeed, we are a special people. Now kindly cease to mind my business."

"Hey, I was paying you a compliment."

"You are most annoying, as Americans are known to be."

"Who told you I was American?"

"Well you are, are you not?"

"How'd you like mocha cream all over that fat Dutch face of yours?"

"How would you like me to sit on dat skinny American face of yours?"

"*Godverdomme!*" escapes Alexander's lips. What an absurd escalation. And it's Americans who allege themselves master players of nuclear brinksmanship? Heaven help us all!

The raised voices have brought the salesgirl up the steps, confusion swarming over her face.

"Dave," says Alexander, "one suddenly feels rather unwell." He stands. "It is time to leave, please."

The flare of Dave's nostrils, the sudden beading of his eyes. A wolf contemplating attack. "Not until I—"

"Now! At once!" Alexander stamps his foot.

Standing, Dave unexpectedly reaches into his pocket and pulls out a wad of guilders, looks at the salesgirl and asks, "How much?"

One's soaring blood pressure finally plateaus. "You're full of sur-
prises," Alexander says. "Thank you."
"If not for you, that tub would have gotten a face full of cream."
Face saved.

* * *

Three blind lice, three blind lice.
Feel how they itch, feel how they itch.
They swing through your pubes in the blink of an eye.
Shampoo and shampoo—yet they never say die.
Don't ask for their purpose; God doesn't know why.
Three blind lice, three blind lice.

* * *

My Darling Boy? or *Sweetheart?* or *My Dearest Dave?*
Dave looks up from the pad of paper to think, up from the sofa,
stares through the sliding glass door, out over his snow-covered balcony, across the parking lot to the other side of the complex. Pee Boy,
that neighbor kid from a condo downstairs, is lying and flapping his
arms into snow angels, struggling up to his feet—poor little fucker's
mummified in thick snowsuit, mittens (not even gloves), blue hood
tied tight, stiff boots. How the hell does his mother expect him to have
any fun?
The sun glares blinding white, reflects nothing. Everything. A
snow mirror. "White is a reflection of every color at once," Mom once
told Davey between spoonfuls of maple-syruped snow. In the
kitchen—round white table, yellow-daisied wallpaper. Dave remembers. So cold on his tongue. "Snow's yummilicious," Mom said, "but
you mustn't ever lick ice or your tongue'll stick and you'll have to rip
it off—boy, will that hurt!" So five-year-old Davey jumped up,
marched straight to the freezer, pulled out the metal ice tray, licked it,
and his tongue stuck. Mom whacked his rump—lightly, not from outrage but from teaching—then poured warm water into his mouth.
Saved!
Eyes back to the pad of paper—come on, Dave, you've a job to do
here. How would she start the letter? What was her voice, really hers
and not Dave's pretend memory of her voice? And her ways . . . her
ass pats and scolding index-finger taps gently across his chin . . . the

page boy flip of her dark hair—does he remember it, really really remember it, or does he just think he remembers because that's the way her hair curls in photographs?

Strain to hear . . . what sound of her tucking-in bedtime voice—lyrical or choppy, high-pitched or low, whispered or even maybe loud in play? A forehead kiss goodnight, this he remembers, but not the lip texture—smooth, chapped, dry, moist? Sweet kiss on the forehead and pinch of big toe sticking up under the blanket and a story about forests and maybe wicked stepmothers. Or sometimes she'd sing him nonsense songs, like that one about a man in combination underwear who couldn't get them off because he forgot the combination. Dave giggles at this now, although he still doesn't know what combination underwear is. And she'd change lyrics to songs he knew, to make them "nice":

> Three bowls of rice, three bowls of rice.
> See how they puff, see how they puff.
> They filled the fat mouth of the farmer's wife.
> She then picked her teeth with a carving knife.
> Did you ever see such a sight in your life?
> Three bowls of rice, three bowls of rice.

All this he remembers, but not whether Sweetheart or Darling or Davey, so maybe all three: *My Darling Sweetheart Davey.* Yes, that's good. How rare for Dave to put thoughts on paper, to hold a goddamn pencil or pen like Mom the would-be/one-day-I'll-be/you-just-wait-and-see-if-I-don't-become famous writer.

Just think of it as a dick, Dave. Ah, pen-dick, OK—fits in the hand, but melts in the mouth?—lame, asshole, shut up and write.

My Darling Sweetheart Davey, Happy Birthday! Don't tell me you're surprised; you knew I'd write. It's your birthday!

Yeah, but you're dead.

So what? Does that mean I don't still think about you? If I were alive I'd write. Well . . . maybe not because if I were alive, you'd have told—but you understand.

Yep. Right. Sure, Ma.

Everything's fine here in good old Hackensack, NJ, just as you left it. Dad's shoveling snow from the driveway. "Hate it when the snow blocks my path." His car's path, to be more accurate, but you under-

stand. Same green Buick as we had right before your sixth birthday, but now it's smashed-up, an accordion look-alike—

Eyes up from the paper. Look outside. Pee Boy's rolling a snow-ball on the ground. Ah, snowman. Where the hell's Pee Boy's dad? Not here to play with his kid—working? No excuse. Such a great kid. Didn't tattle after seeing Dave piss from the condo's rooftop a few months ago. (Hell, Dave only did it that once. Not like it's a sick habit or anything.) Kid said he did it himself, noble little Tom Sawyer. A real pal though he and Dave had never even met.

*Dad's using that same beat-up, bent-edged shovel as you bought him a few years back—*Yeah, Dad, that's right, I'd have bought you a shovel, a man-present—*although it wasn't all so beat up and bent when you bought it at all of fourteen, not that we actually lived to see you grow to age fourteen, but you understand—*

Yeah, yeah, yeah, just write, asshole—Dave, I'm talkin' to you—just write.

If Dad and I had stayed alive, then maybe when you went off to college in Boston . . . surprised I know you did that? I know what you've done in your life. All of it. Every last little bit of it. If we'd lived, you'd have told us because you were always a good little boy who told Mommy and Daddy everything, like the time you pooped little rabbit pellets behind your bedroom door and came down to the kitchen, your face all red and teary and you whispered you'd done a no-no up-stairs. Hit you for messing on the floor like an animal or kiss you for owning up to it? . . . If memory serves, I did both simultaneously . . . We'd have driven up to visit you one day, in Boston. And we wouldn't later have blamed you for that day. You know the day I mean; you've thought about it often enough. In a twisted way you wish it were real, don't you? I bet you wish that we actually did come up, that you actu-ally did hurt us so with your "truth." But you couldn't know what would cause a parent pain; you'll never know that, will you, my dar-ling fatherless son? (Oh, my, but you're rendering me harshly. Is that how you think of me? Like you think of your grandmother? I wasn't like her at all. Not the least little bit. And you should excuse her, you know, after all that poor woman suffered.)

This is my letter so I can make anything happen I want; that's what writers do, we make up things.

It never happened.

It did.

No, Mom, it didn't.

But I say it did. Just like this: That morning started out completely totally normally. Lox and eggs for Dad. Onions and eggs for me (I promised him I'd chew spearmint gum after, to mask the onions, and I did, but did he do anything about that fishy breath of his?) Dad's eggs were dry, mine—moist. My pink suitcase in the trunk beside Dad's blue one. I didn't pack your goodies in the trunk with the suitcases, oh no. In a box I saved from Goldman's Bakery —their cookies were just so-so, but your father liked them for after Shabbos dinner because "they're so festive-looking," your father always said. "Nathan, it's just food-coloring." "Festive," he insisted, "Shabbos should be festive." Oh sure, as long as I was the one who made it so. But I didn't have the patience to fuss with food-coloring and different cookie doughs . . . unless you were here for Shabbos, then I'd force myself to bother for your sake. It would be no bother at all if only you'd come home, but you wouldn't because you said—you would have said if we were still alive to hear, or maybe you truly actually said to your grandmother—you said it was because you had too much studying to do, but I know the real reason: because you couldn't give up an entire weekend of "fun." Euphemism for another f-word, I suspect. I baked for you—ordinary beige cookies, I admit, not pink and green and blue because these were visiting cookies not Shabbos dinner cookies, but sprinkled with cinnamon and sugar just the way you liked. In a box from Goldman's Bakery although, you understand, they weren't Goldman's, they were MINE. Baked with vegetable oil so they'd be parve *and you could have them for dessert right after a hamburger if you wanted, or 6 hours later with milk for a bedtime snack if you were still awake so late (which you shouldn't have been), and it'd still be kosher either way such a good Jewish boy still eating kosher—you do still keep kosher don't you?*

Of course, Ma. Where's my shrimp-stuffed porkchop?

. . . on my lap. Not in the trunk, not in the backseat where they could crumble, but on my very wool-skirted lap, uncomfortable as that was driving 4½ hours to Boston, but they were for you. "The boy can't find parve *cookies in Boston?" your father wanted to know. "It's not the same," I said. "Not the same at all. You're just jealous because I baked these visiting cookies for Davey and merely buy Shabbos cookies for you." Your father shrugged in that way he has—had—and shook his head with a little roll of his eyes to boot, up to heaven as if*

saying to Him, "You see, King of the Universe, what I have to put up with?" As if he expects extra Yom Kippur points when the Holy One tallies up good marks against bad, deciding who'll be killed in a car crash on the way home with a birthday cake for his son's sixth birthday. There's nothing wrong with baking my son cookies! Once a year, twice a year we come to visit? A mother can bake her son cookies!

Dave smiles, laughs even. Mom's rambling. Not that Dave recognized it as such back then, or really remembers it, but Grandma'd imitate her once in a while for Dave, so "your mother you shouldn't forget; a better daughter-in-law there never was, except maybe me." And Dad's frustration gestures—a tense smoothing of his thin hair, a twisting of his neck with a crack to the right, crack to the left, a squeezing shut of the eyes really tight, as if not-seeing equalled not-experiencing. Dave remembers. Sort of.

To cheer myself up when my mind drifts back to that visit, our last visit, I pretend you're here. I baked you a birthday cake today. Didn't buy one from Goldman's like we did back then. Learned our lesson. Your dad never saw that truck rounding the corner—I saw it, but what could I do about it with a sheet cake lying across my lap like a block of cement?

(Watch out, Bub, or I'll toss ya' in the East River in a pair of birthday cake overshoes, heh heh heh.)

Your favorite cake. Imagine stepping onto the stoop—oh, I like the sound of that: stepping onto the stoop—don't you? Do you like the same sounds I do? Do you like word games, too? We used to play them at the dinner table—you, Dad, and I and sometimes your grandmother when we'd be able to pry her out of Washington Heights for a weekend. As much as we loved having her, I had to keep an eye on her when you were around, scaring you with all those Holocaust stories. I mean, for goodness sake, you were just a child. The front stoop. Imagine it still with those chipped concrete corners you'd call "front-step teeth." You sniffing the "parade of aroma floats"—that expression was mine—

Was it? Would she say that?

There's a parade in the kitchen, Davey! Just imagine walking into the house that way, the way you used to after swim practice—not that you were ever really on a swim team. I know. I'm dead, not stupid. But if I'd lived, I bet you'd have been on some swim team or baseball team or some other great American manly team—I was always more

American than your father. I was second generation, after all; he was only first. Although he did play basketball with the neighborhood dads on Sundays, like all good American men. Do you play basketball on Sundays? After swim practice, all ravenous and drippy-haired, whipping your head back and forth to spray me like a wet, shaggy dog, just to chase me out of the kitchen so you could poke around and follow your nose and see what goodies I'd baked. No need to guess about today. A chocolate, chocolate chip cake with coffee icing. Your favorite. Just picture yourself sniffing at it, dabbing at it with your pinky, smoothing a knife over the indent mark your little finger made, thinking I wouldn't notice the icing had been messed with, that somehow my creation had been marred, was not as I'd made with my very own hands, parts of my very own body. The kitchen's still warm from fifty minutes at 350 degrees. Feel the warmth on this wintry day, always winter on your birthday, almost always snow in February but not always, some things you can count on and some you can't. Nature—you can't. See me sitting by the table in the red apron I fashioned from my imagination. Turned out exactly as I designed it, every Martha Stewart stitch in place—was Martha Stewart around back then?—each thread tied tight, the sweetheart neckline revealing just enough of my creamy upper chest to be tasteful but not lascivious (another good word!), pink tulips embroidered on the upper right corner in just the position I'd intended. I'm sitting there waving the Chinese fake silk hand fan you gave me for my birthday when you were just five. Remember? Cold outside but hot in the kitchen. You saw that fan in New York's Chinatown when Dad took you there (not to eat, mind you—nothing there was kosher—but to see how other Americans lived); you told him you wanted that fan for my birthday and Dad looked at you with that wrinkle-eyed look he gives whenever he wants to show you he thinks you're a bit foolish but wants to respect your right so to be. Remember that look? Remember that fan?

Dave had forgotten. He remembers now. Why the hell didn't he ever write this birthday letter before? Never big on celebrating birthdays. Usually, just gets plastered. Last year, Grandma, still alive, telephoned as always. *"Mazel tov!"* and *"Nit far dir gedakht!"* May it never happen to you! A pat on the head as a child, but never a gift, not even a card. His birthday—Dad's deathday. Dave hurls the pen at the sliding glass door where it clatters, then falls.

Up from the table. Socks on. Boots on. Leather jacket and gloves.

Outside.

A fist of cold punches Dave in the face. Across the slippery parking lot, over crunch-crackle ice to Pee Boy.

"Hiya, kid!"

Pee Boy stands from behind a snow wall he's building. He looks up at Dave, blank-faced, then wipes a snowsuit sleeve along his upper lip.

"Yuck," Dave says, "winter snot!"

Pee Boy smiles, wipes his wet sleeve against the side of his jacket.

"Winter snot! Winter snot! I say it is, you say it's not!" Dave winks.

The kid giggles like he's trying not to but can't help himself.

"Come on, pal, say it with me!" Dave smiles; the boy's face goes blank. "Don't feel like talking?" Pee Boy stands frozen, except for his eyes—looking around for . . . Ah, for permission to speak to a stranger. Of course. "I'm not a stranger, kid; I'm your neighbor." Pee Boy looks down at his red boots and his face begins to sponge up like he's about to cry. "Okay, kid, you don't have to speak to me. No problem." Pee Boy wipes his nose again. "What're you building? A fort?" Pee Boy gives a slow nod, like he's wondering if nodding is okay even if speaking isn't.

Dave blows into the air, watches the gray stream dissolve. "Can you do that?"

Pee Boy stares.

Dave blows again.

Pee Boy does too, slowly.

"Great!"

The kid half smiles.

"Want some help with your fort?"

Pee Boy looks around again.

"Alright, forget it." I just wanna play. A little boy to play with in the snow, that's all, who'd jump into my arms for a hug when I come home, who'd drag me to video stores for *Peter Pan* so we could sit on the sofa and practice the songs—"I won't grow up!"—to wrassle with, take to Fenway Park, to buy sneakers for, talk to about sex and girls . . . yeah, it'd be girls for Dave's boy.

Goddamn it. Dave bends, scoops, packs snow into a fist-sized ball, smashes it into his own face.

Pee Boy giggles.

Ahah! "Wanna throw a snowball at me, kid?"

Little eyes wrinkle in hesitation.

"I'll stand behind the fort, and you can let me have it."

Dave crouches down behind the white snow wall, pokes his head above.

A moment, then Pee Boy bends, gathers snow into his mittens, throws—from the elbow instead of from the shoulder . . . like a girl, a sissy . . . even Dave knows that . . . didn't your old man teach you anything? "Missed. Try again, only this time, throw with your whole arm." Dave shows him—like Dave really knows. Pee Boy throws another, harder, while Dave stands tall, leans forward so the snowball can fall against his arm. "Direct hit! Good one!"

Pee Boy grins.

Just look at those red cheeks. Red cheeks to die for.

"Hey, kid, you got it. Great throw!" Now there's no stopping him. Snowball after snowball until pelted Dave crouches down again behind the fort, yells, "I surrender!"

"Hurray!" says Pee Boy.

"Hurray!" says Dave, springing up—the kid spoke.

"Hey!"

Dave spins around. It's the boy's redheaded mother stomping across the parking lot. Wobbly on the ice. Puffy down jacket flapping open, undone boot laces swinging wildly.

"What're you doing with my kid?"

"We're playing," says the boy.

"Didn't I tell you not to talk to strangers?" she scolds her son while staring at Dave.

"We played," says the boy, "so we're friends."

She's out of breath. "You're not friends—" out-of-breath gulp "—until I tell you you're friends." Gray bursts punctuate the air in front of her face. She moves behind her son, grips his shoulders with reddening bare hands.

"Better put on some gloves," says Dave.

"I saw you hide behind that fort. Then jump up."

"It's a game," Dave says, his voice softening. "Just a game."

"You're some kind of sicko, aren't you? Maybe it was you did that from the balcony that time."

Dave looks into this mother's eyes. Rageful eyes, ferocious eyes. He's seen such mother eyes before. Or thinks he has. He whispers, his voice that of a squeeze-toy rubber ducky, "Just a game."

The boy says, "And I hit him with snowballs!"

"That's good," says the mother. Releasing her grip on the boy's shoulders, she brings hands to mouth and blows on them.

"You just leave my boy alone." The edge, Dave thinks, is melting a bit from her voice because of his submission; he wishes he could lick those melting drops, taste her tension's easing.

He nods again—to himself this time—stiffens his shoulders, salutes, turns toe-to-heel crisp, marches back across the plowed parking lot tar, the black ice, a hockey puck blocked by the goalie's protective stick and knocked far afield.

At the building door, he waves to the boy, who waves back. Mother scowls, bends down, mutters words Dave can't hear.

Inside and up to his apartment, gloves off, leather jacket, boots, socks. Heineken from the fridge. Pops it open. Guzzles 'til it's done.

Back on the sofa, he looks out—angels, snowman, fort. Mother and son tossing snowballs. Tossing bent-elbowed. Dave shakes his head.

Come on, you've got a letter to finish.

Don't want to.

Sure you do.

Nah.

Paper. Pen. What else do you fucking remember? What else? *Remember how you used to hold onto Dad's hand when you'd cross the street and not budge until he said it was okay, how you would cross as soon as he said it was okay? He once tested you, remember? Traffic was coming fast and furious but he told you it was okay to go so you started to and he had to yank you back. Remember? He pulled you back and saved you because he loved you. Loves you. Loved you. We never thought you'd wander so far from home. Not for good.*

I'm not the one who fucking upped and got killed.

Never thought we'd not be together on your birthday. I miss night times the most. Oh, I know it's been decades since I tucked you into bed. But I still miss those times. You fresh from your bath—such a big boy, taking baths all by yourself; me fresh from mine. You all talcum-powdered. And you doused in perfume, fresh-smelling and sweet. You'd lean forward so I could sniff your neck, sniff you in really deep, and I'd sneeze. *Remember what you'd make me do every night? So afraid of goblins and demons that you wouldn't let me turn out the light until I checked under your bed and in the closet and sang—well, maybe "sang" is too generous a word—until I chanted, "Demons, devils go away! Goblins, witches, we won't play! We don't like you, never will! If you come, we'll make you ill!" Then I'd swirl around, waving my arms and snapping my fingers, and I'd tell you about sweet fairies enchanting the Jersey pine barrens and you'd fall asleep . . . was that my mistake, Davey, telling you about the fairies? . . . Forgive me. I saw Miss Hochheiser last week in the market, remember her? Your high school drama teacher? Not that I ever really met her, of course, never saw you onstage, but let's pretend. Still talks about you, about your performance in that play, what was it called? Still unmarried, like you, so I have my suspicions. Theater people. You played a retarded child. Amazing how you transformed yourself. Best actor she ever taught, she said. What was that play?* Charlie? Algernon *something? Had I not known it was you who'd become that retarded boy, I'd not have known it was you. Wonderful as a child not my own. You still are. Tonight, to precede your favorite cake, I'm fixing your favorite dinner—what you'd call your "Delish Dish," remember? Sautéed chopped meat on spaghetti—no tomato sauce. "Hold the tomatoes!" you'd say, acting like a waitress in one of our famous Jersey diners. A waiter. Not that I've any idea where you picked up that phrase at all of age five. With mushrooms. Loved to eat while watching TV in the den. Superman. I so loved your dormitory on Bay State Road. It was so Boston with its brick-front and bay windows. Your room was too drab, except for those orange curtains— didn't you learn anything from your old Mom about decorating? And that gold, plastic-framed mirror! From Woolworth's, no doubt, long before they went under. Made your room look like King Solomon's harem or something. You acted glad for the goodies I'd baked with my own hands, carried on my own lap, and I didn't suspect the least little thing when you told Dad and me to sit down on your narrow, creaky bed and you scraped your rickety desk chair over across the room and sat and declared yourself a homosexual. Your old room at home's the same. We haven't changed a thing. Still that royal blue carpet. And that bright blue cloth bulletin board I sewed for you still hangs over the desk Dad built for you out of old plywood pieces and brass handles. Still here. When you were ten, you said you could never work at any other desk but that one because it was filled with nails of magic hammered by Dad's love. You told that to your grandmother and in one of her nightly prayers, she whispered it to your Dad in heaven and he told me. I'd never have predicted such a remark from you so young. Always surprises. A grasshopper-filled music box for my birthday together with that fan. "The music soothes them," you said. Imagine. I don't know which of us all jumped highest when I opened that box! How we giggled over that one. Giggle hug, giggle hug. And those clown faces you used to sit and color with all sorts of bizzarenesses—blue noses, green lips, yellow hair. Always attracted to the freakish. "Homosexual," you said—you would have said, given the chance, right to our living faces, not "faggot" or "ass-packer"— stop, I'd never say 'ass-packer,' that's entirely too crude. I'm your mother, so I wouldn't even know such words. Nor would I ever have heard about rimming or fist-fucking or felching or whatever other perversions you boys have dreamt up after millennia of rabbis and mothers tried to churn out good Jewish boys instead of pagan heathen pigs. "Homosexual," you said as casually as if you'd reminded us you were Jewish, which we knew, thank you very much, because we were there at your bris, remember? No, of course you don't remember diddly. My poor little boy getting his pee-pee clipped. "You're what?" Dad spat out. He looked at you all wrinkle-eyed, as though he didn't find your joke funny, but was trying darn hard to see the humor. "You heard me." So defiant. Where did that come from? You'd always been a sweet boy. "And I'm dating a few different guys." All of a sudden I heard myself scream. It was my voice, I recognized it, but I still to this day can't tell you where it came from, that shriek from Hell. "You're wrong! You're wrong!" I punched your father in the shoulder. "Do something, Nathan! Don't sit there like a lump—do something!" Dad just stood up and slapped you with the back of his hand, crack across the face, knocked you onto your back on the floor—he was a strong one, your dad. Be proud of him. A real man. When you tried to roll away, he pinned your arm with his foot. "Tell me you lie!" he growled. "Tell me you lie!" "Dad, you're hurting me. Get off my arm." "Tell me you lie!" "Dad, stop!" And he stomped and kicked. "Mom, make him stop!" And automatically I stood up and I don't know where I got the idea, but I grabbed that hideous gold, plastic-framed mirror off your wall, held it high over my head. "Hit him with it, Mom! Hit him!" And I looked at him stomping and kicking and punching and I felt the knife twisting in my breast and I just cracked that mirror down hard as I could. Right onto your flailing legs. Twice.*

Do you have a . . . what's the right word? . . . friend? Do you have a special friend by now? You must—you've been dating for more than twenty years. Is he good to you? Do you do it to him or does he—? No, I wouldn't ask such a personal question, although I'm dying to know . . . so to speak. Well, that's about it, I guess. All that's on my mind today. Oh, don't I feel so much better for having shared all that's on my mind? I feel better, don't you? So sign off for me won't you? How do you think I'd end this birthday letter to you?

You'd tell me to blow out the birthday cake candles and make a wish. *You only get one wish a year,* you'd say, *so make it good!* What should I wish for, Mom? Tell me . . . Mom?

A crash against the sliding glass door.

A snowball.

Dave stands, slides the glass door open, steps out onto his snow-covered balcony, feels a hot chill spike through his bare feet, a searing hotcold.

Pee Boy smiles from the parking lot below, gives a little wave, hunches and shakes with a mischievous giggle, dashes inside.

His mother's nowhere in sight.

8

"So where've you brought me this time?"

"Don't tell me you Americans cannot read."

Dave looks up at the yellow banner on this sandy-gray brick building: van Gogh Museum. "I'm not big on museums."

"Tonight's the Mr. Leather Contest. We're in need of some preliminary esthetic balance."

"Well, you just saved me from getting the shit crushed out of me in the café, so I owe you one."

"Indeed. You shall not be permitted to leave Amsterdam without having seen van Gogh." Alexander pronounces the name in the Dutch way, *"Fan Khokh,"* like he's hawking up mucous. "You absolutely will not!"

Dave salutes. "Yes, sir! Whatever you say, sir!"

"I'm not into dominance and submission."

"Oh, I bet you're into submission."

"Hope is free."

As they stand at the end of the line—teenagers wearing knapsacks, gray-haired couples in sensible shoes, geeky men cleaning their glasses—Dave rubs his shoulder against Alexander's. No response.

Why has Alexander been spending all this time with Dave? Doesn't really seem interested in sex. God knows, Dave's given him every possible opportunity. The man really doesn't want it. How weird. "Companionship," Alexander said that one time. He really meant it?

"When we're inside," says Alexander, "you should pay attention to . . . " Dave hears, but doesn't listen. He's looking into Alexander's dark brown eyes, trying to figure this guy out, really studying his eyes for the first time, the corners where they narrow. Does Alexander have the same peripheral vision as Dave? Can he understand what Dave sees, his view of the world?

Does Alexander truly see who Dave is and like him anyway?

Pretty boy eyes. Not Dave's usual type, but then . . . this isn't how Dave usually feels with a guy. Okay, okay, Dave can admit it—he feels a little something. But not sex really. No, if he's honest, Dave's gotta admit he doesn't really feel a sex-pull to this little guy. Strange.

A connection, though. Not like with a trick or a date. But something. Like it would be boring to sightsee in Amsterdam without him. Shooting the shit, goofing around town with a little buddy.

Alexander's fun to tease, the way he pretends not to like Dave's off-color remarks, but always comes back for more. Dave says, "Waiting to get into the museum is like waiting to fuck."

Alexander purses his lips and raises a brow in (pretend) annoyance. "Must you sexualize everything?"

"Can't you sexualize anything? Or maybe you Dutch only like *Amsterbation*."

"You are so droll that laughter completely evaporates before even finding expression. Very well, continue with your typically gross simile. Waiting in line is like waiting to . . . "

"To fuck someone who's shy," Dave says. "You're there doing all the preliminary shit while what you're really thinking is what it'll feel like to get inside and poke around."

Alexander rolls his eyes, shakes his head. "You're impossible."

"Nah, I'm easy." And even though Dave can predict the negative response—no, precisely because he can predict the negative response, he says, "I could prove I'm easy if we went somewhere else, like . . . my hotel room?"

"You never give up, do you?"

"You bang my knee, my foot kicks out."

"There will be no banging today."

It's their game. Dave's sometimes tried playing this game with others, but none have picked up on it like Alexander. Damn fun.

"Save your energy for tonight," Alexander says. "After the Mr. Leather Contest, hormones will be absolutely flooding the city."

Dave grabs his crotch; Alexander lifts his nose in the air and turns his head aside. Yeah, *their* game.

The line begins to move.

Dave follows Alexander through the glass door, inside to the wide-open first floor. Up one flight and they join a small crowd before the painting of a peasant family at table.

"The Potato Eaters," Alexander says, and while he comments on nuances of composition, Dave stares at the unrealistic faces and angular bodies, actually studies them because Alexander thinks this important.

"Look how sad they are," Dave says of the family. "Like they're numb from pain."

"I'm amazed you said that."

Dave wants to spit on the polished wood floor. "Gimme a fucking break—I never said I know shit about art."

"No no. I'm amazed because your remark's so perceptive."

A patronizing little prick, but hey—a compliment's a compliment. Dave turns, wanders the galleries with Alexander commenting at his side, recognizes a painting of tortured sunflowers, tilts his head as he's seen experts do on TV. Dave stands now in front of blue irises on yellow, now in front of a small pear tree blossoming white—these paintings don't affect him; but he's moved by twisted buildings and wheat fields beneath thunderclouds, paintings whose distorted forms, he thinks, capture his own relationship to the world. These thoughts surprise him.

On the next floor, Dave concentrates on studies of peasants: a woman sewing, a woman winding yarn, a man smoking a pipe—all with glassy eyes, looking as though desperate to cry, but too exhausted. Protruding chins, receding chins, dark skin looking as though it's absorbed clouds of soot and ash. Not exactly the way Dave has thought of concentration camp victims, but awfully close. "I'm glad you brought me."

Alexander winks, then points out preparatory sketches and paintings of hands and heads and feet.

"Body parts," Dave says and, trying to lift his own mood, continues, "kinky."

Quiet perusal, then back down the steps to the first floor.

Before a series of four van Gogh self-portraits, Alexander says, "One just adores the way he swirls dabs of paint in these. Strokes of yellow and green and red and orange and blue all part of a cheek, nose, mustache. As if to say this is who he is, a composite of multi-colored bits."

"Looks depressed in this one. And kind of crazy in those."

"Reminds just a tad of Jeroen." Alexander's face darkens.

"Jeroen?"

Alexander turns his back to the portraits. To Dave.

"Alexander?"

"One needs a moment, please."

Jeroen? Who's that? "Who's that?"

Alexander breathes deeply in, turns and faces Dave. "My lover."

Alexander's got a lover? He never said anything about a lover.

"Former lover," Alexander says.

Ah, the guy's been dumped. That explains a lot. Everything. No wonder he doesn't know what he wants. Ok, Davey, you gotta cheer him up. Don't let things get too heavy: "What—did he up and leave you because you played too hard to get?" Wink. Elbow poke in the side.

"Not exactly. One tried to keep him. Truly one did. However, he simply up and . . . " Alexander's lips continue to form words, but without sound or air behind them. He swallows. "Up and d—"

Shit. Shit shit goddamn shit. Fuck up, Dave! You're a royal fuck up! "Hey, listen Alexander, I'm sorry. I didn't—"

"Relax. It's been an entire year. Twelve months and three days to be precise. One is . . . One is perfectly . . . " A sigh from Alexander— the hot desert wind across a caravan from the East. Dry and scorching. Those eyes a wet oasis. Eyes reaching out of Alexander's flat face, stretching toward Dave like eyes he's never seen before. "Tell me," Dave says, wondering if he should, surprising himself that he asks.

Alexander opens his mouth—a line of white mucous webs from upper lip to lower. A soft croak, the creak of a haunted house door.

Dave glances quickly around. "Let's sit." He leads Alexander over to a bench, leads him by the hand, Dave . . . what—a big brother?

"One does not talk about this," says Alexander, "not ever." He's actually pale. He whispers, "He was so sick." Dave concentrates, forces himself to listen—now's the time to pay attention, Davey Boy, if ever. But those eyes. Those eyes those eyes those eyes. Sucking Dave in. Ancient Egyptian mudpits at midnight. No stars, no moon. And Dave—the Hebrew laborer summoned to turn the mud into brick into pyramid, a death memorial out of sludge. Dave's never felt so protective and totally needed. He watches those eyes blink and close, tilt up to the ceiling, down to the floor, fix again on Dave's. " . . . cared for Jeroen every day . . . " Over Dave's shoulders, while the voice mutters, "His bum . . . salve . . . suddenly new medications out . . . but he was so far gone . . . still one can't help but wonder if a year or even half a year would have made . . . " Eyes inviting Dave in, begging, endless night beckoning immersion. "Finally, his brothers show up . . . " A deep swallow. " . . . 'Please change the bed sheets once more, then you can go.' " Forced smile. " . . . the Chink houseboy, I suppose." Deep space eyes. Empty. No stars. No suns. Black. Staring at Dave as torch, as way in and way out. Is Dave doing this right? Is he helping? " . . . the very next day." And the eyes shut tight.

"A lot of shit to shovel," Dave says.

For a short while, Dave looks quietly at the self-portraits now a distance away, sees only bits of color.

Eyes clamped shut, Alexander clears his throat. "An unrefined farm boy . . . tall, blond, muscular. Couldn't have possessed more than five hundred words of vocabulary when I met him (you know me and my little prejudices). Not what I'd expected . . . I'd gone out for a somewhat rough trade sort of evening."

How about that? For all Alexander's prissiness, he really wants the sort of sex Dave can give. But Dave keeps this notion to himself—he's never had another conversation like this, and doesn't want to blow it.

Alexander and Jeroen spotted each other across the bar at The Eagle, Jeroen approached, called Alexander "pretty" and "Little Rijsttafel," little rice table. "An abhorrent name." Alexander opens his eyes, looks straight ahead seeing the past, "But so suddenly intimate—I was his very own Dutch buffet of Indonesian sweetmeats. Before I could say a thing, his Viking tongue . . . all over my face, right there in the bar, tenderly licking my eyes. My eyes, Dave . . . you understand the significance?"

Dave nods.

Alexander pauses, takes quick breaths.

Dave hesitates, looks up at the crowds.

No one's paying attention.

Who the fuck cares, anyway? He puts an arm around Alexander's shoulder—(—is this the right thing to do?

—it feels right

—but you don't want to give him the wrong idea

—but it goddamn feels right!)—gently tilts the man's head to rest against his own.

No resistance. No reciprocal embrace, but that's not what Dave wants.

"Not a heavy licking, just a light fluttering."

"Sounds really great," Dave says.

Alexander takes Dave's free hand. "Don't misunderstand."

"No." Dave squeezes Alexander's fingers. This, too, is adventure in the unknown. This, too, exceeds the limits of everyday life. This, too, is risk.

"My pet name for him . . . I can't believe I'm telling you this."

Dave squeezes Alexander's shoulder more tightly, feels the soft, thin upper arm. Alexander sidles into him. How good this is. How very good.

"I called him . . . 'My . . . '—oh, God—'my Dutch colonial master'. . . . It was just a game." Alexander pulls gently away from Dave. Those eyes again. "Is that just the most terrible thing you've ever heard?"

This little guy wants Dave's approval. Dave's. "No. No, it isn't so awful. Anything's okay in bed, especially if you love the guy." Not that Dave knows about love, but he has ideas. "So maybe you'll show me his picture one day?"

Alexander nods. Nods and nods. Then he sighs, more lightly than before, leans back into Dave, looks down at his lap, becomes obviously absorbed in his own thoughts.

Dave lets him be. More moments of quiet. The sort of sweet quiet, Dave thinks, like in those seconds after cumming, just before drifting to sleep. More fulfilling than the orgasm itself, much more fulfilling, although he'd never admit this aloud.

* * *

Eenie Meanie Mussolini, ooh-aah, Hitlerini
Atcha Katcha Caught ya-Gotcha, ah-ah Jew!
Ish bibblie oten don'ten ver-boten, forgot-ten, why not'n
shhhhhh . . .

* * *

Looking after the guy who just walked out, Dave sings, "Ninety-nine bottles of beer on the wall, ninety-nine bottles of beer . . . you take one down, pass it around . . . Ninety-eight bottles of beer on the wall." Blue Shirt chuckles, the other two act like they don't hear. Tough crowd, thinks Dave.

So many empty waiting room chairs . . . waiting for . . . waiting . . . to be filled by faggot coins—heads you live, tails you die. But they're not all empty. "Hey, guys, wanna play musical chairs?" The other three men look over at Dave. "No? Come on, winner gets to live."

A smile from Blue Shirt, with his hooked Jewish nose, blue T-shirt, muscular arms, a pumped up chest Dave'd like to bite. Smiling—here of all places? Even Dave's not that twisted . . . Yeah, right.

Dave looks up at the fluorescent lights, at the square ceiling speaker—music? muzak?—can never get the difference, though it has something to do with strings. Angels and harps. Like that's what heaven is. "Heaven isn't hearing angels and harps, but fucking without rubbers and swallowing without worries." Mr. Philosopher. Again, Blue Shirt chuckles. The other two squirm in their seats, but oh no, they didn't hear a thing. Ah, it's Kiss 108FM. SWAK. Sealed with a kiss. The envelope, please . . . and the winner is . . . ? Odds are one of them's a winner. At least one. Odds are. But what's the test? That's the question. What's the real test? There's always a real test.

So many empty chairs. Plastic—goddamn cheap hospital—vinyl? What's the difference? Even the filled chairs are soon to be empty . . . of bodies if not already of souls. Fancy thoughts, Dave—thinking like that foreskinned fucker now, are you? Makes sense, now that part of him's inside you. Just don't go quoting goddamn Shakespeare like him. Not yet, anyway. "Literature is truth," he said. What the hell does that mean? Grandma's bedtime Bible stories—truth? Yeah, like some bush really burned forever in the middle of the dessert . . . the desert . . . that's a difference Dave understands, thinks he understands, thought he understood—chocolate pudding versus sand, what feels good in your mouth and what doesn't, what goes down nice and smooth and what churns up your insides slowly slowly slowly making your guts bleed so you don't even know until the grit's imbedded in your stomach and it's too late for anything to save you. Dave knows not to swallow sand. He can recognize sand. But not all sand's created equal. Sometimes the grit's too fine to see, especially if some asshole mixes sand with chocolate.

Blue Shirt looks back at his *People* magazine. The black guy in a suit gets up from under the calendar with its flowery meadow, moves to the window, looks out at Boston's Charles River below—good thing the window's locked or maybe he'd jump. That ol' man river, he just keeps rollin' along. A musical coming to mind now? Yeah, Dave, you're a faggot alright. Like there was ever any doubt. Save me, black man. Take me into the stillness of the night. Absorb me into your darkness. Turn slave into master. Shackle me. Beat me. Anything, if it means I don't have it. "Fuck political correctness!"

All the others look at Dave. Ol' Man River stares, then looks back out the window. Fuck, is this the test—how much Dave can handle? Two weeks of this shit? He's here okay, he made it here. The Rican—

Dominican? Cuban? Who can tell the difference?—looks down to fumble around in his knapsack.

Ol' Man River bites his cuticles, and Dave says, "Hey, buddy, you better stop or you might get an infection." The guy pauses his nibbling, looks over at Dave like *you talking to me? someone talking to me? someone actually caring? and you think I give a goddamn about a cuticle infection?* Dave smiles. "Stop or you might get an infection," he repeats, then gets up, goes over to the Rican guy, about to bother this poor college kid who's pretending to concentrate on some textbook when he's just gotta be thinking about his maybe limited future. "It's a joke—worrying about a stupid fingernail infection. I mean—here, of all goddamn places. Get it?"

Scared bunny rabbit eyes up at Dave. "Yes, I get it," says the kid. "Please . . . " *Go away and leave me alone,* the kid obviously wants to say but is afraid to because of course he can see Dave is whacked out from worry and is standing right over him where he could slap the Rican's face or pummel his forehead or knee his plexus. Nothing in the world's funny now, nothing. Dave knows how the kid feels. They all know how they all feel. Even if the others are just here to get blood drawn and not to get the actual results yet like Dave, they all know. In the same boat up the same shit creek and no paddle, waiting for some tug boat nurse to toss a line and haul them to shore or shoot a hole in the boat and watch them sink, slowly, into shit of their own making— no, of God's, if He exists—melted icebergs of God shit that made the creek in the first place. A friendship test, maybe? Of buddy-buddy survival? Can Dave pass it?

He leans over and even though the Rican kid pulls back in his chair, clasps his textbook flat against his chest, Dave plants a big kiss on the kid's forehead, not a sexy tongue-in-the-middle kiss, but a dry Glinda-the-Good-Witch-protection kiss. Like Dave can protect anybody, but still. What was that elementary school chant—"whatever you do bounces off me and sticks like glue to you"? Dave's gonna pass this test.

Eight years old. In bed with scarlet fever. Naked but for sweaty briefs. Blanket down at his ankles. Floppy-slippered Grandma shuffling into the bedroom and out, now carrying a bowl of ice water and sponges, now a bottle of rubbing alcohol, her nose red, her damp handkerchief half in-half out of her flowered housecoat pocket. Now a tray with a bowl of steamy chicken soup.

"*I'm not hungry.*"

"*You're a Jew.* Me darf zayn shtark vi ayzn. *You have to be strong as iron. You're a Jew. My chicken soup, it will cure anything better than anything.*"

"*Better than prayer?*" Davey-the-ball-breaker even in a fever.

"*Like me you're sounding already. With that Baby Moses face, how could the Holy One refuse you anything? But He works in mysterious ways. Remember about Baby Moses? Pharoah's test—if this baby is really special and a threat, he'll know the difference between jewels and hot coals, no? And if he chooses the beauties, then he's too smart to live. Well he was a Jewish baby, after all, so what do you expect—lentils for brains? Down swoops the Holy One's angel moving that baby hand to the hot coals so he'll fail Pharoah's test and survive, but who knew Baby Moses would stick his burned fingers into his mouth and burn his tongue forever? Survival carries a price, believe me, I know. So drink your chicken soup—it's not too hot to burn your tongue.*"

That's the point of your fucking story, Grandma? No wonder I can't hold onto a thought for more than two seconds.

"*Alright, I know I had a point to make, it fell somewhere between the cracks. Don't ever step on a crack, Daveleh-my-Adam, or you'll break your Grandma's back, hah, hah, hah—my English is pretty good, eh? Alright, another—here, listen: you're old enough I should tell you something. Then maybe at least you'll taste Grandma's soup?*"

If you shut up, I'll taste your goddamn soup. Maybe that was the test of my childhood—surviving her.

"*Alright, so. His Holiness wanted us to find a land flowing with milk and honey. Right? Okay. But . . . Canaanites, Philistines . . . everybody getting in the way . . . scaring off the bees, curdling the milk, so we gotta fight for the land, you see? Even though it's our inheritance, even though He, Bless His Name, gave it to us, even though the heavenly real estate deed listed our name under "Owner," still—Joshua led everybody, remember Joshua? The walls of Jericho we had to make come tumbling down. His help, of course, but our trumpets and the air from our lungs and our sore fiselach did the marching around that city. A test, maybe of our commitment. For us, everything's a test. Ever since Abraham and Isaac—test after test. You're a good student, Daveleh-my-Adam, so you should never worry.*"

Never worry—yeah, right. What the hell's the test this time? The obvious? Just whether I'll live or die? Is that all? Nah, too simple. Remember, God works in mysterious ways.

A woman enters, in nurse whites and a thin, beige cardigan. Dave rubs his naked forearms. Cool for May. She should be wearing a white cardigan. Or a black one. That's it—a code: white for Negative and black for Positive. A signal like color-coding in the bars: red hanky left equals fist fucker, red hanky right means fist fuckee. Yellow hanky. Blue . . . too many shades of blue for Dave to keep straight. Was Larry wearing a handkerchief Dave didn't see that night? Some tattoo on his dick—a plus sign on his foreskin, maybe? A warning Dave missed in the dark of the moonlit reeds. A Jew with a foreskin—right, Dave. Creating a fairy tale about him being some twentieth-century Marrano. Seeing what you wanted to see instead of what was. Fucking moron.

"Your outfit doesn't match," Dave says to the nurse so as to get a reaction, any reaction. "I'm gay, so I know fashion."

She smiles. Dave can't tell if it's sincere or professionally forced or tolerant or full of pity. "Ah," she says, "a man who knows how to relieve tension." Sort of the way Dave thinks of his mother—compassion in her voice, but nothing sappy, an edge. Short red and gray hair a little mussed, like she brushed it quickly before leaving home but not again after the wind had its way with her in the hospital parking lot because she's a nurse for God's sake and has more important things to worry about than hair; thick around the middle the way a mom should be. Her hands? Dave wants to see her hands, looks to see her hands so he can imagine them caressing his forehead with their softness, but can't get at them closely while she reads a name from the chart, "Figueroa."

The Rican jumps up, his caramel complexion suddenly a shade paler than a minute ago, he stands in place, a soldier in the gay revolutionary army, pinky tapping against thigh, tapping tapping for seconds and minutes and hours, and Nursie walks over to him, Dave and everybody watching, Dave and every single one hoping she'll do what she actually does—rubs Figueroa's forearm, yes, touches him, Great Mother touches him, Mommy Mommy Mommy (can Dave change his own name to Figueroa?)—and says it'll be alright. Whatever the hell that means. A lie maybe, to get the poor sucker into an examination room so she can tell him the truth behind closed doors where the rest can't hear him scream or cry. But maybe not. Maybe "alright" is the truth. If his truth, then maybe theirs.

Nursie and Figueroa leave.

"Ninety-eight bottles of beer on the wall, ninety-eight bottles of beer . . . you take one down, pass it around—ninety-seven bottles of beer on the wall." Dave, Ol' Man River and Blue Shirt glance at one another, then quickly away. All three of them quickly away to focus their eyes on some private empty space inside their heads where they watch themselves twist and fall and silently scream and get smaller and smaller and smaller until they crash into a million pieces. What was the name of that Agatha Christie novel—*Ten Little Indians?*

"Hungry, kids? Thirsty? Want the land flowing with milk and honey, asked the One and Only. There's a reservation in your name at the best table in the center of the room, but while you been wandering around forty years in the parking lot with no directions to the front door, another party got to your table first so you gotta kick them outta your seats. His Holy bouncer'll help you, but still, you gotta do the work and you just might get a couple bloody noses—that's His constant test for us: you got the strength to fight for every inch? Thousands of years ago and then again in this century we gotta fight, even though there's a big sign on the table saying 'Reserved for Jews.' Like nobody else can read."

Dave set his bridge table for the first time in years, set it with Grandma's—dead nearly a year, not exactly, but almost—old white china plates trimmed in gold, her ladle-sized soup spoons, pitchfork forks, butcher knives, napkins edged in lace. Grandma's *fleishick* set since Dave was serving chicken and wanted the meal to be really Jewish for the first time in modern memory, for the sake of this man Dave believed, in his twisted imagination, to be a foreskinned Jew. Chicken soup—homemade with parsnips and carrots and sautéed onion, whole chicken that Dave boned after the cooking, and three glugs of kosher Chardonnay the way the Grandma taught him. And basil. Skimmed the top for fat. And matzoh balls—of course matzoh balls! Shaped from matzoh meal and egg and salt and oil and ginger ale— just a shot—Grandma's secret ingredient, secrets for this foreskinned Jew, a descendant, Dave stupidly reasoned, of Holocaust survivors like Dave, reasoned because that's what he wanted to think: that there was another Jewish fag in town who survived a grandmother like his. All Grandma's cooking secrets, the family jewels out of the memory vault to pass the Jew test and please this Dave-like whore he'd met in the Fens months before, a Jew, Dave was certain from his face, a Jew with foreskin secrets. Matzoh balls measured—while Dave was fuck-buck naked—to the size of his own balls, oval spheres rolled in his palm, one larger like Dave's left, one smaller like his right. Jewish soup nuts. Hah! He covered the pot while they boiled— "or the water vaporizes," Grandma used to caution, "and the tops of the *knaidlach* turn brown. Some salt in the water but not too much. You know what happens when you drink too much salt water—sucks pure water out from your brain, and like Lot's wife you'll end up, after she saw the destruction of her past the Holy One told her not to see. Idiot, failing God's test. So not too much salt."

Across the table, lit Shabbos candles off to the side, white and four inches, so he said to Larry, "white, flame-tipped Shabbos mini-dicks on the table in Grandma's candlesticks." Dave thought Larry'd laugh—any Jew Fag would laugh, at least in discomfort if not blasphemous joy—but this one, he gave only a polite smile, a lift of lip corners like he didn't really know whether it was polite to laugh or not and gave one of his fucking quotes, "Ah, 'blessed candles of the night.' " First clue and you missed it, Dave; you just shrugged.

Dave chanted *kiddush* over the wine—hard for Dave to believe he remembered. Not the whole thing, but the one key phrase: "Blessed art Thou, O Lord Our God, King of the universe, who createst the fruit of the vine."

"That's us!" Dave added in uncharacteristic high camp, with left eyebrow raised. "Fruits of the vine." Another half-smile from Larry. "Well," Dave explained, "we met in the Fens, the victory *gardens*. Close enough to vines!"

What kind of Marrano secret Jew was this? Didn't he get it? Didn't he get any of it? If not, then—why the hell did Dave assume this guy was Jewish?

Because he nodded at Dave's question, that's why. Out in the reeds of the Fens six months ago—six goddamn months the bastard waits to call and you don't tell him to go fuck himself—the bastard nodded: when Dave was holding Larry's foreskinned cock in his hand and eyeing that Jewish-looking face, Dave asked him, "Jewish?" and Larry nodded. But here he was not knowing Shabbos candles or *kiddush*. This was a Jew? One more test: "You like the soup?"

"Ambrosia," Larry said. "Food for the gods."

"You a pagan?" Dave half-joked.

"No, just your run-of-the-mill Catholic."

Dave stared at the guy, waited for the punchline that never came. Then, "You fucking nodded, remember?"

Larry dropped his spoon, splashed soup onto the blue cloth placemat. Larry whispered, " 'Oh what a tangled web we weave, when first we practice to deceive.' "

Dave just sat there and squinted like an idiot.

No, Dave wasn't in love, but he'd been in hope that finally on Chanukah with Grandma watching down from heaven, finally he'd met a Jew out for sex under the stars like himself, not lurking about some gay synagogue Friday night *oneg* social, pretending to be more interested in the *ruggalach* or the weekly Torah portion just discussed than his own imaginings about the dick size of the bearded guy who led the discussion, talking of *mitzvahs* and *parshas* and even goddamn *halakha*, as if rabbinic law applied to them at all, rabbinic law that declared them all abominations and exiled them from the Jewish fold, when what they were really thinking about was sucking Jewish dick and fucking Jewish ass because Jewish men get fat in the ass and this makes for a real soft hump and how Dave loves to watch butt cheeks jiggle during a fuck. For six months the guy didn't call for a date or at least another suck, so Dave stopped hoping, but then out of the blue . . .

"Yes, I remember," Larry said. "I nodded."

Another test? To see if Dave could be civil even when bullshit?

"You wanted me to be Jewish," Larry said. "At least I thought so."

"Only if you really were."

"You can't imagine how I've been beating myself up over this." Larry explained: so long since he'd had sex, his Semitic-like looks seemed to turn Dave on . . . so he pretended. "A classic sort of entanglement: *Much Ado About Nothing, As You Like It*—"

"I don't like it. And what's with all the fucking quotes?"

"Titles of Shakespeare's plays, not quotes. I quoted earlier—from *The Merchant of Venice*. And then from Sir Walter Scott's *Marmion*, although many people mistakenly assume it's Shak—"

"Who gives a shit?"

"English major in college." Larry was mumbling now. "Literature . . . . Should I leave?"

"Bart Jenkins?" It's Nursie again. Stone-faced Ol' Man River leaves the window and follows her. Black and white. You're gonna live or you're gonna die.

"Hey, Mother Theresa!" Dave calls after them.

Nursie turns, her face tight now with control, "Yes?"

"What's the scoop on Figueroa? Thumbs up or down?"

"You wouldn't want me discussing *your* privacies with other patients, would you?"

"I wouldn't give a f—" Watch your mouth, this is almost-Mommy you're talking to. Angel without wings. "I wouldn't care."

"Hospital policy, to say nothing of the law. Dear." Nursie turns and leaves with Ol' Man River.

"Ninety-seven bottles of beer on the wall, ninety-seven bottles of beer . . . you take one down, pass it around, ninety-six bottles of beer on the wall." If this whole thing's a test of musical ability, Dave'll win hands down.

Blue Shirt shakes his head without looking up from *Better Homes and Gardens*.

Would it have killed her to say if Figueroa's got it? Poor scared kid. Maybe she isn't an angel, after all. At least not with any power. Just a messenger. Don't kill the messenger, Dave. Probably a former Girl Scout. "Wonder if she's got any cookies."

"What are you talking about?" asks Blue Shirt, looking up.

"Not those mint ones—wouldn't go with beer and we got ninety-six bottles left to polish off. Just you and me."

"I used to think you were sexy, but you're just loony tunes."

"Used to think? What the fuck you talking about?"

"You really don't remember, do you?"

"What—we tricked or something?"

"Something. A little more than a year ago?"

Hooked Jewish nose, pumped up chest . . . hey! Dave didn't even recognize him before, couldn't tell the difference between a stranger and a former almost-trick. "Hey, you're Big Tits."

"How flattering."

"On your knees in the bar." Yeah, Dave's remembering, remembering clearly. "Like to get whipped."

Big Tits smiles, lifts an eyebrow. "But you didn't whip me as hard as you should have, Master Dear."

"You been a bad boy, huh?"

"Yes, Daddy, a very bad boy."

God, we can never turn it off, can we? Not even on fucking death row. "Guess you've been bad, alright. Since you're here."

Big Tits' happy mask slides into one of rage. "It's a germ, not a punishment!"

"Yeah, right—and I'm the Tooth Fairy."

"Oh, fuck off, you sick asshole."

"Don't know yet if I'm sick," Dave says. Big Tits is too muscular for Dave to take a chance on slugging. Play-whipping is one thing; serious fistfighting is another—at least that's a difference Dave understands. "After we find out if we're gonna die, I'll take you home and whip you."

"Don't you just wish," says Big Tits, and he turns back to the magazine.

"Well excuuuuuse me for trying to play nice!" You Dumb Fuck. "Just trying to make conversation." Moronic Asshole. "Trying to make time pass." Scum-sucking Douchebag. "I'm nervous, so sue me." Shit, now the fucker's got Dave shooting his mouth off. Dave's more a basket case than he thought.

"Yeah . . . so . . . I'm nervous too," says Big Tits. Magazine onto the next chair. "Sorry. Edgy, I guess . . . Not your fault . . . My own defensive shit."

"Yeah." Now this is a person, a *mensch,* as Grandma'd say. Maybe that's the test—can Dave finally learn to figure out who's real? "Here for the results?"

"Yeah," says Big Tits. "You?"

"Same."

Big Tits stretches, rubs the back of his neck, twists his head from left to right to left; it cracks each time. "Been a tough two weeks."

"Tell me about it," says Dave. "Only way I survived was to get plastered every night."

"Not too smart."

"I don't need you giving me a hard time."

"Oh, but Daddy Dear, I think you do." Wink.

"Shit!" Dave smiles.

"So tell me, what'll you do if the results are . . . you know?"

"So a little tumult with those intruders who took our table—the Lord helps those who help themselves—we take our rightful seats. (Now I'm not saying you throw those others out in the cold; they're

people, too, and gotta eat—but just not at your table.) Some black
eyes? Of course black eyes. And we don't all survive: since Noah,
some die so others can live. But don't you ever forget them, not for a
day, an hour, a minute, not for a second . . . we'd have gotten Eretz
Yisroel without six million sacrificial lambs? . . . Inflation over the
centuries—the price of Jewish survival keeps going up."

"Just finish your soup," Dave told Larry and then muttered, "My
own goddamn fault for being such an idiot. Foreskinned Jew—yeah,
right."

Loud slurps, soft slurps.

Dave lifted one of the Shabbos candles high in the air over the
bridge table, first vertically, then horizontally, making the sign of a
cross. "I want my guest to feel at home."

"Maybe I should leave," Larry said.

"You don't like my soup? I spent hours making this soup." Dave
knew how to lay on the guilt—he was Jewish, after all. He forced a
guffaw: "Guess I'd've done same as you. Anything for a suck, right?"

Larry nodded, gave a weak smile. "I really should be going. But . . .
before I do, there's . . . actually there's something else . . . the reason I
called . . . I mean, after six months . . . the real reason . . . I've re-
hearsed it, actually."

"What—I gave you the world's best blowjob so now you gonna
drop to a knee and propose?" He's not here because he wanted a date?
So, why?

"You have a great sense of humor." Larry's face looked like someone was pinching his balls.

"What is it?" Dave asked, a little nervous now.

"'Every one of you hath his particular plague, and my wife is
mine; and he is very happy who hath this only.'"

"You telling me you're married?" Yeah, make jokes when serious
shit's going down. He said *plague.* Every faggot snaps to attention at
that word like a dog when his name's called.

"Another quote, admittedly sexist, but at least obliquely relevant—
Plutarch."

"Can't you stop fucking around behind somebody else's words?"

"Literature is truth. Indulge me in one more quote." Larry was
mumbling again, and Dave leaned forward to hear—wanting to, not
wanting to: "'The gods are just, and of our pleasant vices/Make in-
struments to plague us'—Shakespeare again. *King Lear.*"

Dave blinked. Shit. You were right. "A second quote about plague."
Shit. Shit! "Shit!!!"

Larry reddened, stared into Dave's eyes.

"Shit . . . oh shit . . . goddamn shit!"

Larry nodded.

"You?"

Larry nodded again and Dave felt like an eight ball bouncing zig-
zag around all four sides of the billiard table and back again. Don't be
a prick. This guy's got enough trouble. Shit shit shit. Don't be a prick.
Even though . . . even though . . . Oh my God oh my God oh my God . . .
what to say? What to think? What to ask? Don't blame him. Not his
fault. He's a victim, too. Not his fault. And he's telling you. Maybe he
got it after you . . . yeah, that's it . . . calm down . . . after you . . . Goddamn fucking shit! Gotta say something gotta say something gotta
say something. "You just found out?"

Larry shook his head. "I've known for years."

Big Tits stands—shit, he's taller than Dave remembered—comes
and sits down beside him. "So what are you thinking about?"

"What?"

"I asked you what you'd do if the results were Positive, and your
eyes glazed over. So what are you thinking about?"

"Grandma. And an asshole."

"Yeah, my mind's been wandering too. Not sure what I'd do."

"Guns are too messy," says Dave. "Knives are too slow, never
could swallow any kind of pills . . . Run in front of a bus maybe."

"Hey, pal, you don't have to—" Big Tits stops himself, looks
Dave's face all over as if searching for the right thing to say or the
way in or both. "It's not like it was. This is 1996. All those new cocktails. They don't work for everyone, but there's hope."

Dave shrugs. "Yeah, like if they do work, they don't destroy your
liver and your guts, right? Poison, that's what those 'cocktails' are. If
the virus doesn't kill you, the side effects will. Or could. I don't know.
You hear things. Positive equals a slow-burn electric chair. Maybe.
Sometimes. Nobody knows. Living on Death Row and maybe you'll
get a pardon, maybe you won't."

"Don't give up." Big Tits reaches down to Dave's lap, pets Dave's
crotch. Gently, reassuringly.

A touch not meant to lead to a suck or a fuck. Dave damn well
better not look into this guy's eyes or he'll turn into a pillar of salt.

"It's not the end," Big Tits says.

Dave nods and nods. "Yeah. Yeah." He clears his throat. "So . . . so what'll you do, if?"

Nursie strides back into the room, proverbial chart in hand. Like the fucking Book of Life that God writes in on Yom Kippur—who'll live and who'll die? "Sam Greenwald?"

"That's me." Big Tits stands.

A Jewish man has soothed Dave's crotch. For a few minutes, Dave forgot about the Jewishness of Big Tits' face because that isn't really their main connection, not today, not here, even though both are Jewish, of course, but what's connecting them is—"Don't drink all ninety-five bottles by your lonesome." Big Tits winks.

And he's gone.

Dave murmurs, "Ninety-six bottles of beer on the wall . . . ninety-six bottles of beer—" He wonders if, after this is all over, he should hunt around town for Big Tits or Figueroa or even that stuck-up Ol' Man River. They could get together once in a while maybe, shoot the shit about meds or whatever, like war vets who share something nobody else could ever hope to touch, survivors, at least for a while, at least some of them, odds are some of them'd survive a while. Maybe he'd even call that asshole, Larry, and invite him to their group. Now that'd be something.

"I've never done anything like this before," Larry said. "So irresponsible. Shameful. Even criminal. Call the police if you want. I deserve whatever."

Dave recalled the taste of Larry's cum, recalls it in the waiting room now. So sweet with just a tinge of bitterness.

Why the hell couldn't you tell the difference between Jewish cock and *goyish* cock? Oh, shut the fuck up—like that's what this is really all about. Like that was the test. Like it would have been safe if it was Jewish cum you sucked down. Thou shalt be stricken with plague for having devoured a *gentile* man's seed. No such adjective. No such commandment at all—but this isn't about God, it's about life and what the hell does one have to do with the other? Stupid stupid stupid. What's the fucking test?!

Hey, go easy on yourself Davey Boy, you were just being a Jew, right? Everyone knows a Jew's gotta do what a Jew's gotta do. Spin that Chanukah *dreidel;* roll those ancient cosmic dice to find out if it's the rock or the hard place; crowd onto Leon Uris's rickety *Exodus* knowing it's 50-50-50—no, knowing it's 100-100-0—that you'll drown in the Mediterranean or be forced back to Nazi Europe or somehow survive to bathe in that honey and milk. Take the risk, you're a Jew. And if you're not the one destined to survive, then you're a sacrificial lamb and an automatic hero to be remembered and monumented and prayed for by children who never even heard of you while you lived. God's game of Jewish risk. His fault! All you did was swallow the cum and save another Jew from doing it, jumped onto the grenade to save some other Chosen Army faggot who can't recognize his own troop's uniform either—yeah, of course, you hope it won't go off in your belly but if it does . . . Jewish destiny. If it's Positive, you pass the Jewish martyr test with flying colors, a historical winner—a true blue Jew who took risk and lost, one of your people, fulfilling God's defined destiny—

Nursie enters, again the chart in hand. Behind her, Big Tits pokes his head into the waiting room, gives Dave a thumbs-up and another wink. Leaves again.

"Does that mean he's clean or is he just wishing me luck?"

"We've been through this, dear. I can talk to you only about you. You're David Miller?"

Dave nods.

"Follow me, please."

"Can't you just f— . . . Can't you just tell me? Tell me now?"

"I have to compare your ID number with the number in my office. You did bring your card with the ID number?"

Dave stands, reaches into his pocket, pulls out the crumpled cardboard square, hands it to her.

"Come."

How many times he's heard that command, how many times he's given it.

In her office, at her metal desk with its puke-green blotter, Nursie looks at his ID, rifles through sheets and pulls one out of the pile. This is it this is it this is it.

Follow Nursie's finger, her rough-skinned finger, as she points to the sheet, to the word, to the one word that'll change your life, that might force you to decide whether to fight or give up. That's what this test is really about, isn't it? Why didn't you see that before: how much of a real goddamn Jew are you?

"The point is—and here's a point I remember—the point is, you're Jewish: you wanna survive, you gotta fight. So eat your Grandma's chicken soup and be strong."

Dave punched his soup bowl off the table, heard Grandma's gold-trimmed white china crash as he watched the liquid pool and spread, a matzoh ball rolling and stopping on a chink in the floorboards. Scraps of scattered chicken. "Like a chicken swallowed a grenade and exploded," Dave said. "I should kill you," he spat at Larry. "I should fucking kill you."

A hushed mouthing of, "I'm sorry," a shove back of his chair, a rush to the front door and Larry was gone.

Dave stood, tore off his shoes and socks, jumped in a puddled spot free of broken china, squished his toes among chunks of celery, flat squares of onion, thick disks of carrot and mushy parsnip, felt the dead chicken pieces rough between his toes, the matzoh ball rolling out from beneath his sole as if to avoid being smashed to bits, but he ran after it, chased that matzoh ball around the living room floor, down the hall, through the streets of Jewish Brookline-right-outside-Boston to the sanctuary of Grandma's Yeshiva University in New York, up the *bimah* to the Torahs themselves, out all the way across the ocean—Dave running on water—to the old city of Jerusalem, through the Dung Gate to the ancient Temple, the Temple destroyed by pagan Romans, up the Western Wall, the Wailing Wall to the top Holy of Holies forbidden by Jewish Law to Jews because that's where God resides (or used to), but where Dave's matzoh ball rolled anyway—and what guy wouldn't follow his own ball?—to the Al Aqsa Mosque, Dave's matzoh ball rolling around turquoise Moslem tile mosaics and Dave jumps on it—splat—crushes the matzoh ball with a belly flop on top of a red wool Turkish carpet, into it, the grains of wet Sinai desert matzoh meal mixing with the fibers of the carpet, merging two cultures with his very own body, Dave solving the Mid-East crisis, Dave a hero on his people's shoulders, Dave the Savior, Messiah, so Holy, so grand and Holy it's his turn now to die but not on a cross because that's been done, so he runs to the edge of the top of the Western Wall and hurls himself off the mammoth yellow stones, sails over men in *tallesim* and *tefillin,* women in wigs and kerchiefs and wrist-length sleeves, sails and soars and flails and falls until he lands on the cobblestone and cracks his skull like Humpty Dumpty with a yarmulke, Dave's yolk oozing and spilling across the Old Temple plaza to be stepped on and swum in, the way Dave should bathe in Grandma's chicken soup in an effort to help himself, although this time, he's sure, the soup's curative powers would do Dave absolutely no fucking good at all if—

"You understand?" Nursie says. "You're Negative."

9

Bored by the MC's rambling in Dutch, Dave walks around the perimeter of the crowd, buys another Heineken in a plastic cup. The summer sun is still out. He glances back at the stage with the black-and-white banner, "Mister Holland Leather 1997." What a hoot—a leatherman beauty contest right next to Oude Kerk, a stained-glass-windowed, pointy-gabled, gray medieval church smack in the middle of the Red Light District. And across a cobblestone alley, a sign: Prostitution Information Centre. Bizarre town, this Amsterdam.

Dave peers at the prostitutes in their storefront windows—poor bitches, no business tonight, at least not from this crowd. A fat black whore in skimpy white dress smiles at him, demurely. A sweetness in her smile, a willingness to please and boost ego—yeah, if he were straight, Dave'd go for her. And a few windows down he catches the eye of a thin black one in red lace bra and panties. They cluster in whore neighborhoods—black women here, white blondes a couple alleys away, Mideastern ones along a canal. Mini-communities. Good for business or good for security?

Mini-ghettos.

The thin whore sees him, opens her door. "Come in, baby. I give you what you want."

Dave smiles at the Surinamese accent, says, "Sorry, honey, but you can't give me what I want."

"Come on, baby. I like da way you walk; I like da way you talk. You want watch me and girlfriend? Ten guilders. I touch and make her wet. I lick her puss. Ten guilders. You watch. Juicy juicy."

Dave laughs, winks at her. She shakes her dreadlocks and turns to catch some other guy's eye. What a town! Anything's possible, anything!

Dave buys another Heineken and, hearing English over the loudspeaker, makes his way back to the front of the crowd—some men in leather jackets, some in jeans jackets, others in black T-shirts and black leather vests. "I'm dressed all wrong," he says to Alexander.

"I know—black vest and *white* T-shirt? So American. But at least you've bought black shoes—you're learning."

Dave watches the contestants come out onto the raised, makeshift stage and strut their stuff one at a time. A few skinny white blonds in harnesses and leather jocks dance lamely about. A black guy with chaps and armbands—hey, he's pretty sexy, knows how to move his butt, and look at those muscular arms. A hairy-chested white guy in leather vest and pants whips a couple of extras onstage. Dave joins the crowd in whooping. Another guy, with handlebar mustache and tit clamps, dances while tugging on the chain between the clamps, nearly creams.

And then—it's Muscle Dick. He looks like a giant up on that stage. Dave feels a twitch in his jeans. The epitome of masculinity, steroids or not. All that a man should be—bulging muscle upon muscle, inviting attack, yet unconquerable. Unbreachable armor, walls of Jericho that will never come tumbling down. That's what a man should be: hard and invulnerable, a muscled suit of armor.

Boots. Jock. Harness criss-crossing incredibly pumped-hard pecs. All black leather. And a black leather cap. A Nazi kind of black leather cap—no swastika, but the same style.

Dave hates that goddamn look. How he fucking hates it! The look of perverse power. How it fucking gives him a hard-on.

Muscle Dick dances around onstage like the others did, thrusts his crotch at the audience, turns around and bends, spreads his leather-thonged ass at the crowd, that muscular ass, all the while waving the longest zucchini Dave's ever seen. Muscle Dick turns again, stands, tilts his head back, slides the green zucchini far into his mouth, twists it to the left, to the right, to the left and—

"Fucking shit!" Dave yells, ready to laugh.

"He bit it off!" Alexander says.

"What a trip! What an incredible trip!"

Ooohs and aaahs from the crowd as Muscle Dick chomps on the zucchini, chews it up good, then—spits it out onto the crowd.

"What the—?" Dave wipes chewed bits of zucchini from his hair.

"Disgusting!" Alexander says, wiping leather sleeve along his forehead.

And again, Muscle Dick chews and spits, this time at another section of the crowd. Men are laughing, men are booing, men are cursing—even in Dutch, Dave can tell they're cursing. "What the fuck you think you're doing, asshole?" Dave yells out in English, yells loud.

Muscle Dick turns to Dave, takes another bite, chews, sprays the zucchini smack into Dave's face.

"You goddamn fucking Nazi son-of-a-bitch!" Dave lunges onto the stage, hurls a punch at Muscle Dick who laughs and ducks. Two bouncers rush out, seize Dave, twist his arms behind, toss him off the stage.

Dave scrambles to his feet, moves to clamber back up, but Alexander grabs his arm. "Please, Dave. Please! The police!"

Dave looks around; two policemen approach.

"Let's get the fuck out of here."

* * *

Family Matters.

Family—Sada Thompson, the blank-faced mom so buxom and always there the way a mom should be always.

My Three Sons—two men raising the boys, at least for a few seasons ("Uncle" Charley my ass).

A Family Affair—kinky title.

The Brady Bunch—fag for a dad, but nobody allowed to say.

Bonanza—Michael Landon listening to Lorne Greene speak Yiddish on the set, but the world must never know because Jews are good for *shtetl* wimps, not macho, home-home-on-the-rangers.

The Waltons—oh oh oh oh—Goodnight John Boy, Goodnight Jim-Bob, Goodnight Elizabeth, Goodnight Mama, Goodnight Daddy. Orgasmic bliss on the mountaintop, sweeter than on Sinai.

All in the Family.

WE ARE FA- MI- LY!

* * *

Pressed with belly flat against tree, as if bound to the trunk by the need for secrecy, Dave lurks, shadows, spies; an unanticipated recon mission—to monitor those three by the corner chain link fence. They don't suspect being observed by Dave, the all-seeing, all-knowing, omnipresent, omniscient—hey Dave, sounds like you're . . . well maybe I am, maybe I just fucking am. In that case, pity the world. Heh heh heh.

Dave wants to roar like a lion, but mustn't alert them. Them: not his prey, no, of course not; not his victims. Them: objects of reality, subjects of fantasy. (He knows this, pretends he doesn't.)

Apple tree? He rubs his nylon-covered crotch lightly against the bark, feels the roughness against his soft cock, looks up at tiny, pale green fetus fruits dangling overhead. A big strong apple tree rising up from spongy grass like a cock from pubes, a macho tree birthing its young—fucking brilliant idea, Nature. Dave presses harder against the rigid trunk, almost as if to merge into it.

The Fourth of July, a time to be with family like Pee Boy's sprawled out there on a red-white-and-blue striped tablecloth, so cliché, an apple pie family with all the trimmings. Why are they so far from the pool? As far as the perimeter chain link fence will allow, chain link softened by wood chips and azaleas and rhododendron with blossoms and dickhead buds ready to shoot, or maybe more like hot-licked clits (although Dave can't be sure), and stalky forsythia whose yellows have long since dropped and blown away, but the family's not anywhere near the blue-filled pool or its concrete apron covered with flowery cloth lounge chairs. Not "by the pool," just "at the pool," doing what normal families do. A picnic at the pool. Dave can almost hear the redheaded mother this morning, kissing Pee Boy awake, asking if he'd like to go. "Picnic—hurrah!" Pee Boy says and springs out of bed, runs into his dad's arms, so Dad can lift him high to the sky until Pee Boy's head touches the ceiling and everyone laughs.

Sure, Dave could have tanned on his balcony, but better where water reflects sun, where maybe he can glimpse pairs of hairy pecs, a crotch bulge or two, not that he'd do anything about it . . . hell, his straight neighbors'd ride him out of town on a rail . . . might feel good, but still . . . No more balcony, goddamn sick of sitting alone over the parking lot, watching mothers jump into cars and take tiny tots to daycare, fathers rush to meetings, pull in and out, in and out, watching families through plate-glass balcony doors across the way sit down together for weekend brunch or in front of Disney videos so the kids won't squawk. Better outside by the pool with normal American families and old ladies gaggled in the shade of a low-branched pine tree and Russian immigrants whose gold-capped teeth clack in consonant-filled chatter.

So sweet this apple tree sap, Dave is certain, if it is an apple tree, so sweet Dave wants to pierce the tree's flesh with his saber-tiger incisors, stretch out his tongue, lick oozing sap. So sweet baby, so sweet. Dave dwelling in the Garden of Eden, lapping up trickles of botanic orgasms and God saying it's okay, all as He intended. Thanks a lot Adam, you prick, for screwing it all up!

Dave pokes his head around the tree, stares at Pee Boy, the giggler: red boxer bathing trunks, blue T-shirt so as not to burn his shoulders and back, white sneakers with colorful cartoon characters—Dave can't make them out—Goofy, maybe, and Mickey and Donald. 'Atta boy! Be a kid. Enjoy life while you can.

Dad rubs suntan lotion on Pee Boy's exposed arms and legs, rubs the white cream into his boy's skin, white cream that once was his boy before his boy existed, pre-boy Pee Boy; Dave watches the cream disappear into skin, sees Pee Boy hug Dad for no apparent reason and declare, "I love you." What if that high squeaky declaration were made to Dave, if Dave were the one inspiring little boy giggles and fun, if Dave were that father, or that little boy, if Dave could feel those little boy arms around his neck, hugging a big strong man who'll carry Davey and toss him in the air and into the pool and jump and splash with him, only with him, Davey the most important boy in the world for the most important man. Gurgling and giggling and swimming away underwater, doing handstands and somersaults, racing side-by-side across the pool and Davey's heart ready to explode with the joy.

Who's that walking by? Some old jelly-belly Russian man stops at the tablecloth, chucks Pee Boy under the chin, cackles a command of Commie experience, "After food, vait half-hour before go in pool." Then he waves to the gaggle under the pine tree, shuffles off toward them. Pee Boy's face clouds over and Mom's eyes redden to match her hair and Dad's face turns white as if the old Russian's talk about going into the pool was obscene. All three look at the pool in the distance, look for the first time since Dave's been watching, look at wading mothers and toddlers, one kid on a raft, another tossing a beach ball into the air, teen boys doing laps to impress teen girls.

"Let's pack up," says the mother. "We can eat inside."

"We've been avoiding this long enough," says the father.

"I'm not ready for this; I told you."

"We have to get back to normal." He reaches and tweaks Pee Boy's nose. The boy gives half a smile.

Mom shuts her eyes, breathes deep, sighs, breathes deep, sighs—as if she's been practicing—then opens her eyes and crinkles foil off a plate of (Dave cranes his neck to see) fried chicken, scrunches the foil up, looks where to throw it, stares back at the pool, stands and sits with her back to the pool as if to insult it. We're here, her body says, but we're not. Opens the foil ball, scrunches it. Opens, scrunches until Dad grabs it from her, says, "We're on a picnic. Enjoy the present moment." Mom pinches the bridge of her nose, Pee Boy goes over and hugs her; they all hug each other and what the fuck is going on it's just a goddamn swimming pool!

Dad stretches out stiff, hairless legs on the tablecloth, swats a mosquito hard against his thigh—red splotch—scratches his balls through the nylon of his yellow boxer trunks with their blue racing stripe down the side. So, Dad, take Pee Boy into the water *before* he eats; Talmud says it's a father's duty to teach his kid how to swim, Dave's dad did before he died, not that Dave remembers the "hold onto the edge of the pool and kick," the " 'atta a boy!" and "way to go!" But Dave knows how to swim. So it must have happened just like that. And maybe the fog memory Dave has of "one day" was real and not a lingering dream: Davey sneaking up on Dad one day while Dad was showing some neighbor kid how to blow bubbles. Attention to some neighbor kid when it was Davey's Dad! So Davey swam up behind and thought to sneak and surprise with how well he could swim under water, wriggle and swim and Davey approached as he saw Dad stretch back his legs underwater, Davey about to reach out to grab Dad's ankles—he'll get so scared!—and Dad stretching his legs and suddenly showing the kid how to kick—heel smack into Davey's eye. Yowwwwwwww! Daddy's so sorry, poor Davey poor Davey. Daddy holds Davey and cradles him, quick! ice so it won't swell! and Daddy's so sorry would never hurt his little Davey poor Davey, Daddy loves Davey loves him more than any little boy in the whole world.

Mom passes out the fried chicken. Dave can picture her cooking fried chicken—hair up in a Mom-type bun, she in pink dress with flouncy skirt cinched at the waist and in white spotless apron, grabbing chicken legs with tongs, dipping them into egg batter and bread crumbs, frying them in hot sizzle-crackling grease, never sweating, her hair never frizzing or losing its curl, a lipsticked smile whenever she thinks of her boy, blowing kisses onto the chicken as it simmers all bubbly. Turning the pieces one by one, out onto paper towels, piece by tender piece, draining off excess fat to protect her family's veins—so much work, but for her family, it's worth it.

Dave's so hungry for fried chicken, this fried chicken, Mom's, ravenous for it, mouth's watering for it, wants to beg some, but Mom dislikes him as stranger. So no fried chicken for Dave. Unless he creeps up and steals it. Yeah, he could do that, he could dash over and grab a piece and run away before Mom or Dad or police catch him. Yeah, he deserves that fried chicken, Mom-cooked fried chicken, that fried chicken.

But if he goes for it, he might scare Pee Boy, this little fellow who's befriended Dave without condition. And Dave doesn't want to ruin the possibility of pretending to live in Eden, once in a while going upstairs to his apartment and telling himself gee, didn't you have the greatest day with Pee Boy and Mom and Dad, just like old times, as though Dave really had lived it when of course he hadn't, but he could fool himself for just a little, maybe, a minute or thirty seconds or ten if only he drank enough and squeezed his eyes shut tight.

Like now. Like right now. He shuts his eyes tight and Dave sees Dave leave the tree, soar high above himself and the pool and everyone. Dave, the worst that Eden has to offer but Eden's stuck with him—Dave slithers along the chain link fence, across the wood chips, in between azaleas and around rhododendron, slinks over to the innocent family, and in a fleeting instant, a speck of time, dirt on the eyelash, into the eye, sharp like a pin, but just for a second, Dave as desert sand granule in the family's eye as well as God's, an irritation to be blinked away by tears—Dave lunges and grabs a leg alright, but not the chicken's, lifts Pee Boy, holds him momentarily aloft, securely in two hands, as if this trusting giggling smiling little neighbor boy were the Two Tablets of the Covenant, the distillation of divine purity and wisdom. In a guardian embrace, Dave presses this sacred trust to his chest and runs and runs so he can follow the goddamn Talmud, be a good Jewish father and teach a boy how to swim, survive, to find renewal in Noah-Flood-cleansing water, Dave rescuing Pee Boy from whatever inevitable lonely future is to be his, whatever destiny, whether straight or gay, married or single, Dave breaking a link in the boy's chain-future, redirecting it so that somehow in a way Dave doesn't understand but feels in the churns of his stomach, the pumps of his heart, the surges and spews deep within his panicking balls, Dave can save this boy and somehow save himself.

Onto the concrete apron and then—into the pool with Pee Boy, gleeful little-boy arms around Dave's neck. Splash!

Jelly-belly Russian jumps up, hollers and screams; gaggle of old ladies jumps up, hollers and screams; toddlers, mothers, kids, teenagers jump up, holler and scream. Dad in the water and Mom screaming screaming screaming in the water. The Russian and old ladies and toddlers, kids, moms, teens, all in the water with Dave, one big happy family until Dad smashes a fist into Dave's face and yanks Pee Boy away. Pee Boy reaches out to Dave.

Russian bites Dave with gold-fillinged teeth, teenage boys kick Dave in the gut, teenage girls tear at his face with fake nails, kids piss on him, toddlers shit on him, moms stick him with big old-fashioned diaper pins. Police show up led by Captain Larry-the-Foreskinned-Non-Jew—where the hell did he come from?—Larry crawling hands-and-knees on the pool apron with dripping-wet Pee Boy on his back, the Golden Calf carrying baby Moses. Dave yanks away from the hands clawing at him, clambers out of the pool, mounts Larry, wraps his arms around Pee Boy, who's now giggling once again. Dave holds Pee Boy safe and tight, and he whips Larry's ass—Giddiyap! Ride 'em Cowboy!—Larry bucks, gallops, ascends; they fly over Pee Boy's open-mouthed parents, fly like Elijahu in a carriage—Eziekel saw the wheel, way up in the middle of the air, Eziekel saw the wheel, way in the middle of the air. Dave and Pee Boy and Larry-the-Foreskinned-Non-Jew in the middle of a Chagall-Oz twister in the sky, fried chicken legs and gold fillings whirling, apple buds and tablecloth shrouds, everyone and everything reeling above the pool, Dave clutching an innocent boy in his arms, himself, his past, the world's future. Crash!

Larry lands, bucks the outlaw off his back, Mom grabs Pee Boy and whisks him away while Pee Boy kicks and screams, his little hands clutching open and closed for Dave. Dad, face twisted in bullrage and fists clenched to pummel, lurches at Dave, Dad attacking Dave—Dave's Dad—Dad kicking Dave in the balls, and Dave feeling pain as his balls fall off and drop into the water. Dave dives in after them, but they drift out of reach no matter how he stretches and flails, his balls float away from his body out of reach out of sight down a metal drain all the way to burning Gehenna while pain radiates throughout Dave's body, pain from Dad's circumcision-taken-one-step further, a sweet pain from yanking a baby tooth it's time to rip out but you're sorry to lose, yet once it's gone you know another will grow back, a bigger stronger one, a man tooth, a hunter's tooth, a tooth for a tooth, a tooth to use in goring your enemies, in smiting them, extracting vengeance, a pain, so Dave swings his leg in the water, slowly through the water, kicks his leg forward at Dad now in the water, Dave's steel toes right into Dad's balls, then he reaches and rips the balls off Dad in one clean yank. No loss of baby tooth for Dad because Dad's a grown man—a real tooth this time, a man's tooth knocked out, one that will never grow back; the pain sends Dad howling-roaring-bellowing to the corner of the pool and out, to the corner of the yard, clinging to the chain link fence with fingers and toes as if trying to escape over barbed wire but caught in the searchlight beams of Dave's eyes, and how Dave laughs triumphant, Dad balls in his hands, Dadballs to boil and eat so Dave will become Dadstrong—no no no, not to chew and mash and digest turning Dadstrength into Daveshit, but to wear, yes, to replace Dave's own, to dangle low and semenful between Dave's legs, to swing with every step Dave takes so he can feel their weight every minute he walks— no no no, that way nobody else will ever see them between Dave's legs, except men Dave will already have conquered-seduced, and then what's the point?—so: to wear forever around Dave's neck on display, yes his neck, for the world to see who the real man is, Dave, the mannest man in the world not settling for tattoos but for real balls, studballs, Dadballs—no no no, you don't got it yet, Dave, get with it, come on!—preserve them in leather, each of Dad's balls wrapped separately and sealed in leather, two balls attached by a single leather cord, a macho Gaucho bola to fling around other men's legs and fell them, or to hurl about their necks and choke them, a Dadgarrote, an heirloom to pass from generation to generation—but aren't you the last generation, Dave?—no no no, better still: attach separate leather cords to the leathered ball pouches and, every morning, rest one on Dave's forehead, the other on his upper left arm, Dave's holy leather Dad*tefillin*balls on Dave's mind and against Dave's heart whenever Dave goes to a leather bar and every morning, every single morning, even Shabbos, as he prays the instant he awakens, wears the symbols of his God and his faith, for what is a man's faith but his father's, his Father, his father faith . . . or filth, all so close within Dave, opposing parts of Dave, will the real Dave please stand up? father faither filther? filter falter? father feather farther further? where's the meaning Dave seeks, the answers? Dave'll settle for clear questions—every morning he'll pray for Dadessence to seep from the Dad*tefillin*balls through the leather onto Dave's skin, the skin over his brain and his heart, then to permeate deep within, so Dave will *know* Dadstrength and *feel* Dadstrength and *look* like Dad and *smell* like Dad and *fuck* like Dad and *be* a real man just like Dad.

10

Alexander adjusts the white towel over his crossed knee (modesty in public, even in the baths) and takes another sip of his koffie verkeerd. One has standards, after all. There are places and there are places: of course he let the towel casually slip off his waist in the steam room, where one is expected so to do. But no actual groping.

So many new physiques to admire! Alexander ogles a muscular back at the bar, another hairy one, wrinkles his nose at an excessively flabby one (a modicum of firm flesh to hold within one's grasp is sensuous, but so much that it oozes between one's fingers . . . heavens no!).

He wonders where Dave might be. A quick dash away from the police down this alley and that in the Red Light District, two coffees in some hole-in-the-wall café. Then Alexander said he was going to the night baths—"so much cleaner than the darkrooms. Ages since one's been naughty, but even so, there are places and there are places! Would you care to provide company?"

"Been there, done that," Dave said, as though having had his fill of sex with every man in the establishment. Well, in his particular case, anything is possible. He's so free. So free in his conduct. Alexander finally understands the fuss about Americans loving freedom. A bit ironic though, given Dave's inhibitions about things Jewish. Freedom without, but not within? Perhaps that's where Asian philosophy excels, in attaining inner freedom regardless of outer limitations. Or so one assumes, without actually knowing, since one has not paid much attention to Asian philosophy. Hmmm. Perhaps one should pick up a book on Zen or something. Not that one can picture oneself sitting cross-legged on a mountaintop wearing nothing but a loincloth.

Alexander fingers a corner of his white towel and giggles.

That Dave. A rather healthy influence after all. Wishing to see Jeroen's picture. So many pictures. How long has it been since one has looked at them? No matter. One remembers them. Every single one from all the touristy locales he wished to visit, all those places where no sophisticated Dutchman would deign to step foot: Jeroen kneeling on a polder before a Zaanse Schans windmill, *that* windmill, where we . . . to help one recover from the mortification of discovery *in flagrante delicto,* Jeroen then treated us both to pancakes (he ate two orders!). Jeroen, hands in pockets, leaning against a stout tree trunk where earlier that morning we'd . . . by the Edam cheese market scales. Jeroen crouching in front of the Porcelyne de Fles factory in Delft. In Utrecht, gulping down a dish of vanilla ice cream at canal-level. One was constantly taking his photograph in the knowledge that . . . a way of holding onto him for the future, of preserving the present for the time in the future when it would become the past. One knew. We both knew . . . In front of the Frans Hals Museum in Haarlem. Click click—like a couple of foreigners. Shame shame that one has not looked at those pictures in such a dreadfully long time.

Although one has constantly remembered the feel of those calloused fingers. Virtuoso fingers knowing precisely how to strum beneath one's arms to produce harp-pluck tingles, just the right vibrations resonating from nerve fiber to nerve fiber. It's not so much God who works in mysterious ways, as it is the human body. Or perhaps—man in God's image?

"Alexander!"

Alexander looks up and instantly recognizes the bare belly in front of him. He says, directly into the belly button at eye level, "Why Hans, how good to see you!" Hans is the only person in the world, in the universe, who ties his towel in a knot just below the belly button instead of tucking one end in at the hip like everybody else.

Hans bends toward Alexander to give peck on right cheek, on left cheek, then on the lips; he sits on the neighboring cushion, plastic cup of beer in hand.

"Hans, will you please cover yourself!" As usual, his towel front has fallen open upon his sitting. "You do that on purpose, one knows!"

"Hey, if you got it, flaunt it!"

"Well, my dear, everyone knows you've got it. *Everyone!*"

"The same little cat, aren't you. How've you been?"

"Perfection."

"Meant to call or something. Sorry to hear about . . . you know. Thought I'd bump into you here sometime and tell you. You two used to be here a lot."

"A veritable social club."

"Now I understand why Je . . . why your . . . why he never liked to do anything. Why he'd only watch."

"You can pronounce his name," says Alexander. "It's been a year. One will not crumble."

Absentmindedly, Hans fingers his exposed penis, rolls it around in his hand.

"Really, Hans! There are places and there are places! Not here in the café!"

"Sorry. Forgot how prim and proper you are. Any luck tonight?"

"Merely a spectator. A sort of memorial service, one might say."

"Dating anybody? . . . I mean, it's been a year."

Is this an invitation? Why Hans, you boor, one never realized you had any interest. Hmmm. "Well . . . not dating. But one has been spending an inordinate amount of time with an American tourist."

"You're kidding. An American?"

"Yes, difficult to believe, of course. But he has his own sort of charm. All he can think about is sex."

"Ah, a real American Midnight Cowboy. You lucky dog."

How delightful to mislead! Is Hans envious? . . . Envious of oneself or of the American? Hmm. Possibilities to keep in mind for the future.

* * *

Hurray for the red, black, and blue . . .
For the ammo that could be inside me.
Through history they all beat the Jew,
And they never regretted their kill.
So if I wish to wreak our revenge.
And to scare every damn one at random,
I'll stick my prick up their kazoos—
And I'll shoot—inside them; shoot—until they weep.

* * *

Looking for someone. Looking looking. Naked but for white towels. No suits, no ties, uniforms or caps, no torn jeans or hard hats, no polo shirts, no designer slacks. Legs and arms and torsos and shadowed faces. Sweaty parts, cooled in the Boston summer by air-conditioning. Sweaty. Men.

Thump thump thump—the music's bass through his feet, up his shins to his crotch his sternum his heart.

In the dark corner, Dave leans back against a thin Italian, who grabs Dave's ass through the towel. Reaching behind, Dave feels Italian's taut belly, feels his soft inner thigh, his hard outer thigh, a submerged tumor (emerging tumor?) half a hard golf ball growing on the side of Italian's thigh. "Poor bastard." Dave's not looking for him, but turns to embrace him, kisses him, runs his tongue along Italian's thin mustache, runs his hand gently along the tumor. Another's hand reaches from nowhere and tweaks Dave's nipples and Italian's, big hands, a fat body, a belly topped by a fuzzy white beard and straight ponytail, visibly blond even in the shadows of the baths, of the farthest, deepest corner of the baths, the suck corner with glory holes where a swarthy body with dark beard and square pecs is sucking an anonymous cock protruding through a perfectly round hole in the plywood. (A moment before, Dave had tried to touch Sucker's tits, to enhance Sucker's pleasure, but Sucker shoved Dave's hands aside. "The limits of pleasure," Dave thought.) Ponytail reaches down between Dave and Italian, reaches down with two hands, takes their cocks, Italian's uncut *goyish* cock and Dave's cut Jewish one. "What limits pleasure?" Dave thinks as Ponytail squeezes his cock. Pleasure limits itself—too much pleasure; pain limits pleasure, fear limits pleasure, guilt limits pleasure, memory limits pleasure. Fucking memory limits pleasure.

Italian removes himself and walks away, but a short, chubby blond with a large, cylindrical head somewhat reminiscent, thinks Dave, of tyrannosaurus rex, moves in for a kiss. "Whatever," Dave thinks and sucks in Dinosaur's long, lizard-like tongue, feels Ponytail's fingers around his cock. The three go back to Ponytail's room, his cubicle, his closet where Ponytail orders Dave to bite his fleshy tits, which Dave does, gently at first, then with fervor as Dinosaur drops to his knees to slurp on Dave's cock, to make Dave's soft cock hard, to suck and suck while Dave bites Ponytail's tits. Poppers pass around the cubicle, but Dave declines; "give me a headache," he mumbles between chews. Ponytail sticks a condom on his dick and Dinosaur sucks him off. Dave keeps biting Ponytail's tits, hugs him after he's cum. Dave thinks to maybe put on a condom too, for the sake of principle, but thinks that Dinosaur should be smart enough to take care of himself and besides, Dave won't shoot in his mouth. Even if he does, Dave's test showed him clean. But tests can lie, so Dave won't shoot. It's a rule. Dave's rule. A pretest rule, a posttest rule, a Dave rule, Thou

Shalt Not Kill, at least one Commandment Dave obeys. The limits of pleasure despite the allure of risk. To spite the allure of risk. Risk can reach beyond the bounds of fucking memory, can circumvent it, block it, erase it. Enhance it, legitimize it, validate it. Risk redeems— there's its allure and danger. The forbidden apple. Risk. Disobey God, Moses, strike that rock, get the water you seek, lose the Promised Land, become a hero forever. Dave pulls Dinosaur's young healthy mouth off his cock. They leave the cubicle.

Hearing about-to-cum grunts from other cubicles, bare-palm ass slaps, post-fuck chatter, Dave saunters down the dark corridor, avoids eyes yet looks for the one he's been seeking, who will sense the limits of Dave's pleasure, who will understand the nature of risk, who will push Dave beyond the limits of pleasure. He stops in a corner, watches a porno video shown just below the ceiling, and a hand reaches out to his hairless belly, squeezes it as if the belly were a balloon, fondles Dave's balls through his white towel and a voice, a voice soft and ghostlike, ethereal from another world, a biblical angel's voice, the Snake's voice, God's burning bush voice, husky and weighty with authority and risk, that voice whispers invitation into Dave's ear and Dave follows toward another cubicle. From behind, along the corridor, Dave watches Voice's ever-so-slight waddle, the thick muscular arms, Voice's hairy shoulders, the thin ass crack above the waistband of towel. Dave climbs on top of naked Voice in the tiny cubicle, on the doctor's examining table in the cubicle, climbs onto Voice's belly, rubs his cock against Voice's, feels Voice's muscular arms around Dave's shoulders and back, hears Voice order him to "bite those tits to make my pussy wet." Dave wants to leave. "Milk those tits and make my pussy wet. Like a wet pussy?" Dave concentrates on ignoring the words, yet knows that this, too, is risk, beyond the limits of familiar pleasure, so he bites those tits, flat pink disks on a flat, hairy chest, bites hard in anger. "Oh, you make my pussy wet. You like to fuck pussy? I bet you know how to fuck pussy." Dave sits up, thinks to leave but does not because of the allure of risk. "Wanna fuck my hot pussy?" Dave does but does not. "Wanna lick my wet pussy?" Dave does but does not, thinks "risk," then does want to lick this pussy, wants to lick pussy for the first time, this pussy.

Dave rolls Voice's legs up, licks the sweetly cologned balls, so sweet so sweet, and Dave moves down, buries his face in the tasteless, clean ass where risk resides and lurks. Dave licks and licks while

Voice moans thick throaty ancient biblical moans that mean Dave is being a good boy. Dave licks and licks and thinks of his mom, dark-haired and smiling down at him, spraying sweet perfume on her neck for the very last time ever and some of the droplets of spray hitting little Davey's arm and little Davey licking the sweet droplets from his own arm and Mom about to clamp an open gold earring onto her lobe while Dave licks Voice's ass, Dave's mom who has no business being in the baths, Dave's mom, clamping the earring shut as she was about to go out, to go out with Davey's Dad, to go out to buy Davey his special birthday cake from Goldman's Bakery, dear Mom, who never saw Davey grow into a man, Mom who always sprayed sweet perfume, sweet smelling Mom who used to bake colorful Shabbos cookies, Mom who used to chant a nightly incantation to scare witches and goblins from Davey's bedside, all-powerful Mom, Mom who was more than man, than any man except maybe Dad.

Stop, Dad. Stop, Dad. Stop Dad. Stop him. Is that Dad sauntering into a cubicle? Is that Dad with his soft waist and muscular thighs and curly brown hair walking into that cubicle? Dave rushes down the corridor, looks into the room at the man lying face down on the floor with legs open, but that can't be Dad, Dad who died in the car wreck. That can't be Dad's ass, Dad's ass wouldn't be so hairy and wide and flat and open to the world of cocks, it just wouldn't, not Dad's, maybe Dave's in a weak moment, an honest moment, a moment of supreme risk, but not Dad's because Dad was the real man Dave is proud of. No, that isn't Dad, there is no corridor, Dave is in a cubicle, his mouth and tongue lapping at the tasteless ass of this sweetly cologned pussy biblical voice that groans and moans and whimpers and says "oh yes, lick my pussy, oh yessss, lick those lips, oh yesss, be my macho man," and hands Dave a condom, which Dave does not want to slip on because he wants risk but slips on anyway with practiced ease because that's what pussy ass biblical Voice wants and Dave is obliging and because the limits of pleasure supercede the allure of risk, at least the risk for another. Dave fucks this man who is also woman, this man who, this time, is not Dave, but who could be Dave if Dave were to let down his guard and indulge his true self, his true pussy self, his true less-than-man pussy self, risky self, and Dave fucks this voice and fucks himself and feels his own thighs tremble and sweat, his own ass sweat as he fucks this voice with the thighs over Dave's shoulders, the knees pressing against Dave's neck, hard knees, knobby knees,

Voice's muscular left upper arm raised, his left hand clutching onto a water pipe overhead so he won't fall to the floor at each of Dave's pounding thrusts, risking a yank on the water pipe that would drown them all in flood, Voice groaning and jerking himself off with his right hand and cumming in breathless silence with eyes squeezed tight in the shadows, teeth bared, head snapping up, chin to chest and his innards shuddering, Dave feeling the shuddering, the spasms around the base of his cock as Voice shoots all over his own belly, Voice's own semen on Voice's own belly, his own hot lifegiving semen turning cold and dying on his own belly, no babies, no chance of babies, Dave assisting this man in spilling his seed, wasting his seed, dispelling his seed onto the soft infertile belly, Dave assisting this man in group-ocide, in homo-cide, Dave the accomplice. Dave pulls slowly out, tugs the condom off, lifts his towel from the floor, steps out of the cubicle, wanders down the corridor to the TV room, sits with others and watches a rerun of The Bionic Woman.

Dave breathes heavily for a while, then softly, then puts hand to cock and insists he's ready for more. It's a lie that men need lots of downtime between fucks, a lie if the men are truly hot like Dave, if surrounding scents of musk and sweat are strong. It's a lie, he laughs—a phallusy.

Dave wanders. In the shadows, an old man hobbles on arthritic feet; Dave feels an urge to approach, an urge he recognizes, the twin of his urge to run and avoid, his urge to escape the loving care of Grandma and her survivor friends who raised him—old Mr. Katz with his wrinkled bulbous nose, old Mr. Bialik with his wispy long beard and unfocused eyes, old Mr. Greenblatt with his arthritic wrists, all the old ladies with their checkerboard-cheek wrinkles, their wigs. These men who would *shockle* back and forth in the ecstasy of prayer, these women who would pinch Dave's cheek at every encounter, who would deem him one of them because "he, too, this baby, knows the curse of loss." Old Mr. Feinstein—a survivor; old Mr. Silverberg—a survivor; old Mrs. Kessman—a survivor; surviving their brothers who suffered bullet wounds and died, their daughters who hemorrhaged and died, their babies who starved and died, their mothers who grieved and died, their fathers who died from acid sizzling in their impotent guts, their sisters who died, their cousins who died, their aunts—their butchers, their bakers, their candlestick makers. The lucky survivors. Remember, Davey. Don't ever forget.

You're one of us. Don't ever forget, not for a minute, not for a second, an instant. A survivor. Remember remember remember. Make babies for the dead souls to inhabit. You're one of us. A survivor. Give meaning to the loss. A survivor. Redeem their souls, redeem your own. You're one of us. One of them one of them one of them. Dave's childhood sense of belonging and comfort. Dave's adolescent terror of ostracism and abandonment. Dave's teenage longing to flee these people who recited God's words declaring Dave's pleasure wicked, words which would seek to limit Dave's pleasure, to obliterate it, to provide a final biblical solution to the abomination that was Dave, all these surviving people, these surviving men, the many powerful old men, the incarnations of Abraham, Isaac and Jacob in flowing Mideastern robes who crowded around the edges of Dave's teenage fantasies and watched and jeered and hissed and hurled stones every time Dave jerked off at night to thoughts of young men.

To avoid the hobbling old man approaching down the corridor, Dave ducks into a dark, empty orgy room, leans against a wall and waits. A giant enters, a giant so tall Dave can't lick his neck even though Dave stands on tiptoe and tries. Dave sucks Giant's nubby nipples, and Giant sighs. Dave reaches beneath Giant's white towel and feels his thick, bulbous cock semi-hardened by a metal ring encircling the base of dick and balls. Dave licks his own hand, slickens Giant's cock, pumps and pumps until another hand reaches over. Dave does not want to let go, Giant's cock feels so thick and solid and strong in Dave's slick hand, feels everything a cock should be, and Giant is moaning in Dave's hand, but "the limits of pleasure," Dave tells himself, he lets the other hand take the cock from his. Community. Where Dave belongs. No risk of "outcast," no risk of "abomination," no risk of "shame," of "*shandah*," "scandal." No reading of Leviticus on Yom Kippur to atone for sin. No reading of the Bible at all. No Yom Kippur at all. No sin at all. No sin. Community. A community of men. Survivors of a different terror. A terror, still. A mindless terror that does not seek and hunt and select its victims. A random terror. Survivors. Victims. Community. Dave is one of them because he, too, knows the curse of loss.

An athletic twenty-or-so-year-old with red hair and red mustache sits down in a plastic chair and buries his face beneath Dave's towel, sucks Dave and rubs Dave's cock with his hand, so good oh so good and Dave wants no limits and feels the risk swelling inside him, and wants to explode the risk, but this would be another's risk, another's risk in principle if not in reality or maybe in reality, maybe maybe, and Dave is allowed to risk only for himself, although he shouldn't, he's done that, he's felt that terror, yet that's the whole point. The limits of pleasure? He tells Red Mustache to stop and Red Mustache pulls away; but at the very last second, the very last instant, just as Dave snaps back his head, Red Mustache gorges himself on Dave's spurting cock. Dave grimaces, then smirks at another who understands the redemption of risk. Dave feels good; Dave feels bad. Collaborator. Exterminator. Dirty or clean, the principle's the same— Dave has allowed another to take risk. Accomplice. Conspirator. Commandment Violator. Enraged at himself, not wanting to bear the rage alone, Dave plays with the leathery balls of a stocky black body barebacking a skinny white ass. Standing up and fucking without a condom. Thwack thwack thwack. Skinny White Ass leans over a plastic chair, that same plastic chair while Stocky Black Body fucks him hard; Red Mustache on his knees sucking Skinny White Ass off while Dave plays with Stocky Black Body's leathery balls. "No better than the fucking SS." Dave yanks away his colluding hand, slaps himself across the face—now feel the sting. Others glance up but don't pay attention. "Remember the limits," Dave scolds himself. Remember.

Dave stands alone, watches, inhales the scent of sweat and dried cum, struggles to resist, can't resist, struggles to resist, can't resist, is drawn by the hook of scent snaking into his nostrils enticing him to a group grope in the room's darkest corner, and while feeling hands on his chest, Dave reaches out to touch the shoulder of a new one who's walked over, muscled and dry skinned and standing off to the side, white or black Dave can't even tell in the dark, Dave wanting to be sure that none will leave the room untouched by him so that no potential redeemer is left unexplored, unconnected, even though Dave knows that no one muscled or handsome or big-dicked or young can be Dave's redeemer, the redeemer Dave has been avoiding for years, denying himself because he does not deserve it.

A chubby man pulls off Dave's towel and drapes it over Dave's head, over Dave's face, covers Dave's eyes in the dark—"a goddamn kaffiyeh," Dave thinks to himself, allowing the cloth to remain over his face while Chubby moves down, takes Dave into his mouth. Dave feels the warm tongue and silky cheeks and occasional scrape of upper teeth. Dave thinks to remove the towel from his head, then thinks to keep it so no one will see the joy on his face, the grimace of pain that is the expression of ecstatic joy, to keep it on and hide the fact that Dave is taking pleasure, so that no one, not even Dave who is hovering above and watching himself the way others detach and watch when struggling to tolerate pain, will know and feel compelled to admit that he's experiencing pleasure, moving beyond the limits of pleasure, beyond the—"No!" he shouts and pulls out and rushes from the room.

He cinches the white towel around his waist, stomps down the corridor, passes men lying face down, bare-ass naked men in private cubicles with doors wide-open, and more—bare-ass naked men lying on red foam barrels in the middle of a big room, men with faces turned to the wall so that no one would have to see whom they're fucking, these bodies just lying there, empty, not being fucked because fuckers want to seduce, to feel power and what power is there in entering a body so available? "Most men," Dave thinks, "don't understand the limits of pleasure."

Dave walks, flips through a pile of Safe Sex brochures, wanders into an empty dark room—dark, but not completely. Dave stands against a wall, waits for the man he's looking for, one who will finally offer—Dave feels that he can no longer wait, needs the redemption that is risk. Needs it now. A man walks in, muscular and hairy, who stands next to Dave on the other side of a small wastebasket between them. Dave, knowing this not to be his redeemer, reaches over anyway, rubs the muscular hairy chest, feels the muscles he sees outlined only in the dark. Muscular Hairy turns to Dave; they tug at each other's tits, the wastebasket between them. Another hand on Dave, on Dave's back. A hand massaging Dave's neck, a tongue licking Dave's ear, a hand inclining Dave's head, gently inclining Dave's head down, toward mint-smelling lips beneath a snow-white goatee with a soft tongue that fills Dave's mouth, and Dave moans, Muscular Hairy leaves, Dave embraces the short body with the minty, soft tongue, leans into the short body with the white goatee and minty soft tongue, the short body with the thin, loose skin of old age. Dave feels someone lift his towel, a mouth on his cock; he pulls back, looks down at a narrow face on a thin, kneeling body, a body so thin it is like paper, onionskin paper, a sheet of onionskin with a hooked Jewish nose and a mouth fervently sucking Dave's cock. Dave thrusts his hips forward, gives his cock to this last sheet of onionskin from an antiquated, obsolete, discarded ream. Dave kisses Old Minty-Mouthed White Goatee; other bodies with white hair or little hair drift over to touch Dave's firm pecs, squeeze his big balls until they hurt but Dave says nothing because these old men rarely get to squeeze young balls. Dave envisions himself an angel draped in flowing white, with wings; he pictures even a *goyish* halo over his head and knows that he's breached the boundary, has exceeded the limits of pleasure, has begun his approach to the redemption of risk.

Yet another old man, one Dave knows is old by the stiffness of his neck, the hobble of his approaching, arthritic gait, that same old man from the corridor, the oldest old man in the room, in the baths, in the city, in the world, a man who, Dave is sure, would have the most biblical face Dave had ever seen if only the light in the room were brighter than that of graveyard dusk, a Rembrandt face, an Old Testament face, that old man grabs Dave's head in both hands, shakily pulls with amazing strength, and presses Dave's lips to his. Old lips, thin lips, parched lips, forty-years-in-the-desert lips, a darting tongue; he moans old-man moans, ancient moans, moans made by old men lost in the ecstasy of prayer on Yom Kippur at the end of summer when atoning for sin, old men, sweaty, stinky old men with stinky Yom Kippur breaths, unbrushed teeth on the fast day, no water no food no toothpaste to wipe away the prior night's film of muck, old men, the seventy sages of the Sanhedrin allowing Davey to sit among them, to pray with them, to belong with them. The ancient's tongue writhes in Dave's mouth, against Dave's young-man tongue, Dave's young-man palate, Dave's young-man cheeks, and Dave pictures yellow teeth he feels but cannot see, imagines the familiar loose clacking of skeleton-like dentures he does not hear, tastes the stench of the camps in his mouth, the acrid fire and smoke and putrid shower stall gas on Ancient Yom Kippur Breath's tongue, the taste of singed hair and burning flesh in Dave's mouth, snaking down Dave's throat into Dave's lungs, throughout all of Dave, luring Dave, enticing Dave, Delilah in Dave's lungs. Balm the suffering, redeem the dead, take the risk, redeem yourself. Dave cums in Jewish Onionskin's mouth, shoots his risk, his life, shares his risk, his life, his risk of death, returns his life to from whence it came. Ancient Yom Kippur Breath kisses Dave deeply, gently shoves Dave to his knees and Dave obediently laps at Ancient Yom Kippur Breath's small circumcised cock, feels Ancient Yom Kippur Breath's soft circumcised cock gradually harden between Dave's lips, in Dave's mouth, Jewish risk, Jewish pleasure, harder and harder and Dave sucks until fire ignites a bush on Sinai, sucks until the Golden Calf explodes in flame, sucks until Sodom and Gomorrah burn to cinders.

11

Big yawn. No sleep since that nap before the Mister Leather Contest. Dave drops onto the raised, pink marble platform—his ass on a corner of the Homomonument. They really call it that; Dave read the sign by the canal. A huge pink triangle: one corner descending in steps to the canal, one corner inlaid into the ground, the third corner raised beneath Dave's ass. He looks up, in the early morning light, at the Westerkerk church spire, the tallest in Amsterdam and topped by a crown with a yellow bubble, looking like an excited Chinese prick. Nah—Indonesian.

Dave rubs the burning pit of his stomach; maybe he should have gone back and beaten the shit out of that goddamn Muscle Dick, after all. Damn it to hell!

Alexander said the contest got him all hot, so he was going to the night baths. "So much cleaner than the darkrooms." But Dave didn't want clean.

They agreed to meet at seven a.m. in front of the Homomonument, Alexander gave directions, and they went their separate ways for the night.

With bottle of Heineken in hand, Dave wandered the packed, stinky darkrooms—a few gropes in The Eagle (God, but these Dutch are hung!), a suck in The Cuckoo's Nest, a finger-probe deep into the ass of some black-mustached Turk in a sling at Argos. Lots of foreplay but no bang. He wasn't in the mood. Pissed. Kept thinking about Muscle Dick in that black leather cap. This is what happens when you play with Nazis. Only Muscle Dick's not a real Nazi, Dave knows he isn't, isn't even German. But still. And what was that spitting all about? Almost funny when Dave thinks about it now. Chewing up some big dick and spitting it into queers' faces, like saying, "Is this what you want so bad, you fucking faggots? Ain't worth shit." Maybe Dave's pissed because he never thought up the idea himself. He'd have to try that back home.

"Where the hell's Alexander?" Dave mutters. No one around but sparrows. Peaceful.

Boring.

A freaky guy—bushy, muttonchop sideburns and a thin white bone sticking through his septum like some cannibal—obviously wasted from partying all night, walks down the Homomonument steps descending to the canal, sets a giant sunflower on a pile already there, nods at Dave who nods back (we freaks gotta stick together); he walks back up the steps to a green, oval metal structure raised a foot or so off the ground, about five feet high and topped with lacy, see-through metalwork. The guy walks in, stands, Dave hears him piss. A urinal. Right next to the Homomonument. Well whattaya know? A cruising spot?

The freak leaves without looking back. Dave goes to check it out.

Smells like piss. Inside—a single hole in the concrete floor, not a trough, not meant for a group piss. A leak would feel so fucking good. He unzips, lets it flow. Ahhh.

Shakes off the last few drops, plays with himself until he begins to harden—that a boy, you still got it, but don't waste it alone. Maybe you'll go to the day baths; they open when . . . eleven? Noon? If you're still awake by then. See what Alexander wants to do after breakfast. Now put little hammerhead back into his pouch. There you go. Good boy. Pats himself.

To kill time, he walks away from the Homomonument, heads in the direction pointed at by one of the triangle's corners, continues walking until he reaches the next canal, looks at the houseboats, remembers Alexander's joke about whores and American beer. Dave turns, walks along the canal and—

Shit.

Fucking shit.

Goddamn fucking shit!

He reads the yellow sign again, the text beneath an arrow pointing straight ahead: "Visitors: Anne Frank huis."

It's here.

Around the corner from the Homomonument.

He can't goddamn believe it.

You're Jewish; you should see it, Alexander said.

Yeah, well I see it now. Dave looks up at the four-story, brown brick building, a vertical rectangle with typical rows of white-framed windows and a flat, white pediment. Plain and ordinary and just like any other building facing the canal. Simpler than many. Which window did Anne used to peek through?

It's real.

The house is real.

So Anne Frank was real. And if she was, then Grandma's sufferings—they were real, too, her nightmare screams in the middle of the night. Not that Dave ever doubted, not really, just tried to doubt, wished he doubted because if Grandma's sufferings were a little less real, Dave could feel a little less guilty for not having shared them.

Dave could picture Alexander here, hand on hip, his finger wagging, *You're Jewish, you should see it.*

Dave walks over to the ground-level front door, reads the posted list of opening times. Closed for a couple more hours. And by the way, it's open every day of the year except Yom Kippur.

Perhaps you should wait.

I'd bawl my faggot eyes out. So shut up, Alexander.

No one is here to see. Unless it's the potential for being moved, rather than for being observed, which is the problem?

Maybe they wouldn't even let me in.

You were admitted to the synagogue.

Dave peers through the door windows, sees a cashier's booth and a brochure rack.

No detectable signs saying "Sinners keep out."

Hah hah.

What is it you fear, old chap? A little girl's room? Afraid of pink lace curtains and bed ruffles?

Yeah, right—like the poor kid had bed ruffles.

Feel for a moment. Feel your stomach-pit sensation, your gut. Set your mind aside.

Dave feels, alright, feels the need to go in like the need for sex, wild and all of a rush, urgent.

Yes, he needs to know Anne Frank.

You can do this. You must.

He tries the doorknob, rattles it the way the Nazis might have done.

"You speak English?"

Dave turns. On the porch at the adjoining building—a slim woman in blue jacket and skirt. Glasses. Straight gray hair. Mid-sixties? Dave nods. How did she know he spoke English?

"The museum is not yet open," she says. "I work in this other part of the building," she says, nodding at the black door beside her.

She pulls a ring of keys from her skirt pocket. "You will return in several hours, please." Polite smile.

"But I've gotta go soon. To catch my plane." Hey Dave, what the hell is this? "Arrived a few hours ago on KLM. From Israel. A layover." Liar liar pants on fire. "I rushed into Amsterdam from the airport. Just to see the house." You fucker.

"Yes, you look weary. I am sorry for your trouble, but the museum is now closed. You can read the chart of hours." She turns the keys in the black porch door, shoves it open, turns and gives him a look of "You're still here?"

"My grandmother was in the camps with Anne Frank. Shared her bread."

The woman's eyes widen. "Really?" Then they narrow. "I know a great deal about Anne Frank. Your grandmother's name, please?"

"She'd never want me to tell you. 'Anneleh's the heroine,' she'd say. 'My name no one needs to know.'" Dave, you're full of surprises.

Eyebrows curl. "What's real?" you can see her thinking, and "what's a lie?" That is the question, Shakespeare. "The rules," she says—half to him, half to herself.

"But if everyone followed the rules, if that Miep Gies who hid her followed the rules, there'd be no Anne Frank House." You're hot today, Dave. Sizzling.

"I think a KLM layover is not the same as hiding Jews from Nazis." One foot through the door, the other still on the stoop. But she's hesitating.

"Please let me in. You don't know what it took for me to get here. To allow myself to come. After a lifetime of hearing Grandma's stories about the camps. I swore I'd never come, but somehow I'm here and if I don't get in now, I'll never have the guts to come back." If all else fails, try the truth. Yeah, Dave, full of surprises.

Her eyes look down . . . she's thinking. "I definitely should not. The rules." She glances up and down the street, the canal, looking for . . . what—museum police? The kind of look this stoop must have witnessed a lot during the War.

"I should not," she says, then steps aside, walks down the porch steps to Dave, finds the right key, opens the museum entrance to him. "Quick, please, so no one should see." She closes the door behind them. "Ten guilders, please."

He pays, she drops the coins into the cash register. "I must take inventory next door. Follow the signs"—she points to a reddish brown staircase—"and you will eventually reach me in the gift shop."

Dave doesn't know why, but remembers his favorite kids' book: Dr. Seuss's *Are You My Mother?* He leans forward, kisses the woman on the cheek.

Startled, she touches a hand to the spot, then nods without saying a word, turns and leaves him.

He stands at the foot of the reddish brown stairs.

What the hell now?

Really, you Americans. Alexander again. The fucker just can't leave Dave alone. *Such children. First one foot, then the other: this is the way we climb the stairs, climb the stairs, climb the stairs. This is the way we climb the stairs, so early in the morning.*

The Anne Frank house.

One believes we've already established the setting. Now—engage with it.

Up. Up to . . . what? What's in those rooms at the top of the stairs?

Old ladies' wigs, old men's false teeth and tattoos. Mom being dropped into a hole in the ground, and Dad. Both of them boxed (but not gift-wrapped—Goddamn it, Dave, can't you ever stop?!) for God. More than a lot of Jews got. Tattered prayer books and black leather *tefillin*, silver menorahs and Shabbos candlesticks, braided white and blue *havdalah* candles to bid the Sabbath bride good-bye (Jews and fire, a forever combination), kiddush cups for wine, everything tied up in a *tallis* bundle, shoved onto the end of a long *lulav* bunch of sticks— Jewish hoboes, propping our culture over our shoulders wherever we wander, carrying it with us, but always keeping it behind our backs, just out of reach, behind.

He climbs the steps to a narrow hallway, follows an arrow into a room labeled with a small orange sign as "Victor Kugler's office." Then into Miep Gies's. He knows these names. A video screen in Miep's office for some show. Fine, but not what Dave's here for. Out of her office to face a steep flight of stairs.

Up. At a sharper angle even than the pyramids of Egypt, the houses that Jews built.

Up and up Jacob's ladder to . . . where the angels dwell?

One wasn't aware that Anne Frank played the harp.

Shut up! This is serious.

A thousand pardons, oh solemn one.

More arrows and into a room labeled "storage area for spices." That's right, this building had been a warehouse business. Dutch merchants. White linen coverings on the windows facing the canal. Gauzy. Dutch and English posters explain Nazi persecution of Jews. Interesting, important. But where's the place? The place. The Secret Annex of the diary. THE PLACE!

Following a sign, he walks down another hallway and finally sees a movable bookcase. The bookcase. Three shelves. He touches it, the old nicked wood. If he saw it in an antique shop, he'd laugh that anyone thought they could get a dime for something so worthless. The bookcase that saved their lives for years. He measures it against his body; nearly as tall as he. Each shelf 2½ hand-spans high. Old, empty binders on it. It's been pulled aside to reveal a high step and the Secret Annex beyond.

Inside.

Into a room at the back of the house. Black gauze covering the windows. Tree shadows through it. Did Anne look out at those very trees? Right here in the middle of Amsterdam yet no one knew. How easy to be a part of the world while so apart from it.

Chills along the skin, iceberg skin to match an iceberg heart. Shit. They were all killed, right, except for the father. What gave you the right to survive so long, Mr. Otto Frank? Some fathers die so others may live? Cosmic balance? Maybe Mr. Frank and Dad were a cosmic pair. Like Grandma and Anneleh, "that baby with a wise soul," as Grandma would say.

He glances at the model in the middle of the room, the model of the Annex's first floor. Why study a model when he's actually here?

Into the next room—the shrine. The Holy of Holies.

Bigger than Dave expected. Anne's room, just as Grandma described it, with peeling beige wallpaper, newspaper photo clippings of movie stars on the wall: Deanna Durbin, Greta Garbo, Ray Milland, Ginger Rogers—the real clippings Anne had or museum curator substitutes?

Grandma never said, but maybe she wished she could have hidden here, spent years with Anne . . . only to be eventually found, anyway. Walls of hope. Walls to hide behind for a while and catch her breath.

Anne Frank's closet, different from Dave's.

Not entirely.

A black bust in the corner. Bust of Anne. He knew it would be there.

Dave peers for a moment, then walks over, reaches out to touch it, pulls back, looks around . . .

Go for it, as you Americans would say. You're finally here, for Heaven's sake—go for it.

Dave reaches out again, touches, feels the cold of her bronze nose, the nose that would give her away anywhere in the world, like Dave's nose, and his cock. So maybe she was *his* cosmic twin, across an ocean, across time and the barrier between death and life. Although she'd be old by now. But she's not—just look at her, she's younger than Dave.

The bust takes on a torso, grows legs, sprouts arms which extend to Dave for a waltz, not that he knows how, but they dance around this room anyway, this room that could have been Dave's, depending on when Hitler was. A sweet little voice in Dave's ear, not Alexander's voice this time, but Anne's: *how glad to meet this grandson of a survivor. As a Jewish homosexual, you would have worn a prisoner's insignia star half pink and half yellow.*

Yes, Dave's cosmic twin.

Was it worse, she asks, *to be homosexual than Jew? Is it still? What is the hierarchy of abomination?*

It depends, Dave tells her, on which god's writing the rules. But nothing's worse than being both homosexual and Jew.

Or, she whispers, *maybe nothing's better. It depends on which god's writing the rules.*

Dave looks at her Jewish smile, her dark eyes and graceful Jewish nose, so distinctive and innocent and beautiful and wise. Jews should have saints.

She curtsies in thank-you for the dance, steps back to her pedestal. Arms and legs and torso withdraw so it's just her head again—that face, black and hard and forever there but not really.

Bravo, mon chèr. Alexander applauds. *How good you are with children. Quelle surprise.*

Dave breathes in deeply, caresses Anne's black bronze hair, plants a dry kiss on her forehead. He backs slowly out of the room.

Then he rushes through the "Washing Area" with its toilet in a separate little closet, up yet another flight of stairs, these so narrow he can climb only sideways; a model of the second floor in this, the Annex's living room; through to Peter's room, and across a glass-covered bridge to the adjoining building, into another video room and beyond it—Anne's original diary under glass, her very own careful handwriting, and cases with the text in English, French, Spanish, German (!), Russian, Chinese, Icelandic, Greek, Arabic, Portuguese, Persian, Finnish, Serbian, Hungarian, Hebrew (of course), Yiddish (double of course), Thai, and even Indonesian.

Down more stairs and more until finally he reaches the gift shop where the slim older woman stands behind a counter piled high with postcards and books. "So quickly?" she says.

Dave moves toward her and, thinking to shake her hand, reaches out his own, leans forward over the counter.

She pulls back, holds her hand up like a stop sign. "No kiss, please."

Dave just shrugs. Whatever. "Thanks," he says. "I can go home now."

She lets him out.

He hears the door close tightly shut behind him, hears the bolt click in place.

Down the porch stairs and across the narrow street to the canal's edge. To a statue of Anne flanked by violet beds. He hadn't noticed it before. He looks up at her, a simple statue, hands behind her back. Not in the mood for dancing now? No problem.

Reflections on the canal of buildings, trees, parked cars. The air smells clean and cool. Still no one else on the streets. A dark green houseboat moored behind Anne's statue grows grass on its roof, wild and unkempt like an untended cemetery. A pigeon pokes through the grass, goggles its head at Dave. Or Anne. Or both.

Dave stretches, feels the muscles in his shoulders ache with a new ease. He met Anne Frank. Neck twist left, neck twist right—crackle crackle. He did it. He really did it. He bends to touch toes, hangs there. Better. Much better. Upright again. Another look at The House, a wave good-bye to the statue, then hands into pockets. He really did it.

He saunters back around the corner. Looks up at the black gauze-covered windows in back. He really did it.

Walks to the Homomonument.

Right around the corner from the Anne Frank House.

Did Grandma know that? Did she ever stumble onto the Homo-monument by accident? Or did she ever maybe . . . on purpose turn that same corner after leaving Anne in order to—

Next you'll be saying she laid flowers on one of the pink triangle's
corners.

Well? Might she not have?

Dave considers for the first time: fellow victims of persecution.
Dave following in Grandma's liberated footsteps, shuttling between
monuments to the dead, to heroes persecuted by the same villain.
Possible?

He walks down the third corner of the Homomonument, the pink
marble steps creating a platform at the canal's edge. He stands beside
the sunflower pile, looks over at the brick archway of the nearby
bridge, and from beneath it, Dave sees a long, glass-windowed tour
boat approach and strangely pick up speed, veer sharply askew toward the opposite side of the canal, head directly toward a parked,
wood-planked houseboat, a flimsy white thing attached to the pier
merely by electric cables, and no one seems worried, not the tour boat
captain in his white shirt with blue epaulettes, not the houseboat
owner sunning himself nude on the roof; yet watching the trajectory,
Dave predicts, and: CRASH! tour boat prow into houseboat side—
CRACK! wooden planks splinter to the heavens. Flames—WHOOSH!
an explosion—KABOOM!—and Dave's parents fling high into the
air like Hollywood stuntmen or Three Stooges scarecrow dummies—
too floppy to be real people yet everybody buys into their being real
for the effect, the fictional disaster that makes every safe watcher feel
so clever for having out-maneuvered random fate—his parents fling
high into the air, then land—SPLASH! KERPLUNK!—into the far
side of the canal. Sirens, the EE-AW! EE-AW! of SS vans rushing to
capture clandestine Jews, a swirling red light atop a white van, white-
coated men fishing Dave's charred parents out of the canal with but-
terfly nets, tossing them into the back of the van like corpses into a
pit, shutting the van doors—SLAM!—zooming away with that same
EE-AW! EE-AW! to warn off potentially onlooking crowds. A few
shutters from neighboring fourth-floor windows snap closed—
CREAK!—and Dave shouts to no one that he didn't have time to cry
out warning! GIVE ME ANOTHER CHANCE!

So the SS van AW-EE's AW-EE's backward, the white-coated SS
men open the van's rear doors, dump Dave's charred parents back
into the canal and Dave dives in—balm the suffering, redeem the
dead, take the risk, redeem yourself—swims frantically across to
them, rushing to deliver breech birth Mom and Dad from the canal.

He cups palms under chins, back kicks across the water, drags them to safety, to the Homomonument marble, heaves them onto the pink platform, Dave saving Mom and Dad under the sun, longing to feel their embraces of gratitude and missing, but first—revive them, press lips against theirs, taste bitter near-death, breathe air into their mouths, his air, pray silently to God that if they sputter through their blackened lips, Dave will believe again, he will he will. Dave blows air from his lungs into their lungs, his lungs which are really theirs, his lips really their lips; his lips against their amniotic wet cheeks, gentle fingertips along Mom's soft cheek, along Dad's stubbly cheek, cheeks so shiny and pure, skin whose feel Dave has long since forgotten, Dave's cheek against their skin, Dave's cheek separated from Mom's by a mere sheen of water, from Dad's, Davey so close to Mommy and Daddy, the three of them snuggling on pink Homomonument marble.

Dave breathes deeply in. Out. A fresh morning smell. How still the canal water. Too early for tour boats. No one sunning on any of the houseboat roofs. No one about. Dave alone. Ripples on the water's green surface. Wind ripples, nothing more. A few bubbles . . . of a fish? . . . the last mumbled gasps of a drowning man? Or couple?

Dave wants to jump to the source of those bubbles, to immerse himself in the canal for purification, as if in a *mikveh,* a ritual bath. He went to the Anne Frank House. He can't believe it. Finally, after all these years, he—

Footsteps behind. Real footsteps.

Dave looks up from the canal and turns. What the—?

It's Muscle Dick.

* * *

You say *kigel,* and I say *kugel;*
  You say *chatchkees,* and I say *chatchkas,*
    Kigel-kugel, chatchkees-chatchkas . . . let's call the whole
      thing off . . .
You say *shayna,* and I say *yofie;*
  You say *kipah,* and I say *yammie,*
    Shayna-yofie, kipah-yammie . . . let's call the whole thing
      off . . .
You say Moishe, and I say Marky;

You say Yankel, and I say Yankee,
Moishe-Marky, Yankel-Yankee . . . let's call the whole thing
   off . . .
You say *emes,* and I say *emet;*
   You say *babkas,* and I say *bubkes;*
   Emes-emet, babkas-bubkes . . . let's call the whole thing
   off . . .
You say *kiddush,* and you say *kaddish,*
   I say neether and I say naither,
   Kiddush-kaddish, neether-naither . . . let's call the whole
   thing off.

* * *

Dave squints, looks up again at the wrought iron curlicues—they
were vines a year or so ago, he's sure of it. Wrought iron vines and
flowers and leaves when they buried Grandma here in Newton, MA;
so she could be near her Davey-run-away-to-Boston. But now the
vines have disappeared from the cemetery gate, have twisted and
transformed into words: *Arbeit Macht Frei.* "Work makes you free."
Right construct, thinks Dave, but wrong particulars. It's pain that
makes you free. Grandma always said so. Grandma, the only one of
her family to survive the Nazis.

He enters, walks through the light morning fog. Azaleas and rhododendron with their spring buds, willows and maples and oaks, pine
trees, even a stream. A fucking Garden of Eden. He crunches gravel
on the path, passes a clump of mourners on a hill, visitors to the grave
of some other dead Jew—one more's gonna make a difference? He
pauses, watches them place stones on the headstone for remembrance
and respect. Like the dead will really know that Aunt Selma and Uncle Izzy and little cousin Shmulik were here. Like the dead can really
see and care. And there go the flowers—what? Daffodils. Cute.
Grandma loved daffodils: "little cups of sun reflecting to God so He
should see the beauty of His creation." Stones—the stuff of idols and
ancient punishment; flowers—of love and tenderness. Perfect combination.

Walking, Dave looks from the white shadow moon to the yellow-
orange sun. Shining over us Jews for centuries, indifferent. Watching
us swim in our pain. Laughing at us? Swim, you stupid little Jews—
paddle away in a pool of blood you can't see through. Blood you can

taste but aren't allowed to drink. Blood they said we spilled, the blood of Jesus, a good Jewish boy with ideas. You arrogant grandson-of-a-bitch, comparing yourself to world famous Jesus just because you both betrayed the same ancient tradition. So where are your fucking disciples, Dave? I know where—wrapped in towels at the baths, in leather at the bars, in each other behind the bushes. Yeah, sure, you and Jesus both have the same Golden Rule: "Do unto others as you'd have them do unto you," but Jesus didn't mean it *that* way. No, he didn't, but there is a similarity—he, too, understood Grandma's lesson.

"Pain *macht frei*." She said it each morning as she chose a finger to jab with a needle (her finger, never Dave's). A breakfast ritual: her thin, leathery face turning from its usual grimace into a grin as she first stuck the sewing needle into a match flame "to sterilize, so I shouldn't get infected. Remember, Davey—the body that His Holiness, blessed be He, gave you, you should always treat with respect." (A year ago, Dave went to get his dick pierced, but wimped out last minute. Sorry, Prince Albert.) The tip of the needle gleamed red, then blue, then cinder black. Then red with her blood as she cringed and reminded Davey of the Torah's prohibition against drinking blood—which she then proceeded to do.

Dave pictures her now, her flesh gone, her sagging jowls gone, her gray wisps of hair gone, all gone but bones, synthetic wig—"Never human hair, never!"—and those fiery eyes, still gleaming their vengeance—"Survival is our revenge." Sayings for every occasion, as if she'd distilled her starving years in the camps into maxims she'd feed upon for the rest of her life.

Around an oak tree to Grandma's headstone. Dave drops pink carnations—he knew before he came that she'd prefer daffodils—onto what was, more than a year ago, a mound of dirt. Onto what is, now, a flat plot of grass. Crabgrass. Wide, thick blades growing from the nutrients of Grandma's flesh and blood. Just like Dave, forever sucking her energy and soul. Always begging for more stories of her misery in the camps, stories of deportation, starvation, torture. Stories he loved to hear; stories he hated to hear. Stories she loved to tell. A clump of crabgrass, a tuft here against the cold gray headstone, a tuft there surrounded by thinner blades, straighter blades, lighter green blades. Aryan grass, he thinks and laughs. "Why the fuck am I here?"

Because you love me.

Startled, he looks up at the declaration from nowhere, looks around. He's alone hearing voices. Moses on Sinai.

Because we're blood and I raised you. I was both mama and papa to you so of course you love me.

Dave shivers, crouches behind a bush of white-belled andromeda, hides as though having just eaten from the Tree of Knowledge.

You're here because you love me.

He looks around for better refuge from this crackling voice he has not heard for more than a year, climbs up the oak tree, sits in its crotch beneath a swath of pubic leaves. He snickers.

Because you love me love me love me.

"Shit!" He jumps down from the oak, shouts at the sky, "I shouldn't have come!" He runs back along the gravel path toward the cemetery gate, to the wrought iron vines that no longer are wrought iron vines. Pain *macht frei*. Conscience, he thinks, is a grandmother-installed, barbed-wire fence around impulse and thought—the trick is to break free without ripping yourself to shreds.

Survival is our revenge.

"What the hell you need revenge against me for, old woman?"

Two things in life you can never escape: hate and love.

He bites his lower lip, thinks she's right. He's here because . . . be-cause . . . he needs to say good-bye. Fine. So he needs to. Never really said it. Nearly a year of shouting things he never voiced while she was alive—about her rigidity, her Orthodoxy, himself. But never an actual goodbye. He hadn't meant to come even today, had promised himself he never would. Nearly a year of baiting her, of summoning her—without success—to watch him have sex with men at home, in bars, in the bushes. Sick of baiting her, sick of thinking about her, of feeling her watch him every time he shoves his dick up another man's ass. He loves her and wants to get rid of her.

Back to her grave; he no longer has a choice.

Again, he speaks to the sky. "What is it you want from me?" He smells her rose perfume. "I want to forget you."

You'll remember everything. Always.

He sits on her headstone. "Fine. You're tattooed into my memory. Happy now?"

Finally, Davey, here we are, together again.

"I'm here, I don't know where the hell you are."

Do you pray for me, Daveleh-my-Adam?

"No."

Even kaddish *you don't say?*

"I don't believe in it."

But I *believe in it. My soul, you don't want it should fly, join Him?*

Silence. Silence. Silence.

So tell me, then—what do you pray for?

"Won't set foot in a synagogue. Don't pray for a goddamn thing."

Watch your mouth. But when you were a little pitseleh? *You prayed for what back then?*

"For Mom to come back to life. And Dad. So I could be with them and away from you."

The Holy One, blessed be He, works in mysterious ways.

"So that's who God is, Agatha Christie."

With soap, I'll wash out your mouth.

"Gotta catch me first. Rise from the dead and do it."

Not until the Mashiach *comes.*

"You don't consider me the Messiah? What kind of grandmother are you?"

With soap! With soap!

"Is that Ivory? Dove? Nazi-made, Jew-fat soap?"

A finstern yor oyf dir! A dark year on you!

"You're curse has already come true."

You're plain wicked.

"You don't know the half of it," he says. "I spared you."

Me you spared? Or yourself?

Had he told her while she lived, she'd have said *kaddish* over him, would have exiled him from her life, from the life of her people, his people. So instead, he hid the truth and later ended up exiling himself.

When the Mashiach *comes, my bones will roll beneath the earth to Jerusalem. Then I'll rise.*

"Like your yeast cakes. My grandma, one big sour cream coffee cake. Have her for breakfast. Taste her for a bedtime snack. Mmmmmm, tasty Grandma."

You disgust me.

"You want to talk disgust? Exactly how was it you managed to survive in those camps, Grandma?"

Such a mensch *to visit your grandma's grave.*

"For the first time in over a year; tells you something. You're changing the subject."

Tells me you've been busy.

"Busy fucking."

Klap mir nit in kop arayn! Don't bang into my head—stop talking so much!

"Fucking and sucking and licking ass." In your face and on your face and under your face.

Your shit I need up my nostrils?

"Ooooh, Grandma, good one. Now who's gonna have her mouth washed out with soap?"

For what reason you're doing this?

"Is it so goddamn awful that I want you to know me? Finally?"

So you do love me.

"Like the darkness and cold of night. I'd miss it if it were gone. Yes. Alright. I miss you." There, he told her. He misses this woman who hugged him and fed him and . . . encouraged his mourning tears with "Pain *macht frei*," who baked burned banana cakes just for him . . . "Why are they always burned, Grandma?" "At a wedding, the groom steps on a glass to remind of the Temple's destruction. When you eat my cake, it's burned to remind that it was your birthday cake killed your parents." . . . This was the woman he missed? This woman? No way. No fucking way. "Yeah, old lady, I suck and I fuck and I lick ass." Dave flares his nostrils, shoots a fist of victory up over his shoulder.

With soa—

"Fuck you." He ducks the breeze as though it were a slapping hand.

But you're my baby and I wish I could pinch that shayna punim *of yours.*

"You'd pinch it hard, wouldn't you? So hard I'd need to massage my cheek with my fingers after. Supposed expression of affection; actual infliction of pain."

Love-pinches. Pain macht frei.

"Yeah, right. Like your pain made you free. Like you were ever free of the camps. I mean really free . . . Like I can be free of the closet just because I stepped out of it."

I always wanted you to be free. Like a bird, free.

"Free from what? The weight of tradition? I'm not a Jewish Atlas."

Who's he?

"A *goyish* Samson."

So who told you to cut your hair? . . . I remember your first haircut from when you were two. Your parents didn't want, so I sneaked you—what did they know from raising a child? Like a girl you should look? The sound of the scissors frightened you. And the electric clippers—don't ask! I sang to soothe you. Sing with me, Daveleh-my-Adam—Yidl mitn fidl, Aryeh mitn—

"Stop! Yiddish is dead."

An actress like Molly Picon, you'll never see again. In Yidl Mitn Fidl—

"She's dead."

She's alive if we remember her.

"You're all dead."

Nasty. That's what you are. You're such a nasty little . . . !

"Say it."

I'd never hurt you that way.

"Say it."

A nasty little feygeleh.

"Grandma, how could you hurt me so?"

You made me!

"Did the Nazis think you were pretty, Grandma?"

Gay avek fun mir, *Daveleh.* Gay avek.

"Gay—what?"

Get away from me! Get away!

"I want to know."

I'm leaving!

"Where you gonna go?"

There are other cemeteries.

"But your bones are here. And they've got to rest here until the Messiah comes, remember?"

A prisoner of my own beliefs.

"We all are . . . of your beliefs." He shifts on the headstone.

So maybe we're not so different, after all.

This is what he's come to hear. This. He didn't know it, couldn't have predicted it. But yes. This is why he's come. "Maybe we're not so different, Grandma. We're both whores."

Shame on you, shame on you! No, we're not the same. I was forced.

"You weren't forced. You volunteered. Just like I do."

That's a lie!

"Mr. Katz told me. Mr. Katz from *shul,* also with those ugly green numbers tattooed on his arm." As a boy, Dave often imagined what she must have looked like—wiggling her bony hips, winking a sunken eye, running shredded fingers over her shaved head, all in an effort to entice a sex-starved Nazi. "Mr. Katz said you volunteered, for extra bread." If Grandma were alive right now, her entire face would be whore-lipstick red.

I never volunteered! I had no choice! How dare you compare—

"Why would Mr. Katz lie? I'm not saying it to blame you. Just . . . "

To get even. How would Katz know even? They kept men and women separate. To get even. Once, just after the end of the War, we spent one night together, then nine months later, your father—

"What?!!!!"

The War ended, Katz was sent here, your father and I were sent there . . .

"What?!!!!"

Decades later, In New York we met, but by then, Katz had his family, I had mine. Too confusing.

"What?!!!!"

Eventually, after his good wife died, bless her soul, Katz wanted to marry me, but I said, "It's enough I have my grandson to take care of. We had our night, now I have my grandson to take care of."

What? Really? Was any of this true? Mr. Katz? Had he lied about Grandma out of hurt and anger? No. No!!!! "Don't distract me, Grandma. Don't even try. Bullshit about Katz. Well . . . so . . . maybe you didn't exactly volunteer. Maybe he lied about that for whatever reason . . . but even so, you whored to survive, Grandma. That much I know is true. You whored to survive."

And you don't?

Willow branches sway in the distance.

You want us to be the same, don't you, Daveleh-my-Adam?

The oak leaves rustle. "I know we're different, Grandma." Would the Nazis dress her up before fucking her? Would she really get extra rations of bread? "I give it away for free. Your hell had so many more rings than mine."

Thank you, Daveleh-my-Adam. Such a good Jewish boy.

"I don't mean to compare my life to yours. Mine could never be as miserable as yours."

Your respect—I appreciate it, thank you. So, you want to be just like your Grandma? I see now. That's not so terrible.

"No?"

We whored to survive. Me, to survive them. You, to survive your-self.

"You understand."

We're the same . . . Like a bird free, I want you. Like a bird.

"*Me krikht oyf di glaykhe vent,*" Dave whispers. "You're climbing up a straight wall"—"you're asking the impossible."

The fruit of my loins, the same.

From the ground between his legs, a mist rises, a mist that is Grandma, a shadow figure, transparent. Dave stares through her, at the pile of stones left on the headstone up the hill. He thinks to go grab those stones and hurl them up at heaven, to expose his face so he'll feel them rain down upon him from Grandma and God. The same. Pain *macht frei.*

He continues to stare and through her sees the headstone rows, the stars of David—once symbols of glory, later badges of death. Six-pointed stars, six days of Creation, six million Jews—destined since Creation to suffer? 666—the Christian sign of the Devil. Connections in the universe Dave cannot understand. Connections beyond coinci-dence, too painful to consider coincidence yet even more painful to consider possibly preconceived.

Grandma's mist takes solid form, stretches its arms wide and high, dances away from him and through the cemetery, her curly wig fall-ing off, her shroud, and for the first time, Dave sees her seams. Fran-kenstein Grandma, a walking mass of six million bodies. He stretches a hand so as to touch her seams and all her six million parts, but can't reach.

Remember, Daveleh-my-Adam—pain macht frei, Grandma calls out from the distance.

"I'll remember. I'll be the freest creature on earth."

That's all I ever wanted for you.

He watches Grandma leap high above the headstones, above the shrubs and trees, the clouds, above the blue of the sky and the white of the shadow moon, so high into the sun that she merges and melts into its yellow and orange, joins her soul to the fire she escaped in life, joins the source of light and life to shine her hot sweaty hateful loving countenance down upon Dave, to cast his shadow, her shadow onto his, to burn them both clean forever.

He crouches, picks a few blades of the crab grass growing above Grandma, sniffs them, smells their freshness, rubs his fingertips over their sharp edges. Later he'll . . . he'll—who the hell knows what he'll do? Weave the blades into a cockring? Nah, he probably won't do that. Nah. Whatever. He shoves the grass into his pocket, shuffles toward the gate and home.

12

Standing beside Westerkerk, Alexander gawks at the two men: Dave at the bottom of the Homomonument, his back to the canal, and that zucchini spitter leaning against the green *urinoir.* The muscleman from the contest. Oh my, how intriguing!

A stare of stag-like challenge between the two. Or, more likely, if one knows Dave, a stare of macho, I'll-kick-your-bum, cruising. What might they be contemplating—a quickie in the *urinoir,* perhaps? *Très* vulgar and crude. How could . . . how . . . Oh, Alexander, please cease and desist! Enough enough! As if you and Jeroen had not experienced all those places . . . well . . . never a public *urinoir,* but . . . is your haste to condemn because you have forgotten the joy of shared naughtiness, or precisely because you so very clearly remember?

Alexander takes a step back, as if to give the two men more private space. Such pleasure in secretly observing. Just look at them. Envy? Not a—well, a twinge, yes. At the chance of feeling the zucchini spitter's muscles . . . Oh well, one—yawn yawn—I've had my fill of cavorting for the evening. More attention than I could handle, to be sure, especially when one returned to the steamy sauna. Smooth and hairy, thin and thick. Yum! So many Dutchmen appreciate the exoticism of what colonies could offer in times past; or rather . . . the varied range of what postcolonial, fully integrated Dutch society offers today. Yes. A veritable rijsttafel of men. A Dutch rijstaffel.

Look how the two stare at each other, without the least of flinches. Statue-like, although by no means statuesque. A match of sorts? Oh my! To have been the one to introduce them! In an indirect sort of way. The matchmaker. A very Jewish profession, is it not? So terribly multicultural. Multifaceted. Diamond-like. Alexander, you're a virtual gem!

I would venture to guess that this incipient *rendezvous au pissoir* will turn to naught of consequence, but just imagine if it should become something! Hmmm . . . what to wear to their wedding? Black leather chaps or white evening gown? Goodness, how silly . . . well, perhaps not . . . Nothing too revealing. After all, every eye would be upon me as best man. Best! And a bouquet of purple gloxinia in hand, held discretely at crotch level . . . Hmmm. A cake in the shape of an old tower, yes, from the Taart van Mijn Tante bakery, and . . . Jeroen always teased me for wanting . . . How ridiculous.

Oh look, the spitter's not only grabbing his crotch in the most cliché of poses, but also slipping tongue between lips and . . . ever so subtly shifting weight from one leg to the other so that his hips rock just a smidge in suggestion. Such a whore; they're made for each other!

And Dave—howling like the animal he is. But which one of the two is he deriding? . . . And that laughter! What's that laughter about? Not mockery laughter, as I would have expected. No, not mockery at all. Laughter from joy, it seems. Joy and Dave together? Speak of your improbable matches!

Ah! I have been espied. Wave wave.

Step back farther, Alexander, do not intrude on this delicious *liaison*.

* * *

Dave looks up from the canal and turns. What the—?

It's Muscle Dick.

Muscle Dick in jeans, a T-shirt clinging to every ridge of bulging chest and abs and arms. Black boots.

That same goddamn Nazi cap. Dave should knock it off, bite the cap's visor and hurl it into the canal, throw stones, watch it sink. But, shit, why pollute the canal?

Muscle Dick tosses a large sunflower onto the pile. The men's eyes meet, hold. Who'll be first to break the stare?

Muscle Dick turns his back on Dave, walks up the steps.

What the hell's he doing here? Following Dave? Taunting Dave more?

No, that's paranoia bullshit.

So why isn't Muscle Dick at the baths or some place? He could have any goddamn faggot ass he wants.

A sunflower on the monument, that's why. Whattaya know, the fucker's got feelings.

Muscle Dick steps into the urinal, and through the green lacy metal screen up top, Dave sees the man's shoulders move as fiddles with his zipper.

This is your chance, Davey Boy, you could catch the guy helpless in the middle of a piss . . . But . . . maybe the sunflower was for someone special he lost . . . ah, leave the asshole alone.

Dave looks back at the canal, at sunlight rippling on water.

A weariness in his eyes, a throb at his temples. His belly feels hollow. Hunger maybe, or something else?

A gull caws overhead. Behind Dave, the sound of piss hitting concrete.

A bitter taste in Dave's mouth . . . stale beer, stomach acid. Dave hawks up a mucous gob, weighs it on his tongue, leans toward the canal—nah, don't ruin the ripples. He looks around—for sure can't spit onto the marble steps of the monument.

Should march over to the urinal and spit right in Muscle Dick's face to return the zucchini favor . . . Yeah, Dave could do that . . . but shit—not worth the fucking energy. Asshole.

Dave swallows the gob.

He hears throat-clearing behind him, turns to see Muscle Dick, now leaning against the outside of the urinal. Either the guy's aching for a fight or—hey, what's with this guy? Grabbing his crotch? Yeah, right, like Dave's really gonna spread his legs for a ballbuster in a Nazi cap . . . Say what?—what's he doing? . . . licking his lips? . . . He wanna do something with that tongue of his? And what's with the . . . moving his hips? Nah, couldn't be . . . but yeah, he is.

So that's what the taunting's been about? To get Dave's attention, to get him so riled up Dave would wanna nail the guy? So that's what this muscleman—fuck, a muscleman!—wants from Dave: Dave's macho attention.

Dave had it wrong all along.

He grins, curls hands into fists, releases, repeats, tilts mouth up as if to bay at the sun: "Aaaaaassssshoooole!" And Dave feels, from deep inside, a welling up of laughter. A guffaw bursts out, loud and ringing and echoing off the canal. Shit, almost as good as shooting a load! Dave laughs again and grins, shakes his head.

He spots Alexander.

Alexander waves, then steps back.

Dave looks over at Muscle Dick, those muscle hips solid and round, that tongue, hand on crotch. Hot temptation, damn hot. In a flash, Dave pictures himself grabbing Muscle Dick by the shoulders while the man's strong arms reach around Dave, and—Muscle Dick pulls Dave in close for a kiss, a deep kiss, a soft wet tender long kiss like Dave's never . . . Is that what would happen? And their cocks would press hard against each other, each man grabbing the other's ass, and they'd kiss and kiss, Davey and Goliath playing nice.

Crazy ideas, Dave's so fucked up.

He laughs again, tentatively this time.

Dave looks at Muscle Dick, thinks, looks again over at Alexander, who's still backing up. Such a good little guy, giving Dave space.

Eyes back to Muscle Dick.

Maybe Dave could try this hunk some other time . . . but . . . Dave's in Amsterdam only a couple more days . . .

You don't mess around with this one now, Davey Boy, you might never get another shot.

Like there won't ever be other muscle studs to mess with, right? No other men maybe to hold someday back home and . . . kiss?

Shit.

Dave calls out to Alexander, "Hey, you little fuck, where you think you're going? I've been waiting for you!"

Alexander, hands cupped around mouth, says in a loud stage whisper, "Don't be a dolt; the man wants you for what surely will be a most delicious *tête-a-tête*. Go, but remember every detail!"

"You little twerp, get your butt over here."

Alexander scurries over, glances at Muscle Dick. "Heavens, Dave, this is not an opportunity to be missed!"

"Forget him. I'm only here a couple more days. And I'm starved." Dave makes a fist, taps Alexander lightly on the chest. "So let's you and me get something to eat. Just us."

Alexander stares at Dave, speechless.

Dave slings an arm over Alexander's shoulder, looks back at Muscle Dick. "Sorry, guy," Dave says, giving him the finger and a friendly smile. "Already got plans with my bud."

ABOUT THE AUTHOR

Dozens of **Daniel M. Jaffe**'s short stories and essays have appeared in literary magazines and anthologies such as *Harrington Gay Men's Fiction Quarterly, The James White Review, Christopher Street, Jewish Currents, Kosher Meat* (Sherman Asher Publishing), and *Rebel Yell* (Haworth). He is a widely recognized literary translator, and the editor of *With Signs and Wonders: An International Anthology of Jewish Fabulist Fiction* (Invisible Cities Press).

Order Your Own Copy of
This Important Book for Your Personal Library!

THE LIMITS OF PLEASURE

_____in hardbound at $24.95 (ISBN: 1-56023-372-9)
_____in softbound at $14.95 (ISBN: 1-56023-373-7)

COST OF BOOKS_____

OUTSIDE USA/CANADA/
MEXICO: ADD 20%____

POSTAGE & HANDLING_____
(US: $4.00 for first book & $1.50
for each additional book)
Outside US: $5.00 for first book
& $2.00 for each additional book)

SUBTOTAL_____

in Canada: add 7% GST____

STATE TAX____
(NY, OH & MIN residents, please
add appropriate local sales tax)

FINAL TOTAL____
(If paying in Canadian funds,
convert using the current
exchange rate, UNESCO
coupons welcome.)

❏ **BILL ME LATER:** ($5 service charge will be added)
(Bill-me option is good on US/Canada/Mexico orders only;
not good to jobbers, wholesalers, or subscription agencies.)

❏ Check here if billing address is different from
shipping address and attach purchase order and
billing address information.

Signature_____

❏ **PAYMENT ENCLOSED: $_____**

❏ **PLEASE CHARGE TO MY CREDIT CARD.**

❏ Visa ❏ MasterCard ❏ AmEx ❏ Discover
❏ Diner's Club ❏ Eurocard ❏ JCB

Account # _____

Exp. Date_____

Signature_____

Prices in US dollars and subject to change without notice.

NAME_____

INSTITUTION_____

ADDRESS_____

CITY_____

STATE/ZIP_____

COUNTRY_____ COUNTY (NY residents only)_____

TEL_____ FAX_____

E-MAIL_____

May we use your e-mail address for confirmations and other types of information? ❏ Yes ❏ No
We appreciate receiving your e-mail address and fax number. Haworth would like to e-mail or fax special
discount offers to you, as a preferred customer. **We will never share, rent, or exchange your e-mail address
or fax number.** We regard such actions as an invasion of your privacy.

Order From Your Local Bookstore or Directly From
The Haworth Press, Inc.
10 Alice Street, Binghamton, New York 13904-1580 • USA
TELEPHONE: 1-800-HAWORTH (1-800-429-6784) / Outside US/Canada: (607) 722-5857
FAX: 1-800-895-0582 / Outside US/Canada: (607) 722-6362
E-mail: getinfo@haworthpressinc.com
PLEASE PHOTOCOPY THIS FORM FOR YOUR PERSONAL USE.
www.HaworthPress.com

BOF00